OBSESSION OF THE EGOIST

EGOIST BOOK II
THE THREE KINGS WORLD

NERO SEAL

All rights reserved. No part of this book may be reproduced in any form or by any electronic or mechanical means, including information storage and retrieval systems, without written permission from the author, except for the use of brief quotations in a book review.

Obsession of the Egoist is a work of fiction. Names, characters, businesses, organizations, places, events, and incidents are either a product of the author's imagination and/or are used fictitiously. Any resemblance to actual persons, living or dead, events, or locations is entirely coincidental.

Edited by Emma Jaye
https://www.emmajayeauthor.com/
www.sublimenovels.com

Cover design:
www.sublimenovels.com

Copyright © 2019 by Nero Seal
http://neroseal.com/
author@neroseal.com

TRIGGER WARNING

Obsession of the Egoist contains explicit sexual scenes between men, strong language, dubious permission, scenes of violence, and is intended for adult readers only. This book isn't meant for people with weak hearts or people easily offended or shocked.

THREE KINGS WORLD READING ORDER

LOVE OF THE EGOIST (BOOK 1)
ACCEPTANCE OF THE EGOIST (EXTRA 1)
OBSESSION OF THE EGOIST (BOOK 2)
PURSUING THE EGOIST (EXTRA 2)

DEDICATION

To The Queen of Angst, Emma Jaye, who gives the best writing advice, spiced up with a lot of sarcasm.

To Azur, The Master of Hamsters, who never fails to make me laugh.

To Regine, The Badass Alien Queen, who gives the best feedback ever.

To my lovely Niece Tida who put her immense efforts into everything she does as she did with this book.

To Janet, who mentally murdered me more than a million times for leaving the book 1 with a cliffhanger.

To my Badass Bodyguard, Stina, who always has my back and front.

To the awesome Karen, who always provides the best and deepest input, and who had been there for Yugo and Kuon from the very beginning.

To my kickass beta readers and friends: Kirstin, Tay, Susan, Isabel, Debbie, and Millicent. Your feedback has been invaluable. I had so much fun working with you.

And all the members of my group Nero's Seals who supported, loved, spoiled, and kicked my ass!

Without you all, this book would have never been published. Thank you all for being in my life.

I love you! <3

TABLE OF CONTENTS

PROLOGUE 1
CHAPTER 1 8
CHAPTER 2 19
CHAPTER 3 32
CHAPTER 4 47
CHAPTER 5 58
CHAPTER 6 64
CHAPTER 7 72
CHAPTER 8 84
CHAPTER 9 93
CHAPTER 10. 103
CHAPTER 11. 114
CHAPTER 12. 122
CHAPTER 13. 138
CHAPTER 14. 152
CHAPTER 15. 160
EPILOGUE. 173
ABOUT NERO SEAL 177
ALSO BY NERO SEAL 179

THE THREE KINGS WORLD:

THE S-SYNDICATE—a criminal organization that specializes in illegal weapons, drugs, murders, kidnapping, pornography, sex trade, organ trafficking, slavery.
 YUGO—The Black Duke of Vienna and the head of the S-Syndicate.
 KUON LEIRIS—ex-police detective, and Yugo's kidnap victim.
 MIO—Yugo's nephew.
 GREG—Yugo's right hand.
 YUGO'S PARTNERS:
 TOBIAS—weapon division executive.
 GUSTAVO—drug division executive.
 RUDOLPH—human trafficking division executive.

GRAY GROUP—a criminal organization that runs the best brothels in Vienna, deals in weapons and drugs, and shields the best hackers in the world. Gray Group owns a network of banks as well as their own crypto-currency.
 GRAY—The Kingmaker and the head of the Gray Group.

RIX INC.—a criminal organization that deals with weapons and drugs, as well as information trading.
 PATRICE—The White Prince and the head of RIX Inc.

THE AL-AMIN GROUP—a military organization in Afghanistan which deals in drugs. One of the partners of the S-Syndicate and their main heroin supplier.
 AHMAD AMIN—the leader of the Al-Amin Group.
 ALI AMIN—the third son of Ahmad Amin, executed by the ILO.

THE ISLAMIC LIBERATION ORGANIZATION (THE ILO)—a military group and terrorist organization with the goal of creating an Islamic caliphate within several countries in the Middle East.

PROLOGUE

The caustic smell of antiseptic irritated Kuon's nostrils. Cringing, he rubbed the corner of his mouth with his fist and opened his eyes. The effort drained him of all strength and pushed a groan out of his throat. Despite just waking up, the lethargy dragged at his body and mind. His veins buzzed, and something toxic fermented his blood—something that filled his mouth with a disgusting medical taste.

In the gloom, unlit tube lamps were mere shadows against the low, white tiled ceiling. The bare window on his left glowed with dead moonlight. Streaming into the room, it licked the corner of his bed, coloring the white sheets with neon blue.

Where am I? The thought stirred at the corner of his numbed consciousness then faded into the white silence.

His senses stirred; his raw throat screaming for attention. It burned, and his swollen tongue stuck to the palate in his parched mouth. He tried to swallow, but his salivary glands refused to work, depriving him of fluid. Forcing his lips open, he winced as the skin on his lower lip broke. The metallic flavor of blood seeped into his mouth and mixed with the foul medical taste. He turned right wanting to spit or rinse his mouth with water, then froze.

A tall IV stand loomed over his bed. In the night, a pulse oximeter monitor flashed green, connected to his body via a clip on his right index finger. A guest leather chair took all the space between his bed and the white plastic door.

"Yu…" His mouth opened to call for Yugo, but he bit his lips closed in a heartbeat.

Right...

Shards of vague, misty memories surfaced in his cotton-stuffed mind. So distant, so unreal, as if the events had happened to someone else in the long-forgotten past.

Swirling snow, landing on his feverish skin ... the pier stiffened in ice ... biting frost, and Yugo's cold eyes ... the black muzzle of the gun ... the warmth of the shaking shoulder under his palm, and the sweet smell of freshly baked bread coming from Mio's body.

Have I died and now I'm in hell? Why the fuck is everything always white?

He took a deep breath and leaned up on one elbow to take a better look around. Sharp, nagging pain bloomed in his right shoulder, washing him in heat. Draining the remains of his strength, it pinned him down to the mattress.

A weak groan escaped his throat. It sounded so pitiful and miserable that for a second Kuon felt sorry for himself. Giving up, he rested against the pillow and swallowed a lump in his throat.

I had a gun. I pulled the trigger. Lifting a hand, he touched his head but found no wounds under his fingers. *I didn't dream about it, did I?*

He recalled the gunshot and pain. The deafening reanimated memories ricocheted in his head, and he squeezed his eyes several times, trying to clear his thoughts and figure out what had happened. No reasonable explanation came to mind.

I must have died, and now I'm in hell, in this empty white room. I bet if I open this door, the same room will greet me on the other side, and there will be no escape from the mind-fucking, white nothingness. Sparks of agitation died in his soul as desolation took over. *This is the hell I deserve for not living up to my principles... for involving other people in my business. I used Mio. I am the worst.*

"Oh, fuck, Mio!" He sat up so fast that blood draining from his head darkened his vision. Acute pain shot through his shoulder to his arm and the pit of his stomach, forcing him to hunch forward. Drenching in sweat, he fought the saturating exhaustion. His shaking fingers fumbled across his chest as his brows drew together. Confusion morphed into amazement, as he discovered tight bandages wrapped around his right shoulder and collarbone under a hospital gown.

Jagged pieces of the puzzle clicked as the logical chain of events trailed in front of his eyes, making his lips twitch. Somewhere deep in the pit of his stomach, a throbbing ball of powerlessness formed. It swelled then exploded. Rippling through his body, it pushed a gurgling noise out of his throat. The bed shook beneath him, and he fisted the sheets, anchoring himself to sanity.

A funny feeling tickled his stomach; the room smudged as his laughter grew, and tears rolled down his temples.

He shot me, so I didn't shoot myself! He really did... He wouldn't let me die. He squeezed his eyes, when opened, rainbow circles stained the ceiling. *He will never let me escape...*

He didn't know why he was laughing, but somehow his life was funny. His determination to become a cop and hunt down murderers, his desperate wish to protect people, his resolve to lead a normal life—the life his parents had been robbed of. Now all of that lost significance as realization descended over him—he no longer had control over his life. He didn't own his body—Yugo did. *Then why should I bother? This isn't life, this is existence. The sooner it ends, the better.*

Gone within a heartbeat, the laughter died, leaving his body void of emotions and his head heavy, hot, and pulsing with intensifying headache.

From the outside, a screech of tires reached his ears. The edge of a tube lamp caught the headlight beam; glinting in the dark, it trapped his gaze.

No thoughts, no feelings visited his head. The emotional vacuum replaced his whole being. It didn't matter if Yugo killed or sold him. He didn't care about anything anymore. He just couldn't be bothered.

The light faded. Kuon let out a breath and closed his eyes, submitting to the growing fatigue. His limbs grew heavy, and he would have fallen asleep, but a rustle reached him from his right. He instinctively snapped his head toward the noise. The door swayed on its hinges, but stayed half-open, letting in the night whispers of hospital life and Mio's slender form.

Despite his emotional paralysis, Kuon found himself smiling. Mio looked fine—pale but unharmed. The fleeting relief that Yugo hadn't raised a hand to Mio warmed his blood. He propped himself up on a shoulder to take a closer look. Thin, beige jersey hugged Mio's bony frame as azure eyes sparkled in the dark. Oddly bright, they reminded him of a vampire.

Mio stomped toward his bed; his hand gripped the white rail as he doubled over, catching his shallow breath. The smell of freshly baked bread washed over Kuon as flaxen hair veiled Mio's face. Up-close, even in the gloom, Kuon noticed his flushing cheeks and dark, almost black lips.

It took Mio a few moments before he raised his eyes and pierced Kuon with a cutting glare. Kuon's smile dimmed, anxiety twitching in his chest. *Is he mad? Of course, he is... He must have felt responsible for my actions. I would have if I were him. He gave me a gun, he helped me escape, and I tried to commit suicide. Anyone would be mad.*

"I never expected this," Mio said, a blizzard in his voice. "I thought he would kill you."

"M-me too…" Kuon stuttered as the guilt aggravated. He hoped that an apology and explanation would soften the sharp notes in his visitor's voice but he couldn't find the words. Throbbing pain behind his eyes intensified, mashing his thoughts. Instead, he offered a hesitant, apologetic smile. *Was Yugo so harsh with him that now he hates me? Does he regret helping me? Of course, he does.*

"Such a pity…" Weak, breathless words reeked with hate.

Kuon frowned, feeling stupid, then croaked, sure he'd misheard. "What?"

"I said, what a fucking pity that Yugo didn't put you down, you idiot!" Mio growled, leaned into Kuon; sharp fingers found the bandage and dug into the wound. Kuon hissed, watching red stain the pale fabric of his hospital gown.

"I'm sorry… too." Kuon hissed, breathed through the pain. The realization that he hadn't lied about wanting to die didn't disturb him, but Mio's words did. *He hates me now…*

Mio scowled, let go, and recoiled to the window so fast, only the faint smell of bread remained.

"It was a perfect plan. You're a fucking detective, so tell me, what went wrong?" Mio demanded. Not waiting for a reply, he carried on, pushing cold, thought-through words out of his plump mouth. "I didn't know you… I didn't know what you could do once your back was against a wall. The risk was too high, so I gave you the unloaded gun, and you're such a trusting idiot, you never bothered to check. No wonder Yugo caught you that easily. How were you even a cop? If I'd known that you're this stupid, I would have loaded it for sure." Kuon's eyes followed Mio as he tried to focus on the voice, dripping with venom. He expected to feel a pang of betrayal, but nothing disturbed his vacuum, only the pulsing burn behind his eyes and the sour taste in his mouth. "But you… You fucking ruined everything! You were supposed to hate him! You were supposed to be aggressive! You should have provoked him! He would have realized that he could have lost me. Then he was supposed to kill you with his own hands to save me! Do you understand? He would be mine and mine alone! Why didn't he put a bullet between your fucking eyes? Why?" Mio yelled, and a coughing spasm hit him, crushing his body.

A minute later, still shaking after the fit, with his face red and eyes glistening in the dark, he shuffled back to the bed, put his knees on the mattress, and straddled Kuon. Grasping the front of Kuon's hospital gown, he yanked it toward him; the fabric stretched, then ripped.

"I'm sorry..?" Kuon offered, feeling no anger at all. More than that, looking into the huge azure eyes, stormy with distress, he felt sorry for this young man who craved Yugo's attention to the point of committing murder. Kuon remembered the spikes of jealousy that had hit him the first time he saw Mio. How he'd believed that Yugo cared for this boy. Looking back, he realized that Mio was yet another victim of the Black Duke. How hurt Mio must have been, knowing that Yugo had been sleeping with someone else all this time. Kuon's cheek flinched, as a mixture of guilt and regret darkened his thoughts.

Peering up at Mio, he said, "You should have mentioned it before. Do you want to try again?"

"Idiot! You fucking ruined everything! Everything!" Mio yelled, as his shaking fingers flew to his face, and child-like sobs broke out of his chest.

Kuon smiled. Reaching forward, he put his hand on top of Mio's head, his fingers entwined with the locks of his flaxen hair.

"Come on... Yugo loves you. I saw how he looks at you. He might have fuck toys, like me, but he'll always return to you. Isn't that better?" Kuon didn't know why he said this. The boy wanted him dead; he set him up, yet Kuon wasn't mad. There was no point in getting mad. He would be dead or sold to the brothel soon enough to waste his emotions on things he couldn't fix.

"Why didn't he kill you?" Mio asked, wiping his wet face with his sleeve.

"Good question..." Kuon whispered and looked up, trying to find answers written on the ceiling. Remembering Yugo's eyes, full of frost, he rejected the hope that the Black Duke avoided harming him. "Probably because you set the rules. You played him. He will not be manipulated so he refused to follow along. He wants to be the one who decides when and how I die. Don't you know him, Mio?"

The door flew open. Kuon's heart halted as liquid fear settled at the back of his head then streamed down his spine. Spreading the tension throughout his body, it chased away the vacuum. His vision focused on Yugo's face, seeking any kind of emotion.

The man looked calm and well-rested. The moonlight reflecting off his skin sharpened his features. Yugo ran a hand through his hair, bringing attention to his white shirt that glowed with neon blue in the night, and his dark suit. His piercing gray eyes, never granting Kuon a glance, fixed on something in front of him. Kuon instinctively followed his gaze.

Fuck me...

Kuon's hand, still caressing Mio's flaxen hair, froze in the air, as he realized the image he presented right now. Mio sat on top of him with his knees on either side of Kuon's hips and shaky fingers tangled in the front of his hospital gown. His face, puffy and red, wore fresh evidence of tears.

Kuon gulped, withdrawing his hand from Yugo's lover. *He will kill me for touching Mio…*

"Get out," Yugo rasped, and Mio flinched. His azure eyes widened, lips trembled.

"Y-Yugo…"

"I said, get the fuck out!" Yugo's voice dropped to a sinister whisper, as he seared Mio with his inflamed gaze.

Fingers, trembling over his chest, returned Kuon's attention to Mio. Plump lips quivered, and tears streamed down his cheeks. He released Kuon's gown and hid his face in his tiny palms. Kuon wanted to pat his head to calm him.

"Mio, you can't fool me. I know about the gun and your plan. Get out and wait for me in the car. My car. You lost all your privileges the moment you challenged me."

Mio winced and rolled his eyes; his tears dried as if they had never been. He jumped off the bed and strolled toward the door, wiping the remains of the moisture off his face with his sleeve. Yugo smacked the back of his head with his palm before he threw a razor-sharp glance at Kuon.

"You preferred death to my bed and my embrace for the second time…" Yugo's long fingers flew to his hair, and his ring glinted with the moonlight. Kuon's heart dropped. He knew the next words would be '*so be it*'. He waited for them to fall from the man's lips, but the pause stretched, agitating him even more.

Yugo sighed. His cheek flinched, indicating his inner conflict before he pushed the words out, "Once you heal, you're free to leave. I have no need of you anymore. I don't need to warn you about what happens if you talk, right?" Holding Kuon's confused gaze, Yugo finished, "Good. Farewell, Kuon."

Something snapped in Kuon's chest as he watched the man turn and leave the room. The door shut behind his back. The night murmurs died out, and the haunting emptiness in his chest aggravated.

Is he for real? The words stuck in his throat. He wanted to call after Yugo, ask what he meant, but his lips stayed glued together refusing to open. The hospital room, so lively a moment ago, stood empty, cold, and too narrow to even breathe.

Did he just throw me away? He thought, watching the white ceiling.

'*Once you heal, you're free to go. I have no need of you anymore.*' Yugo's words replayed in his mind. He couldn't suppress the laughter. A sharp pain shot through his bleeding shoulder, but he didn't care. Shaking and coughing, he had to grab the pillow to contain the emotions gushing out of him. Tears ran down his temples, and he hit the bouncy mattress with his fist a few times in an attempt to calm down.

Life is hilarious… He thought when the last spasms of laughter died in his chest. He wiped his face with his palm, staring up at the tiled ceiling.

Didn't I want this? His icy fingers covered his eyes, bringing slight relief. *So why am I not happy? God, life is so fucking funny…*

CHAPTER 1

Slamming the car door shut, Yugo started the engine. Mio, sitting on the front passenger seat, bumped his fist against the glove box and fished out a cigarette pack. His thin fingers dove into the brown wrapping and pulled out a cigarette. Irritation arose in Yugo's chest. Not caring if he hurt Mio, he slapped the pack out of his hands; flipping in the air, it disappeared under the seat.

"Ouch!" Mio's head snapped to the side as he pierced Yugo with a sharp, unhappy stare. He shook his hands in the air with exaggeration and knitted his brows together.

"Don't provoke me, Mio," Yugo warned, driving the car out of the gates of the private hospital his organization had an agreement with. "You don't want to upset me any more than you already have."

"Upset you?" Grabbing the wheel, Mio jerked it to himself.

The tires screeched as Yugo hit the brakes, nearly crashing against the gates. Grinding his teeth, he turned to the younger man. Mio looked paler than usual, but that only emphasized the hardened line of his mouth and the glowing determination in his eyes.

"What about me? I wait and wait and wait until you fucking look at me. See me. Love me. But all you do is an occasional, half-assed blowjob. You don't even let me touch you, but you let him sleep in your bed. I'm tired of waiting. You treat your fuck-toys better than me, and I was supposed to be your lover. That was the deal."

"You are my nephew." Mio flinched as if Yugo had slapped him with the words. "If you are this unhappy, maybe it's time for you to stop waiting and move on."

The dark, full lips trembled, biting back a painful grimace before Mio attacked again, "I only did what you taught me to do. You always said that I have to fight for what I want. I did!"

"You did. And it's time you understand that every decision has consequences. Pick your enemies wisely, Mio. You challenged me. You plotted against me. You took from me. You disrespected me, insulted even. What did you think would happen next?" Yugo pushed the words through gritted teeth. His blood boiled, and he gripped the wheel tighter, hoping that it would stop his brewing outburst of aggression.

"I did it because I love you." The ardor drained from Mio, and his ashen face whitened even more. "I just wanted you to look at me…"

"Well, you got what you wanted. You have my whole attention," Yugo rasped, never looking away from the black mirrors of Mio's pupils. "Pick your punishment."

A light headshake sent small ripples down Mio's bony frame. "N-no. You can't do that. I'm not a kid anymore."

"Pick. Your. Punishment. Or I will." Yugo pressed, dropping his tone to an eerie whisper.

"No, Yugo, please… I only did…" Grabbing the man's arm with his toothpick fingers, Mio trailed off, crashing against the cold, uncompromising glare Yugo granted him.

"One year with Tobias." Yugo gave his verdict.

"A whole year?" Anger flushed Mio's pale cheeks as his nails sunk into Yugo's forearm. "Because of a fuck toy? You can't do that to me…"

"Keep talking and I'll make it two." The dead, emotionless voice rolled out from Yugo's chest. He smirked at the dread settling in Mio's eyes. "You're forbidden to go home. You aren't allowed to use a car, credit cards, or to leave Tobias' place without his permission. You aren't allowed to visit me unless I call for you. If you disobey, I'll send you away to a place you wouldn't be able to escape. Maybe a year with him will make you smarter."

"No. That's too long…" Mio shook his head. Azure eyes welled up with tears. He blinked, and two shimmering drops, broke free from his long, colorless lashes, trailed down his cheeks. Yugo squinted, wondering if they were real.

"I'm in the middle of the war. I have enough on my shoulders without dealing with the spikes of your jealousy." Yugo said, as cold as he could, watching the corners of Mio's mouth drop. Unable to hold back, he said, adding a fair amount of sarcasm to his voice, "Maybe Tobias can teach you how to pick your enemies or, at least, how to look around for security cameras. Stupidity is unforgivable, but hopefully, curable. Next time you plot against a stronger opponent, make sure your plan succeeds, and don't get caught, because your next opponent might not be as kind." Yugo slammed his palm against the wheel; Mio jerked with the loud outburst. "What were you thinking? I didn't raise you to be this stupid! I'm not even talking about you backstabbing me or nearly getting Kuon killed. You risked your own life, and for what?"

"The gun wasn't loaded. I risked nothing."

"Idiot, you risked everything. You risked my trust, your life, and the lives of the people who failed to protect you. Have you thought about what would have happened to them if your plan succeeded? Do you think I would have forgiven them for losing sight of you? For allowing someone to kidnap you from under their noses? What do you think I would have done to them, to Greg?"

"I didn't care..."

"You didn't care..." Yugo squeezed the wheel harder as the itch to hit Mio grew. "We're only as strong as the people around us. If you think they will follow you because you're a Santelli, you're mistaken. There will be people like Gustavo, but friendship is a rare phenomenon in our kind of business. There will be some you can control with fear, but most of your followers will be like Tobias—powerful, resourceful, and smart. You can buy their loyalty with comfort and support. As long as they're happy, they will go through a lot to stay by your side, but don't expect them to go broke or die for you.

"There will be people like Rudolph. Do you think you're lucky he is your uncle? Use your brain. What value do you offer him except another pretty face and ass he can sell? Although maybe I'm mistaken, you might hold some sentimental value; after all, he wanted to marry your mother. But unlike you, Milana wasn't an idiot. She knew he would use her and chose your father instead. Since it was an arranged marriage, it didn't matter which Scarsi brother she married as long as there was a merger. Listen to me, if you don't learn how to control him, he will whore you out to old perverts to gain influence and wealth the moment I die."

Mio swallowed.

"You think you're smart because people let you manipulate them? They only allow it because you're my nephew. Because they're scared of what I could do to them if something happened to you. Do you think you can afford Tobias' services? Do you have enough money for that? Do you have enough connections to keep Rudolph in check? What would you do if I die, Mio?"

"If you know all this, why do you keep them?"

"You're stupid if you ask this. I can't kill everyone who crosses my path, but I can keep them close where I can watch, control, and use them. You see, after all, we have a common goal. They want to earn, so do I. They're powerful. Not too powerful to stand each on their own, but powerful enough to be taken seriously. I'd rather have them as my allies than enemies.

"Remember, loyalty is a rare quality, but if you gain it, it's worth more than money. You were small so, of course, you don't remember how we moved here from Sicily. How we had nothing but a handful of people and a burning hatred. How Gustavo milked a cow to feed you. When I had to start over, I had nothing but their loyalty. What do you have, Mio? Maybe one year with Tobias will teach you something."

Mio lifted his chin in a defiant gesture. His lips pressed together, losing all color. It took him a moment before he managed to choke his pride. "Not him. He hates me... Please, let me go to Gustavo."

"You had your chance to pick your punishment." Yugo's head tilted to the side. "Not anymore. One year with Tobias will do you good."

PROPPING HIS ELBOWS AGAINST THE DARK polished surface of the desk, Yugo rested his forehead over his linked fingers. The dark atmosphere in his office aggravated with every second of silence. Even without looking up, he could picture the pale-gray, almost colorless eyes that now drilled his head with pinpoint pupils.

"I wasn't the one who took away your puppy. If Mio fucked up, why are you punishing me?" The rough voice dripped with displeasure, and Yugo raised his eyes. Pensively scratching his unshaven cheek with his nails, Tobias sat cross-legged in the deep leather chair. His messy, yellow hair stuck out in all directions. The pocket of his black hoodie bulged with a familiar shape, suggesting that he didn't bother to hide his gun. "How is that my problem?"

"I make it your problem." Yugo's voice sounded odd even to his own ears. Dull and tired, it lacked strength, and Yugo wondered if he had picked the right time to have such a difficult conversation.

Standing against the door, Greg frowned and folded his arms over his chest. A sharp vertical line split his forehead as his bushy brows drew together. Yugo saw that something bothered him, but the man refrained from voicing his concerns. Greg didn't often withhold his thoughts, which made Yugo wonder if it was Tobias' presence that glued his lips shut or something else.

"No, you don't. Ask Gustavo or leave him with Rudolph." Tobias chapped lips twisted in a wicked smile when he granted Yugo with a challenging stare. "I'm not babysitting the little shit."

"If I had a choice, I wouldn't be asking you." Yugo's eyes peered into the ever-tiny pupils as he wondered what would be the right thing to say. Unwilling to lay his cards on the table, he asked, "What do you want for your troubles?"

Tobias scrunched up his face and ruffled the hair with both hands, messing it even more. "You know I don't like Mio, right? The kid is rotten."

Yugo smirked. "That's exactly why I want you to take care of him. Rudolph's morality and values are shattered. Mio can't stay with him any longer. Gustavo is his godfather. He has a soft spot for Mio and can't educate him properly. Greg is getting married." Tobias' head jerked in Greg's direction, a weird expression in his tense eyes. Yugo shrugged it off, continuing, "That leaves me with you. You're smart; you have some moral values, and you respect loyalty. Also, you're the only person Mio failed to wrap around his finger. I want you to educate him. He has to grow up and step into the business."

Tobias winced, his head bobbing from side to side. "That's a whole fucking year of torture…"

"I will write off your share of the lost cargo. That would be… forty million?" Yugo offered, watching a suspicious smile stretch Tobias' lips. The light eyes squinted with curiosity, and Yugo raised his palm. "And…I'll make sure you get the permission to fly that military aircraft you bought a week ago."

"Are you spying on me?" Tobias squinted. "Anyway, how do you know I wanted to keep it?"

Yugo smiled, pleased he'd hit the spot. "Twice a month, Tobias. You'll be allowed to use polygons. Even fire rockets… with supervision, of course. You know, without me you'll spend years getting that permission, right? This is a generous offer for a year of inconvenience."

Tobias side nodded, smirked, then murmured, "What do you want me to do?"

"Fix him for me. He has to learn respect, responsibility, and loyalty. He thinks he is untouchable and smarter than everyone. I want him to be independent. He has to grow up. I also want him to learn the business and strategy. He is smart but too careless to execute a simple plan. He has valuable traits but lacks self-control. Fix that, and I'll be grateful. Try not to break him. I don't want him to act out of hatred. Greg will forward his psychiatric profile to you."

"How tied are my hands?"

"No physical violence for obvious reasons. No starvation, sleep deprivation, dehydration, or any kind of health or mental damage. You have to be creative. I'll arrange his weekly medical checkups. Other than this, you're completely free. Treat him carefully, he is still my blood."

"That doesn't sound simple or fun," Tobias noted.

"If it was, I wouldn't be paying you this much." Yugo folded his arms over his chest.

"True…" A razor of a smile sharpened Tobias' predatory features. His eyes narrowed as a wicked expression settled over his face. "This makes me curious: are you mad because Mio went against you or because you lost your puppy?"

A pang of irritation shot through Yugo's core, but he said nothing, allowing Tobias to elaborate.

"And now you want to get rid of Mio so you can get your puppy back, right?"

Yugo smirked as his fists itched to wipe the grin off that mouth. "Aren't you watching too many soap operas? Mio is in the library. Pick him up now; his things will arrive tonight."

"Am I?" Tobias got up and tugged the hood over his head. "Then I'll see myself out. Send my best wishes to your puppy."

Sinking his canine teeth in the side of his thumb, Yugo watched Tobias' head snap back in a silent, suppressed laughter as the man moved to the door. Stepping aside, Greg let him slip out of the room. He waited for a moment, watching the corridor, before closing the door and facing Yugo.

"Boss, are you sure it's a good idea to burden Tobias with Mio right now?" Greg's booming voice sounded tired, and a pang of guilt shot through Yugo's chest. He hadn't slept for the last two days, drowning himself in work, which affected Greg's work rhythm as well. "Mio is a piece of work. Tobias hates the brat. Mio is everything he despises in humankind. Will Tobias manage to operate with him in his hands?"

"This is why I need them to bond now," Yugo replied, blinking with heavy lids. Resting his head against the backrest, he covered his eyes with his left palm. Cool fingers met with the burning skin around his eyes, providing some relief. "Recent events prove that anything can happen. I have to think two steps ahead. I have to secure Mio's future and the future of the S-Syndicate. The day might come when Mio will have to take over. I want to make sure he's ready, and people respect and follow him."

"Is there anything I need to know?" Greg's massive fists disappeared into the pockets of his black baggy pants as he shifted from one foot to the other.

"The war is unpredictable. By supporting the Al-Amin, we represent a great threat to the ILO. To weaken the Al-Amin, the ILO has to eliminate us, and for that, they only have to kill me." Yugo sighed, picked up a cigarette pack that lay on the desk, and pulled out a smoke and silver lighter. Squeezing the filtered side between his lips, he lit up the cigarette and sucked in the bitter, acrid smoke. "Mio isn't safe here, but Tobias is cautious. With the right mindset, he will protect Mio. He used to when Mio was a kid. He can do that again. However, that's not what's bothering me. Let's imagine that the ILO eventually succeeds in killing me. Who would stand in my stead? If Rudolph takes over, the S-Syndicate is doomed to drown in a civil war. In the best scenario, Mio will end up dead or out on the streets. I'll do my best to prevent that. Gustavo would be a great leader, and he would keep Mio safe, but he has no drive nor wish to do that. Tobias? He wouldn't want to be bothered and, if I'm completely honest, I'm not sure where he stands. More than that, he hates Mio. Once I'm dead, he will split off and look for another powerful ally—one who would make him comfortable. That would weaken the S-Syndicate a great deal. That leaves me with Mio and the question: who will stand by his side? The man he is now is a dead man. No one will follow him."

Taking another draw, Yugo pushed the smoky words out, "Mio has to grow up—the sooner, the better. I need him to be strong enough to lead the S-Syndicate and oppose Rudolph. After all, I didn't build the empire to gift it to Rudolph." Twizzling a cigarette between his index and middle fingers, Yugo watched thoughts swirl behind Greg's intelligent eyes. "But I don't think Mio will ever be ready to lead the S-Syndicate if he is left on his own. Letting him stay with Rudolph was an unforgivable mistake. That bastard did nothing to educate him, quite the opposite. He did his best to ruin the potential opponent in Mio."

"So, what are we gonna do?"

"Exploit the opportunity. For Mio to stay strong, he needs all the support he can get. For now, he only has Gustavo, but that's not enough. My best hope is that Tobias will mold Mio into something he would want to follow. A year is long enough for him to grow attached. Mio is naturally smart and flexible. He will do his best to wrap Tobias around his finger. Worst case scenario, Mio will learn some business and return home. If Tobias succeeds, it will be worth the money I invest, and it will secure Mio's future. And while Tobias is watching after Mio, I hope Mio will watch Tobias. Either way, it's gonna be interesting."

Yugo smiled, crushing his unfinished cigarette in the crystal ashtray and got up from his chair.

"Go, catch some sleep. I need to rest too."

"Should I fetch Kuon, Boss? He's feeling better."

"Forget about Kuon. Make sure the investigation into his disappearance is closed; say he reported to a police station, I don't care where. I'm sure we have enough cops in our pocket to make it convincing." Their gazes linked and lingered. Greg dropped his first. He shook his head, opened his mouth, as if wanting to say something, but didn't. Shaking his head again, he left the office.

YUGO'S PALM LANDED OVER the bronze handle. He halted for a brief moment before pushing the bedroom door open and stepping over the threshold. He looked around. The dark silhouette of the tall canopy bed loomed in the darkness. The window stood draped over, but weak light still made its way through the split. Reaching the chandelier, it played with heavy crystal drops.

Yugo cocked his head. Two days of absence made him feel alien in his own domain. Even the brisk lemon smell of antiseptic he'd never noticed, felt extraneous now. Too clinical, too impersonal; it washed out the last remains of Kuon's presence.

He cringed. *Why the fuck do I keep thinking about him? I've already made my decision...*

Shaking off the unfamiliar sensation and unwanted thoughts, he approached his favorite ostrich chair and threw his jacket over the armrest. His wandering glance jumped from the wolf pelt that sprawled its hollow paws across the floor to the bumpy leather of the chair, and the small, barely visible scar Kuon had left with a meat knife. Even in the darkness, he could clearly see it. His memory provided a vivid recollection of Kuon's cocky smile and shiny dark eyes that challenged him. Yugo reached out and pressed his fingers to the scar. The rough texture of stitches abraded his fingertips.

Only a year has passed, but it feels like it happened in another life. His heart made a small flip. *I wish he was here.* The thought made him angry. He dropped his hand and turned toward the bathroom.

Dropping one piece of clothing after another onto the floor, he entered the ensuite, shook off his pants and shoes, before stepping into the shower cubicle. Turning the water on, he closed his eyes, enjoying the warmth wrapping around his body. He tilted his head to one side, then to the other, stretching his stiff muscles and cringed as his neck cracked. It'd been two long days where he had to make too many decisions and chase away too many thoughts. The work helped him keep his mind calm, but now the train of his thoughts inevitably rushed to Kuon.

Yugo clenched his teeth as the pain of betrayal ripped through his chest. He remembered the black eye of the muzzle aiming between his eyes, and Kuon's burning, feverish gaze. A slight furrow between Kuon's brows had brought to his features a painful, disappointed expression as white snow dusted his long lashes. He remembered how his blood turned cold as Kuon pushed Mio away and pressed the muzzle to his own temple. Yugo's body had reacted before he realized what was happening, and for a few moments, he wasn't sure the peal of which gun deafened him.

"Fuck it!" He shook his head, sending myriad sparkling droplets flying in all directions, and turned the water off. Slamming the foggy glass door open with his palm, he went out, splashing the water all over the dark Emperador marble floor. Yanking the towel off the holder that hung on the beige tile wall to his right, he carelessly pressed it to his face, then wiped his hair and chest, before wrapping it around his hips. Slapping barefoot toward the bedroom, he dropped the towel on the floor and slipped into his bed, under the blanket. The black silk, absorbing the moisture, stuck to his skin, aggravating his discomfort.

After two sleepless nights, he expected to fall asleep as soon as his head touched the pillow. Instead, he lay there wide-awake. Blinking into the darkness, he couldn't help but listen to silence. Nothing disturbed the night: no soft rustle of linens; no sound of rhythmical, barely audible breathing; no short, painful moans of an upcoming nightmare he'd grown used to while sharing his bed with Kuon. It'd been a long time since he slept alone, and now his body ached, missing the comforting warmth of another body by his side. He stretched his arms over the cool bed sheet, trying to enjoy the freedom of movement, but something was amiss. He felt it with his skin, with his restless mind, and with that invisible bullet hole that appeared in his chest the same moment Kuon pointed the gun at him. That hole grew bigger with every passing hour, making him feel hollow, incomplete. Irritation crawled under his skin, stirring anger. He turned to his side, wiping his wet hair against the pillow, then to another, but the movement only aggravated his annoyance. His fists itched, as the anger grew stronger, demanding he destroy.

Fuck it! Anyone would do. I'll just revert to my old habits and wipe him out of my mind.

Sitting up, he grabbed his cell phone and dialed Rudolph. A few long, gloomy beeps sounded before a harsh, unpleasant voice greeted him with an unhappy "Yes?"

"Send me a hunk. Now."

"UNDRESS," YUGO SAID, letting a thick cloud of aromatic smoke out of his lips. The scent of tobacco and vanilla eventually overtook the smell of lemons, but something was still lacking. Caught in his thoughts, Yugo almost missed the moment when the muscular man tugged off his white t-shirt. Knotty fingers folded the fabric before the hustler glanced around.

"Drop it," Yugo said, forcing his focus upon the man's masculine features. The hazel eyes glinted from the shadows of his protruding brow bones. The powerful jaw accented the sinful bottom lip that was darker and thicker than the upper one. The dirty blond hair, falling over his right eye, emphasized the shaved left side of his perfectly shaped skull. The man made a small movement with his chin. Yugo squinted, wondering if he polished his skin with oil. It looked too smooth, too tender, too tidy. For some reason, he didn't find it appealing.

"I don't like things messy. May I put it on the table?"

"I don't care what you like. Drop it." Yugo didn't know why he said it. Kuon had always been messy with his clothes. He'd never folded his t-shirts, leaving them crumpled all over the place, and he had no problem with wearing the same, wrinkled t-shirt for several days straight. That habit had always annoyed Yugo, so why did he miss it now?

The man shrugged, and the shirt landed by his polished black shoes. Squaring his sun-kissed, muscular shoulders, he faced Yugo.

Propping his elbow against the armrest, Yugo rested his cheek on his fist as he examined the brawny torso and pumped-up, hairless chest. In his early twenties, the man was about Kuon's build, approximately the same height, but the atmosphere around him was different, and Yugo wondered what caused it. Leaving the unfinished cigarette smoldering in the ashtray, he pushed to his feet and approached the younger man.

Their eyes leveled when Yugo stepped into the hustler's personal space, making him tense up. The overpowering mix of soap, toothpaste, and bergamot washed out the natural scent of his skin, making the man even more impersonal than he appeared at first; therefore Yugo didn't care to ask for his name or his preferences.

"Wasn't I clear? Undress."

Fingers found the belt and threw it out of the loops before the younger man tossed it aside. Never looking away from Yugo's face, he dropped his pants along with the underwear, then stepped out of his shoes. With the corner of his eye, Yugo saw a long, uncut cock, smooth groin, and a small star-shaped tattoo on his right hip, but none of this touched his curiosity.

"On the bed, on all fours."

Without waiting for the man to comply, Yugo grabbed his elbow and pushed him on the bed face down. Palms slamming against the mattress, the hustler glanced over his shoulder, his eyes wary, questioning.

"Look down. Stay still," Yugo ordered and tore his belt out of the loops.

AMBER LIQUID, SWIRLING IN THE GLASS played with sharp edges of ice, trapped Yugo's gaze. Gray morning crept up behind the window. Overtaking the darkness, it splashed fog over the forest, coating the naked birches in a thick blanket. Yugo barely registered it all. Sinking into his thoughts, he couldn't help replaying the events of last night in his mind. How he'd crammed the hustler's face into the pillow, preventing him from turning around, and how he'd twisted his arm up, bruising it. His knuckles had been sliding up and down the smooth back, failing to find the thick, bumpy scars of the whip. When the man started moaning, Yugo cringed—short, needy, loud sounds provided a sharp contrast with Kuon's quiet gasps and suppressed groans. Wanting to quiet them, he'd clasped the hustler's neck and squeezed as hard as he could. When the orgasm cleared his head, Yugo released the deadly grip. He remembered how the wet, sweaty sheets made him feel revolted, and how he'd left the hustler in his bed, coughing and gasping for air.

Yugo wasn't sure how long he spent in his office, but when he returned to his bedroom, the hustler was gone, the bed—freshly made, and the brisk smell of lemons washed out the stench of sweat and sex. Yugo's head buzzed with alcohol when he approached the bed and sprawled his tired limbs over the mattress. He didn't care about undressing or removing his shoes. He just wanted to stop thinking about the swirling snow, and the black void of Kuon's dilated pupils, that begged him for something. At that moment, Yugo would have given anything to get into Kuon's head to understand what the younger man wanted from him.

CHAPTER 2

Two weeks had passed. Two long, dreary weeks, filled with monotonous square tiles of the white ceiling. No one came to visit, as if no one knew he was alive, or maybe no one cared anymore? He didn't care himself, and he wasn't sure he wanted to see anyone. The only people he interacted with were doctors and annoying, flirtatious nurses.

Back then, with Yugo, he would have given anything in exchange for human attention or a simple conversation. Now, lying on his back in the hospital room, he felt lonelier than in the isolated white room, next to Yugo's.

The flow of medical workers never subsided. Nurses used every moment they could to touch his bandaged chest, stick his arm with needles, and take samples of his urine. Not wanting to invite a conversation that would raise unnecessary questions, he'd never asked what month it was, what day. At some point, he managed to steal a glance at the clipboard with his medical records. It had no name, no date, just S-Syndicate and a number.

The wound on his shoulder was closing and soon skinned over. Three days later, Kuon, sick of the idle, clinical air, left the hospital. No one asked for his insurance or his ID, and he assumed that his name would never appear in the hospital paperwork.

The provided clothes bore a faint smell of tobacco and woody cologne. Kuon couldn't help but wonder if they belonged to Yugo, or if they had just spent enough time in his room to absorb his smell. Along with the clothes, the nurse handed him a fat envelope containing his apartment keys, a no-name debit card, and money, enough to pay for his living for a year.

Looking at the old metal keychain, he wasn't sure if he wanted to return to his apartment. His old life had closed its gates before him, and there was no way to forget all that time he'd spent with Yugo.

Under the bright winter sun, he strolled along streets powdered with fresh snow. Everything felt surreal. No wind disturbed the air, creating the illusion of warmth, but his breath misted in the air. Kuon bent over and scooped some snow to feel the cold. It melted in his fingers, leaving his palm wet and pink.

Feeling like an alien in this bustling city so full of life, he stared at the laughing faces and wondered why he felt nothing. *Didn't I want my freedom back?*

Trying to mimic people around him and stir emotions he used to have before the abduction, he stopped by a coffee shop, but perpetual noise and the overwhelming amount of people chased him away. He'd grown used to isolation to the point his mind couldn't tolerate noise anymore. He didn't want to use the subway or take a bus, so he kept walking until his legs brought him to his old, small apartment.

It took him some time standing in front of the door and staring at the keyhole before he could push the key in. The rumbling of the lock vibrated in his fingertips. Combined with the emotional numbness, it provided him with an illusion of a weird dream that would end anytime. He expected to wake up in Yugo's bed, wrapped in the man's arms, but that never happened. The emotion came later, but not the one he welcomed. A weird longing for something familiar settled in his empty shell.

He stepped out of his tennis shoes and onto the dark-gray plank floor. Clean and polished, it informed him that someone had taken care of his place in his absence. Maybe they wrote him off as a dead man, and someone else lived here now. Someone careless enough to keep the old lock?

He frowned, entering the living room where everything remained the same as he left it. The ghosts of his past lurked about the apartment, reanimating unimportant memories. The picture of his mom and dad in the amusement park hung on the gray painted wall. The memory of that day brought pain to his chest, the same as always. His mom looked so happy, so full of life. A bitter taste filled his mouth, and he turned away.

The ugly driftwood lamp, every one of his girlfriends hated, loomed at the far corner by the balcony. It took a lot of space but barely provided any light. Kuon couldn't explain why he liked it, or why he never gave it up, but now, staring at it, he felt a weird kinship with it. It didn't fit anywhere, just like him.

He ran a finger along a small table standing in front of the old brown leather sofa. No dust.

Did Yugo do that? Hope twitched in his chest but instantly died. *That's stupid… Why would he do that? He threw me out like a broken toy. He even gave me money, as if paying off a whore… What for? To keep my mouth shut?*

The thought stirred something in his chest, but it wasn't strong enough to spark any real emotion and instantly died out. His old self would have narrowed down the circle of people who might have taken care of his flat then he would call and thank them. Now he hoped they wouldn't notice his return and leave him alone.

Emptiness filled his soul to the point where he couldn't tell if he even possessed a soul at all. Maybe it was located where the bullet hit him, and now it was gone forever. He couldn't tell.

The walls were closing in on him. The overpowering smell of floor antiseptic and furniture polish stirred a headache. He opened the balcony, but the brisk wind didn't bring in the smell of vanilla and tobacco that a part of him wanted to detect. The thought that he didn't belong here crossed his mind. He'd never felt this alien in his own home, in his own life before. He had to remind himself that this was his real life, the life he wanted to return to for so long. The life where he wasn't limited to Yugo's bedroom.

He rubbed his temple with his hand and looked out at the busy street. Colorful cars rushed about their business as flocks of young girls laughed out loud, nudging each other with their elbows. Before the kidnapping, this view would have recharged him, but now he felt exhausted merely by looking outside. His hand reached for the black curtain but stopped halfway. Closed curtains were everything he'd looked at while confined at Yugo's. Dropping his hand, he decided that he would never close curtains again.

His gaze slid around the gray room and stopped at the phone. The black plastic handset glinted under the electric light. He hesitated. He didn't want to hear or see anyone. He didn't want to explain where he'd been and what had happened. He never wanted to talk to anyone about Yugo. He wasn't sure he could face anyone anytime soon, and he certainly couldn't return to his job. That path had perished, and he didn't feel he had the right to reclaim it. He'd failed as a police officer, as a man, as a human being.

Guilt and a sense of duty, buzzed in his head, forcing him to pick up the phone, but he dropped it the next second.

I'll do it tomorrow. One day changes nothing.

The mere thought of hearing someone's voice and forcing a conversation made his stomach roil. He picked up the remote control and turned on the TV. The screen flashed with the news channel. He froze when his eyes caught the date—January 17th.

"Ten months..." he breathed, watching the people talk. The TV was set on mute.

Someone paid for electricity and TV. Who hoped I'd return? He wasn't close to his adoptive family; he hadn't seen them in ages. *Then who paid for all this? Was it Yugo? Did he plan to let me go from the beginning? Is it some kind of a sick joke?*

He turned the volume up and clicked through the channels, not paying much attention to what was showing. He needed a distraction—from thoughts, memories, emptiness, and life.

During the time he'd spent with Yugo, he'd never worried about what he would do once he escaped. Now he had his freedom back, but he had no clue what to do with it. Decisions had been made for him for too long, that he'd forgotten how to make his own. He didn't even know which channel to watch.

The flickering screen trapped his eyes, throwing his mind in a half-hypnotic state. But a part of him kept thinking about what he would have to tell his family. Why he had been missing? Why he couldn't go back to the police? How could he be normal ever again? How could he have another relationship in his life?

Maybe I wouldn't feel this useless if I killed him? Would his death release me? Why have I never been able to kill him? He did so many things to me, yet I couldn't pull the trigger. Why?

His finger kept switching channels until he found the news again.

"The public execution of Ali Amin, the third son of Ahmad Amin, the leader of the Al-Amin group, triggered a civil war that is drowning Afghanistan in blood. Dozens of innocent people died in the crossfire," said a female anchor with a sorrowful face, tucking a lock of slick black hair behind her ear. The screen changed, showing devastation and destruction reigning on yellowish, sandy streets. Now and then, gunfire disturbed the clear day as the camera focus traveled from stone buildings to United Nation soldiers, and then to bodies, piled on the dry ground, covered with white sheets. Among them, red poppy flowers bloomed.

The anchor kept reading the news, but Kuon stopped listening. His eyes focused on a child's hand, showing from under the dusty fabric, and the small text, running at the bottom of the screen.

Mindlessly he reached for the phone and dialed the number on the screen. He introduced himself to the female receptionist at the other end of the phone, barely registering what he was saying, while his mind concentrated on a single task—*don't think…*

"THAT'S TOBIAS, BOSS." Greg's voice, coming from the speakers, sounded a tad worried. Putting a whiskey glass aside, Yugo frowned. The civil war in Afghanistan shuffled his cards. More than three weeks had passed since Yugo's position became muddied. Communication with the Al-Amin was cut short, and no matter how hard he tried to reach Ahmad Amin, he always met the same, emotionless answer of his secretary: 'He is out of the office. I'll pass the message.'

"Put him through."

A sharp click reached Yugo's ears, signaling Greg had switched lines.

"Speak," Yugo said, as the low hissing of a long-distance call inhabited the air.

"I'm in Kabul. We got a new deal." Tobias' voice sounded restless, strained even. Yugo wondered what caused his distress, but the course of his thoughts changed. He frowned.

"If you're in Kabul, where is Mio?"

"He is fine. Locked away." Yugo's senses spiked as he imagined a scowl of dissatisfaction on the weather-beaten face.

"Alone?"

"Relax, he's under surveillance. Nothing will happen to him." Tobias snorted, but his voice dropped when he continued. "We got a proposition. We need to give our reply as soon as possible."

"Then start talking."

The pause stretched, filled with a low hissing.

TAP. TAP. Yugo frowned, as all his senses came to attention. The sharp sound of something hitting the speaker repeated, and he realized that Tobias was warning him of a tapped phone.

"Start speaking," he repeated.

"Today Ahmad Amin made an official statement where he promised to create an Independent Emirate of Afghanistan and restore the country to its former glory by implementing full Sharia law and clearing the country of the filth and foreign influence. In his public speech, he demanded the president of Afghanistan to withdraw from his position and hand the reins of power to him within three days. If his demands aren't met, a civil war will start."

Yugo pinched the bridge of his nose with his thumb and index finger. "Did you give any promises?"

"Not yet." Tobias cleared his throat but said nothing else.

Biting a side of his right thumb, Yugo sank into his thoughts. Even if Ahmad Amin had enough resources and men to overthrow the existing government, he would have to retain the power, as well as receive diplomatic recognition from influential countries. Throwing out foreign influence would be a nearly impossible task. Afghanistan has a great geo-location. The United Nations will never give it up. *Why did Tobias call rather than return and discuss it in person? That doesn't seem like him at all. He hates phones, yet he is using a tapped one. Was he asked to provide an answer today? What's the rush?*

Leaning back into the chair, Yugo folded his hands behind his head.

Supporting such a huge war would bring lots of money, power, and enemies. However, it was only a matter of time before the United Nations would stop calling the Al-Amin a group of separatists and start calling them terrorists. If he wasn't careful, the S-Syndicate would share this fate.

"Thank you for the update, Tobias. I can't give you anything right now." Yugo squinted at the colorful flicker trapped in the edge of the crystal ashtray. "Maybe in a week. There is nothing left for you to do in Kabul. Return. Now."

A PIERCING GLARE IN THE LIGHT, almost colorless eyes shot through Yugo as Tobias rocked in the guest chair. His gray jersey showed dark patches under his armpits and in the middle of his chest. "Couldn't we talk tomorrow? I'm freaking exhausted. I look like shit. I need a shower."

"Huh? I didn't notice. You look usual to me," Yugo said, and Greg, who stood by the door with his hands in his pockets, snorted.

"Fuck off," Tobias snarled, but his shoulders relaxed as he wriggled himself into a comfortable position. Cracking his neck, he shut his eyes and let out a prolonged moan of relaxation.

"So?" Yugo urged, and Tobias cautious eyes popped open.

"Something big is going on. We aren't talking about guns only. We're talking about a complete military regime: C-4, tanks, helicopters. I was promised, if we manage to fulfill all of the Al-Amin's needs, they won't enlist anyone else. That's billions."

"Can't remember you ever asking for my permission to make such a deal. What are you afraid of? Can we cover what was asked?"

"We can." The air shifted as Tobias spoke in a careful, well-considered tone.

"Spill it, will ya? Do I have to torture you to get to the point, or what?"

Tobias grinned, showing Yugo his rounded, crooked teeth. He plucked a crumpled paper out of his pocket, spread it over his knee, and smoothed wrinkles with his palms before tossing it onto the desk. "Check this out."

Yugo leaned back. His lips curled as he gave the paper a long stare before he pushed through his repulsion and picked it up.

"What is it?" Skimming through a long list of armor and weapon models, Yugo scowled, glanced up. "You wrote their order on a piece of paper?"

Tobias shrugged, scratched his neck, then yawned.

Written in small, rounded handwriting, the list contained everything to equip a decent army. "Cyanogen chloride, Tabun, Chlorine… Why the fuck do they need chemical weapons? Five tons of C-4 and trotyl? This doesn't look like a coup d'état. This looks like…"

"Terrorism?" Tobias asked, yawning again.

"Is this the reason you didn't close the deal?" Putting the list aside, Yugo linked his eyes with Tobias' ever-tiny pupils.

"No." The unshaven chin went to Tobias' chest, as the corners of his mouth curled up in a wicked smile. "Full Sharia law? Stoning for adultery? I kinda fancy their girls. They are… shy."

A creepy smile transferred to the colorless eyes, and Yugo shook his head, unable to tell if Tobias was serious.

"Implementing Sharia law is a political move to gain powerful allies. How many countries promised Ahmad Amin diplomatic recognition if he succeeded?"

"Four for now."

"More to come?"

"Probably."

"Which ones?"

"I don't know."

"Then find out."

Greg's head bobbed, as his attention jumped from Yugo to Tobias. He approached the desk and picked up the crumpled sheet. His eyes strained as he read through the list.

"Does Ahmad Amin intend to fight two wars at the same time?" Yugo rubbed his forehead. "What about the ILO?"

"A funny thing…" Tobias' head snapped to the side as he brought his hand to his face and tapped his unshaven cheek with his index finger. "Their presence in Afghanistan has diminished. My informant said that after Ahmad Amin claimed his rights, at least five ILO's bases were mothballed without any explanation."

"Why would they do that?" Yugo muttered, squinting up at Greg. The bulky man shrugged without looking up. "The civil war will weaken the Al-Amin. Why leave at such a time?"

"Why not?" Tobias' smile widened as he leaned forward and put his elbows on the dark-wood desk. "When two people quarrel, the third rejoices."

"Huh? Why waste people and bullets when there are United Nations soldiers to do that for them? Most likely they will gain more with occasional, unpredictable subversive acts than with an open war, but that will bring them no fame. That doesn't look like the ILO's MO." Yugo finished.

"Everything changes," Tobias murmured, "if profit is involved."

"Can it be that Ahmad is playing a double game and has already closed a deal with the ILO?" Greg's low bass boomed in the room.

Yugo shook his head, doubting the idea. "The ILO's influence is strong in Syria, Iran, and Iraq. Check if any of them offered diplomatic recognition."

Tobias side-nodded. "Ali was his favorite son. Ahmad's insecurity and paranoia grow day by day. He wants to make sure no one will ever touch what's his again; this is why he is doing all this. His hatred for the foreign presence grows too. He can't forgive the foreign involvement. His intelligence works day and night to discover who sent the soldiers to kidnap Ali. He doesn't trust anyone, even us. Honestly, I don't think he would deal with the ILO."

Yugo picked up the lighter from the desk and flipped it around his fingers. "Who will support their war? Any promises?"

"Uslan, the Chechen Separatist Leader, agreed to provide soldiers and weapons. Ahmad promised to support them in their fight for independence from Russia. The vice-president of Pakistan agreed to supply soldiers, weapons, and medical assistance, as long as his involvement remains hidden and, when the time is right, he expects the favor returned. That's all I know for now," Tobias said.

Pushing his chair back, Yugo got up and approached the window. A heavy veil of impenetrable clouds enclosed the sky. Shuttering the sun, it mish-mashed the dull colors of the passing winter. Occasional birds hurried toward the forest, fighting the gusts. The first, heavy raindrop crashed against the window with a dull **THUD** and slid down the glass. Fetching a cigarette from the pack that lay on the windowsill, Yugo lit it up. Sucking in the thick cloud, he closed his eyes, enjoying the bitter-sweet taste of strong tobacco and vanilla.

"Greg, find out what's going on with the ILO, and I want to know who else is in the game. Which countries promised support, which countries are considering the offer, and what was promised to them. If someone rejected Ahmad's proposition, I want to know." Clearing his throat, Yugo turned to Tobias. "How soon can you fulfill their order?"

"Armor and weapons within two weeks. I can get five Russian tanks and two Mi-6 helicopters by the end of the week. I don't know why they want a jet, but it will take a month."

"Give them yours," Yugo said.

Tobias stabbed him with an acute glare of mistrust. "No. The rest of the military hardware wouldn't be a problem. But even with the plane, they don't have pilots. Finding the right people will take time."

"Work on it. But tell Ahmad that no chemical weapon will be delivered. This is suicidal. The United Nations might overlook a civil war if Ahmad is being reasonable and cooperates; that will never happen if he uses chemicals. Move the pickup points to Turkmenistan. Make sure Ahmad understands that we make no permanent commitments, and will be handling every order as a separate deal. We won't be openly involved, but we will keep supplying the Al-Amin, as we did before. Also, the deal with heroin stays. Don't rush with the answer. Give it at the end of the week, as we agreed. And start working on recruiting his secretary. Threaten or promise him money—I don't care, but make sure he works for us. If you get any more information by the end of the week, let me know ASAP."

"Got it," Tobias got up from his chair. He made a first step toward the door but froze. Half-turning to Yugo, he tapped his cheek with his index finger.

"What?" Yugo asked, disliking the evil sparks flickering behind the pale eyes.

"Your puppy…"

"Save it." Shooting his palm in the air, Yugo cut Tobias off. "I'm not interested."

"Is that so?" Lips stretching in a predatory smile, revealed a white row of crooked teeth. "Even if…"

"I said, I don't care." A pang of irritation twitched in Yugo's chest as he crushed the unfinished cigarette in a crystal ashtray. "If you're done, get the fuck out."

When the smile grew bigger and Tobias' lean frame tilted to the side, as if he listened to something with his whole body, Yugo clenched his teeth.

A second passed, then another, before Tobias' spine snapped upright. He squinted, opened his mouth to say something, but changed his mind. Humming, he passed Greg and slapped his wide shoulder with his palm, before slipping out of the office.

Yugo turned to the window as his hand grabbed the cigarette pack, crumpled it, then tossed it back at the windowsill. The mental turmoil he'd been fighting for the last two weeks returned with the bitter taste of defeat. Despite making the final decision of letting Kuon go, he felt robbed of his choices, and every day, the growing dissatisfaction poisoned his blood.

"You too," Yugo said, but no rustle, no footfalls reached his ears. Subduing the first impulse to throw something at Greg, he bypassed the desk and approached the bar. Entering the hidden, rounded niche, he grabbed a bottle of whiskey from the nearest shelf before picking up a square glass.

"Boss…" The low, booming voice radiated concern. "Tobias is right. Why don't you check on Kuon?"

"Have you nothing to do? Go. Now."

When the sound of a closing door shuttered the silence, Yugo pushed a breath out of his lungs and slammed his palm against the polished surface of the bar.

A LONG WEEK HAD PASSED since Tobias closed a new deal with the Al-Amin. A silent, boring week, filled with occasional minor news and monotonous preparations for another delivery. The week where Yugo couldn't keep his mind occupied with his business anymore, as the rush of inevitable thoughts he had been trying to fend off for the last four weeks stormed back into his mind.

He couldn't help remembering the sleepless nights, filled with torn breathing, suppressed moans, and dark eyes glistening with emotion … the sweet smell of Kuon's skin … the softness of his insides. Then the piercing wind and the brief triumph in Mio's eyes, as he stood on the pier watching Kuon bleed.

Squeezing the glass in his hand, Yugo swallowed the rising anger. Many years ago, he had promised himself that no one would take from him ever again. That no one would ever walk away from stealing from him. Now, he couldn't even punish Mio. One year with Tobias wasn't nearly enough to make Mio pay for the old, open wound in his chest. Making the best, logical decision had never been this hard before, as his blood boiled with the need for vengeance.

Sitting in the ostrich leather chair, in the darkness of his empty bedroom, he picked up a bottle that stood on a small coffee table on his right and refreshed his drink. He hoped that the alcohol would keep his mind off Mio and the dark haunting eyes he couldn't forget.

The door of his bedroom opened, showering the floor with a bright light, then closed.

"Boss?" Greg's rusty voice disturbed the silence.

Granting his subordinate with a long stare, Yugo pushed his glass toward him. Slipping across the polished wood, the glass stopped at the edge of the table. "Drink."

"Boss, it's been four weeks already..." Greg's sulking voice irritated Yugo. He lifted the glass in the air and slammed it against the tabletop. Amber liquid, splashing inside, ran overboard and soaked his hand along with the white cuff of his shirt.

"Shut the fuck up and drink!" The room swam in front of Yugo's eyes, as lightness settled in his head. Sitting in the dark, he hadn't realized how drunk he was.

"I refuse!" The firm notes in Greg's voice made Yugo's blood boil.

"Then get the fuck out of here!" he roared, picked up an empty bottle that stood on the floor by the chair, and threw it at the splitting image of the man jiggling in front of his eyes. Leaning right, Greg evaded the bottle. The glass smashed against the doorframe and crashed down onto the dark wooden floor.

"If you miss Kuon this much, get him back." Greg innocently shrugged. Yugo blinked and rubbed the back of his neck with his palm, disappointed that he'd missed. "Should I order him caught again?"

"What for? So one day he can blow his brains out just not to see me again?" Grabbing the half-empty bottle that stood on the coffee table, Yugo gulped from it then scowled as alcohol inflamed his throat.

"You like him, don't you?"

Whiskey rushed back up his throat. Yugo hunched forward, bumping his chest with his fist as he coughed. When the first fit passed, he glared at Greg.

"Are you an idiot? I will fucking fire you!"

"Why don't you talk to him? Tell him you like him."

Yugo snorted.

"Why? So he can laugh at my face? He hates me." He closed his eyes in an attempt to stop his head from spinning. From the moment he released Kuon, nothing had been able to catch his interest. The days dulled and lost color. Only the burning sting of alcohol helped him forget those eyes, full of hatred, and control the rage the betrayal caused.

"I think Kuon likes you," Greg said and wiped his palms against his dark baggy suit. His gaze glued to Yugo's hands, ready to dodge another bottle. "Anyone with eyes could see it. Talk to him."

"He doesn't." Yugo pushed the words out; a small muscle twitched under his left eye. Sinking his fingers into the leather arm, he continued, "He had no other choice than to believe he does. This is how a human brain self-protects. Left without information, he looked for any kind of connection, communication, kindness. This is just simple psychology, nothing else. Do you know what white torture is? In full force, it makes people forget the faces of their parents within a few months. Isolation overwrote his mind, emotions, morality. Having no one in his life, he concentrated on me. That's it. His feelings weren't real. I gave them to him, and he took them, simply because he had nothing else left. As soon as he had a chance, he snapped back to his old self. Because I didn't push him; because I didn't want to break him."

"I don't think that's the case, Boss. I watched him, you know? I think he likes you." Strolling toward the window, Greg jerked a crimson curtain open. The bright morning light stabbed Yugo's sensitive eyes. Opening the window, Greg let the fresh air into the room. "Why don't you take a shower? You look no better than Tobias. The room needs cleaning; it stinks in here. Go and talk to him. What will you lose? In the worst case, kidnap him again; just treat him nice this time." Greg shrugged again.

Unable to keep sitting, Yugo got up, hope warming his fingers. "Greg… If you're wrong, don't come tomorrow, or better yet, leave the country."

Grabbing the cell phone from the small escritoire, he dialed the number.

"Find Kuon. Now," he said to someone, hung up, and stomped out of the bedroom.

"Wait! Where are you going? Boss, you can't drive like this!" Pushing an irritated breath out of his chest, Greg rushed after Yugo.

"HE DID WHAT?" Yugo breathed as his gaze roamed all over the black passenger compartment. Energy draining from his body, he dropped his hand onto his lap but kept staring at the lackluster screen. A heavy wave of exhaustion crushed his spine, and he rested the side of his head against the window. When his gaze found the rearview mirror and linked with Greg's attentive eyes, he ordered, "Stop the car…"

Giving a light nod, Greg pulled over. Pushing the door open, Yugo got off in the middle of the road and approached the gray, dusty railing that once was white. His hands patted the pockets of his white suit, then the black button-up, before he found a cigarette pack.

Stroking the lighter, he sucked the smoke in, and the soft sound of fire consuming tobacco leaves reached his ears.

So quiet. No car disturbed the early morning, no bird dared to chirp, as if the world had died, leaving him and Greg behind. He looked up at the morose, colorless sky, and a few fat snowflakes landed on his face.

Just like that day… He closed his eyes. Yugo wasn't a fatalist. He had always believed that the weak looked for a reason, and the strong for a method, but at the moment, the snow erasing the ground made him wonder if everything was destined.

"Boss, what happened?" Greg's usually emotionless face radiated concern as he approached Yugo.

"Two weeks ago, he sold what he could and transferred all the money to charity. He joined the United Nations peacekeeping troops. He is not coming back."

"What d-do you mean he is not c-coming back?" Greg stuttered, and Yugo peered into his deep-seated eyes, full of puppy loyalty.

"I don't think he will ever return to Vienna…" Sticking his fingers in his hair, he turned away and kicked the gray, rusty railings. "Fuck!"

CHAPTER 3

TWENTY MONTHS LATER. THE NETHERLANDS.

"All rise. The international court of justice of the Hague is now in session, the Honorable Judge Steiner presiding," the bailiff announced, and Kuon got up. Hands icy and numb, he didn't hear the judge enter the courtroom and take a seat. He heard the judge talk, and how the bailiff called the day's calendar. The noise in his ears grew louder, erasing the following events. He didn't hear the name of the prosecutor or the attorney introducing himself. He didn't hear anything at all, just the drumming of his own heart.

"Sergeant Kuon Leiris, you are charged with violations of the Military Criminal Code article 202 subsection (a)—Intentional Failure to Comply with an Order. Which reads: Intentional failure to comply with a lawful order is the intentional refusal to implement the orders of a military supervisor on repeated occasions. If committed during time of war, combat, or mobilization, this offense shall be fined under this title or imprisoned not more than twenty years, or both.

"You are also charged with violations of the Military Criminal Code article 202 subsection (b)—If two or more persons conspire to violate subsection (a) of this section, and one or more such persons do any act to effect the object of the conspiracy, each of the parties to such conspiracy shall be punished as provided in said subsection (a). Do you understand the charges?" The judge's voice was emotionless, monotonous, and disinterested as if he'd already made his verdict. Kuon knew he had. He even knew the sentence. Eight years of imprisonment without appeal. The trial was a pure formality.

He got up. "Yes, your honor."

"Would you like to make a statement before the trial begins?"

There was no reason to stretch out the hearing, so Kuon said, "I want to plead…"

Someone cleared their throat, muffling his words.

"My client will not be making a statement." The unfamiliar, male voice sounded abrasive and assertive. A hand landed on Kuon's shoulder, pushing him back into his seat. Using the brief pause, the man said to Kuon, "Be quiet."

"What's going on?"

"I would like to inform the court that Herr Leiris is requesting a change of defense," the same voice said. Whispers ran through the courtroom. "As his new attorney, I must ask for a continuance in order to run a properly defended hearing in respect of my client's best interests."

"Who the hell are you?" The bile of irritation rushed to Kuon's throat as he realized that he was flat out ignored. "I didn't request a change in defense."

"I said, shut up." The sharp fingers sunk into Kuon's shoulder, pinning him in place. "Your honor?"

Seconds ticked. A heavy sigh sounded before the judge banged his gavel. "Granted."

THE CHILLY ROOM MADE Kuon clasp the coffee mug in an attempt to borrow some warmth. His knee bounced as he grew tired of waiting. It felt like at least an hour had passed since he was escorted into this room, but his coffee was still warm. Taking a sip, he sighed. The door behind him opened, and someone entered the room.

Kuon turned around, "I didn't request the change."

"No. No, you didn't." The abrasive voice came from above, and a paper rustled in front of him. "But someone else did. Sign this contract."

"Who?"

"Lis-sten…" The chair was dragged against the floor, and the man slumped down by Kuon's side. The airwave he produced washed a strong smell of aftershave and menthol cologne over Kuon. Just like the man, his scent was overpowering, sharp, annoying. "Don't complicate my work, okay? Sign the contract, and you will be a free man by the end of the week."

"No. I'm pleading guilty."

"You don't understand... Let me describe your future. Without me, you will spend years in prison. Even if your eyes are fucked, you're still kinda cute. Ex-military, ex-cop—what do you think will happen in jail to such a pretty boy? I'll tell you what–"

The mug rattled against the metal table as Kuon pushed it aside. He had no intention of taking the insults from the stranger who never bothered to introduce himself. On his feet, he struck before the man could finish, but his fist swished through the air, missing the aim. The chair banged, falling, and Kuon pushed an angry huff out.

"Ha-ha, that's the spirit." The man didn't sound scared at all, but now he kept his distance. "Sign the contract."

"Fuck off."

"You're a sacrificial goat, you know that, right? By the end of the hearing, you will not only be charged with insubordination, but with intentional actions that brought grievous harm. Every family of every dead kid will curse you for the rest of your life if you let them hang this on you. Sign the contract, and I'll make it all disappear."

"I don't know who you are or who hired you, and why you think I should trust you, but you're wasting your time."

"Stubborn idiot..." Kuon heard a nail hitting the glass, then a sequence of tiny, barely audible phone tones before someone answered the call. "It's me. We've got a problem."

"Who hired you? Give me your phone." Patience running thin, Kuon stretched out his hand, palm up. "Now."

The rattle of the lock and a metal screech preceded footsteps coming into the room. Kuon instinctively faced the door.

"I did."

The mix of emotions washed over Kuon as he recognized the voice. Even though he hadn't heard it in years, he could have never mistaken it. Husky, low, charred, it brought back memories.

"I'll wait outside," the lawyer said, and the door closed with a quiet click.

"Long time no see, Kuon. I wish I could say you look good, but you look like shit."

Kuon sighed, "Don't waste your time, Gray. I won't sign it."

"It doesn't matter. It's just a formality." A hand touched his cheek, slipped up to his temple. "What have you done to yourself? If you don't care about your life, think about Mom. She has been restless since you enlisted in the UN. You could have at least called her."

"Don't." The needles of Gray's words pierced Kuon's chest, instilling guilt in him. Gray had always known what to say to manipulate his feelings and reactions. Hating the power Gray had over him, Kuon jerked his chin away, but the persistent hand found his skin again.

"Mom can't wait to see you. She prepared your old room. Can you imagine she still keeps your old toys?" Gray chuckled, and Kuon's guilt aggravated, feeding his now ever-present anger. He clenched his teeth, trying to control himself. "She blames herself for you leaving. She thinks she wasn't a good enough mother to you."

"Stop…"

"Kuon, whatever happened before, it's over now." Gray's arms wrapped around his torso and squeezed him in a painful embrace.

The harsh smell of tobacco and menthol brought back fragments of memories of his fuzzy childhood. *Dad used to smoke the same brand…*

"I'm here now. Nothing bad will ever happen to you again, I promise. I have already arranged a good clinic. Relax and let me fix everything, okay? You're going home with me."

Palm against Gray's chest, Kuon tried to push him away, but for some reason, his hand shook. A part of him wanted to trust Gray, just like in their childhood; he wanted to accept his offer and let Gray fix everything. To feel protected, loved again. To be surrounded by family and the care they provided. He couldn't. He wasn't a kid anymore, and Gray was no longer his family. Biting back the weakness, he blurted out, "I'm fine. I don't need your help."

"Yes, you do. You're lost, I can see it."

"I'm not lost! Stop treating me like a kid. It makes me sick!" Kuon pushed harder.

"Fine!" Gray easily gave up, releasing him from the embrace. "But I'm not going anywhere. You will go home with me. This isn't negotiable. Now, let me see your eyes. I've read that the healing isn't going well, and you're facing the risk of corneal perforation."

Persistent fingers chafed his cheek with ice. The only thought of Gray pitying him made his guts clench.

"What are you, a doctor? Let go!" Anger breaking out, Kuon slapped Gray's hand away, before throwing a punch forward. His knuckles burned with the impact of connecting with soft flesh. "Stop acting like you care! You aren't my brother! I don't need your help! I'm not coming home!"

"Yes, you are. Whether you like it or not, I'm your brother."

"Is that so? Where have you been when I needed your help two years ago? Where have you been when I was kidnapped and tortured? Did you even notice I was gone?" Kuon's lungs burned from screaming; he turned away and slammed his fists down on the metal table. Pressure built in his eyes, and his head buzzed with a rush of blood. "Back then, I needed your help. Not anymore. Go home."

"Kuon, calm down." The sweet, patronizing notes disappeared from Gray's voice, revealing the worry. "We can talk about it at home. All you need to know is that I tried to help you. I understand you don't trust me, but persuading you isn't my priority right now. I'll explain it to you later if you let me, but we've got to get you out of here first."

"Are you deaf? Someone got arrested because of me. I'm pleading guilty."

"No, you won't," Gray said, "I've read your report. His too. No one forced him to follow you. It was his choice."

"I'm not going anywhere."

"Yes, you are. I won't allow this."

"I'm not asking you."

"Kuon, you can make my life easy by keeping your mouth shut and letting Stephan do his work. Everybody will be happy. Or you can plead guilty and make things hard for me. This way, no one will be happy, you understand? Either way, you'll go home with me." A hand cupped Kuon's throat, demanding he turn around. "Now, remove it. Let me see."

"Guards!" Kuon called. Gray's hand clasped over his mouth, another wrapped around Kuon's abdomen. The heat of Gray's chest, pressing against his back, seeped under his skin.

"Easy! You don't want to make Mom cry even more, do you? Neither do I." Gray's voice lost all the warmth, picking up business-like notes. "Let's make a deal."

Kuon's chin rose, escaping the tobacco-smelling fingers. "What deal?"

"You cooperate. You go to the clinic I choose. You behave and meet Mom." Kuon snorted and shook his head. "In exchange, I'll let you kill Yugo. I knew one day you would want to, so I've got things prepared." When Kuon didn't answer, Gray continued, "If you don't want to dirty your hands, I can destroy him from afar. You can sit back and watch him writhe in agony."

Hearing Yugo's name again felt weird. It stirred something in his stomach. For a short second, Kuon listened to the hissing knot of emotions but instantly shook his head. He didn't want to think about Yugo. He had left him in the past and had no intention of bringing him into his present. The whole conversation was unpleasant and made him feel uneasy. Gray's intrusion into his life added to his heightened anxiety and rage.

"Listen..." Kuon dropped his voice, making sure the man would take his words seriously. "Whatever I have with Yugo, it's my and his business. You weren't there two years ago, so don't start playing a concerned brother now. I'm not a kid. Stop protecting me."

"Hmm..." The painfully-familiar hum provided Kuon with a clear image of the handsome, young face, with unnaturally silver, old hair. Gray pulled back. "Don't you want him dead? Don't you want him to suffer?"

Kuon replied before he could think, "No... I don't."

"Huh... Rudolph told me he treated you well. I guess it was true, after all. Fine. What do you want then?"

"Rudolph Scarci? From the S-Syndicate? How are you connected to that sick fuck?"

"I'll explain later. This can wait. Kuon, I need you to cooperate. Please, concentrate. I don't have all the time in the world, neither does Stephan. What do you want?"

"Rick. He was arrested because of me. Fix it, and I'll do whatever you want."

"Kuon, he has already been convicted..."

"If my case is dismissed, you can appeal." Kuon lowered his stubborn chin. "Fix it, or no deal."

"Fine..."

THE PROCESS STARTED A WEEK LATER AND ENDED the same day, leaving Kuon with a filthy aftertaste of bribery and corruption. He didn't know what kind of strings Gray pulled; he didn't want to know. It didn't matter as long as Gray kept his word.

Sitting in the car, Kuon opened the window. The warm breeze, breaking in, washed his face in the mixed scent of mown grass and heated dust. "What's next?"

"We'll spend a night in a hotel. I have some things to do tonight, so we'll fly to Vienna tomorrow. You'll stay with mom for a day or two, then you go to Switzerland."

"What about Rick?"

"He will be free before you know it."

"Fine…" Kuon leaned back against the backrest and clasped his arms around his shoulders. After long minutes of silence, Kuon yawned. He felt tired and wanted to sleep.

Gray sighed.

"Kuon, two years ago…" Gray's quiet voice merged with the faint purr of the engine. The vestiges of sleep gone, Kuon became all attentive. "I knew you were working Yugo's case. I wasn't worried, at first. I knew he had lots of people bought, so you wouldn't be able to get close enough to him to get hurt."

"Tsk…"

"After your disappearance, it took me a month of investigating to find out what happened."

"If you knew everything, why did you never help me?" Hand slapping the door, Kuon suppressed the wave of anger.

"I tried. What did you expect me to do? Hire an army and storm his house? Offer him money? Start a war? Have you ever thought what Yugo would have done if he knew we're related?"

Under the bandages, Kuon's eyes burned with frustration as he faced Gray. "What would he have done? What could he possibly ask for that is more important to you than your family? If I am… your family."

"You know why. He would have used you against me. He would never have let you go. I had to play smart. I waited for the right moment. I recruited people. I got a deal with Rudolph. If not for that stupid boy, I would have gotten you. I knew he let you go, but no one knew which clinic had you. When you came home I wanted to visit, but the S-Syndicate had you under surveillance. I couldn't risk exposing our connection."

Why did Yugo put people on me? Was he scared I would talk? This is stupid. As if I could ever talk about him… Kuon rubbed his chest as the dull pain spread behind his ribcage.

"What deal?"

"Rudolph gets you, gives you to me. I make you disappear. He gets ten million."

"Just like that?"

"Just like that."

"I don't believe you." Kuon breathed, swallowing the lump at the back of his throat.

"Your call, but that's the truth." Hitting the brake, Gray added, "Arrived."

PROBING HIS WAY OUT OF THE BATHROOM with his foot, Kuon ruffled his wet hair. Gray had left half an hour ago, promising to return late at night. Kuon didn't mind. Being alone was better than keeping that uncomfortable conversation going; at least, he thought so. The memories hurt his pride and dignity. He wanted to sink into the serenity of emotional numbness he had been in for the last few months.

The conditioner, blowing cold air, dried the droplets of water on his skin, making him shiver. His first thought of looking for a remote disappeared as he realized its impracticability. The room was big and unfamiliar. It would take him hours to search. Turning around, he stumbled back to the bathroom. Hand slapping the wall, he found a bathrobe and tugged it on. Wiping the trickle of water off his neck with his sleeve, Kuon plodded to the room again.

"Kuon, I thought you might get hungry, so I orde… My fucking god." Air shifted with the motion, and icy hands cupped his face. Kuon flinched away from the touch, realizing his bandages were off. "Open your eyes."

"No." The burn, starting somewhere behind his eyes, transferred to his face, to his throat, until it inflamed his lungs. Biting his lips to stop them from quivering, Kuon shook his head.

"It's okay, baby brother. Let me see." The fear and concern in Gray's voice felt real, and for a second, Kuon wanted to trust him. "Please."

Gulping back the sour saliva that flooded his mouth, Kuon opened his eyes but saw only swirling gray fog clouded around him. For the first time since the reunion, he hoped that Gray would say something, but minutes passed in silence. Only when Kuon closed his eyes and shied away, did Gray's gravelly voice break the stretched pause.

"Change of plans. You won't meet Mom. We'll go to the hospital tomorrow."

WHEN A GUARD SAID THAT HIS LAWYER waited for him, Rick shrugged but followed. After entering the prison meeting room, he glanced over his shoulder, expecting the guard to inform him that he'd entered the wrong room, as this posh man couldn't possibly be here to see him. When a manicured hand pushed a contract toward him over the metal table, he grabbed the back of the chair, bolted to the floor, and took a seat. For a long ten minutes, he stared at the man, examining his freckled face and red hair, expensive designer suit, and gold watch.

"This must be a mistake," Rick finally said, pushing the contract back with two fingers.

"There is no mistake, Herr Kainz. Sign the contract." The smile on the thin lips didn't reach the light-green eyes of the man who never bothered to introduce himself.

At that moment, Rick thought that if there were a devil out in the world buying souls, he would look exactly like this. Arrogant, disinterested, even bored.

"I can't afford you," Rick said, pushing the paper back.

"Oh, I know you can't." The lawyer's lips twitched as if Rick had said something funny before the man pushed the paper toward him again. "My fee has been covered by someone else. You only have to sign the contract."

Rick didn't believe him, and for the next hour, he read the contract three times, but failing to find a scam, he eventually signed.

Hearing after hearing, he was dragged in and out of court before the charges had been dropped and he was released. Standing at the gates of the federal prison, he stared at the sky, unable to believe that he was once again a free man. He'd made his peace with his sentence months ago, expecting to spend eight years in prison, eating shitty food, and sleeping on a bad bunk. Now, a world of possibilities lay open in front of him, making him appreciate this unexpected second chance.

The screech of tires brought his attention from the cloudless blue sky to the black Cadillac CTS that stopped in front of him. The passenger door flew open, and a husky, charred voice invited him in, "Hop in, Sergeant Kainz. Let me give you a lift."

Here it is, Rick thought, remembering the old proverb: 'Free cheese only comes in traps'. Still, he got in, thinking that whatever the man had to offer, most likely it was worth eight years of freedom. Getting comfortable in the seat, he examined the luxury atmosphere of the ivory and mahogany interior, before he linked his eyes with the silver ones of the stranger. The sharp clean-shaven chin and angular cheekbones only accented his x-ray-like stare. Rick would have estimated the man to be in his early thirties, if not for his completely silver hair.

"I've been looking forward to meeting you, Richard," the man said, smiling. "My name is Gray. I'm Kuon's brother. Mind joining me for a ride? I'd like to show you something."

"Kuon has a family?" Rick asked, frowning. They had served together for more than a year, but Rick knew nothing about it.

"He doesn't talk much, does he? I figured that I'll get a better chance of understanding him if I talk to you." Gray's unblinking eyes made Rick feel uneasy. He shrugged, and Gray continued. "I'd like to know more about what happened to him there, in Afghanistan. Would you enlighten me? How did you two meet? What was he like there?"

Is this why he pulled me out of jail? To ask about Kuon? He could have just visited... Confused, Rick glanced at the man again. Gray's wolfish face with thin, aristocratic features had nothing similar to Kuon's honest and open lineaments. But Rick couldn't find another reason why a stranger would be interested in Kuon's service years unless this was a provocation.

"How do I know you're Kuon's brother? You look nothing alike," he finally asked.

Gray laughed. When he stopped, a glint of curiosity settled in the depth of his eyes. "I like people who think before they speak. You're right, Kuon and I aren't blood-related. He was adopted into my family when he was little." Fishing his phone out of the pocket of his gray suit, Gray swiped the screen, tapped it a few times with his finger, before showing Rick a picture of two kids. The older boy was around fifteen and already had salt and pepper hair, another one was about eight and wore a gloomy expression. No mistake—it was Kuon.

"I met Kuon during his first year in Afghanistan." Rick started, feeling uneasy. To ease the discomfort, he rolled his shoulders and looked out of the window at the gray winter streets. "That year, we had lots of fresh meat. The lines of the peacemakers thickened with cannon fodder—young and stupid boys who could barely reload a gun. And that's in the country where six-year-old kids are already professional murderers. It was a bloodbath. When Kuon was assigned to our division, I thought he was one of those young idiots who romanticized the war.

"Our first raid proved me wrong." Rick turned his attention to Gray. "He didn't romanticize anything, and he knew how to handle the weapons. 'Crazy Kuon', that's what we called him. He was insane; everybody hated him. No one wanted to be paired with him because he didn't seem to have any respect for life. He didn't follow protocols. All he did was pull the trigger. At first, he was lucky. The bullets avoided him for some reason, and people thought he was possessed." Noticing the smirk on Gray's lips, Rick added, "It would be funny if you aren't in the middle of the war where everyone has a gun and can shoot at your back. I can't remember all the times our own people had a go at him, thinking he was cursed. At least three of the attacks were genuine attempts on his life."

Gray's smile dimmed, and Rick continued, "People avoided him, but it didn't bother him. He never talked to anybody unless it was necessary. He never smiled. He was the same as the gun he held. He just wanted to kill, or that was what we thought."

"It sounds like you hate him." Gray's eyes glinted with ice as his voice became smooth, oily.

"I did, for a long time." Rick didn't lie. "Not anymore."

"What changed?" Gray's predatory eyes bore into Rick.

"Six months before the terrorist attack, we were assigned to guard The Arg, the citadel that serves as the presidential palace. We were told to protect the government body at any cost. That day we also received the order 'in case of crossfire ignore civilians and complete the mission'. At first, everything went according to the plan. We secured the perimeter, and despite the increasing attack, we were able to hold our positions. But in the middle of the crossfire, a little boy appeared out of nowhere. Kuon ignored the direct order and left his position. A bullet caught his shoulder, so he was sent to the hospital.

"No one knew what to do with this child. His family was dead, and there was nowhere he could go, so he stayed there too. It's so weird how war and death bring people together. The boy came to visit Kuon every day. They didn't have anything in common. They didn't even speak the same language, yet the kid managed to change him. Kuon started smiling. In a few weeks, the boy was sent to France to his new family, but Kuon had changed. Little by little, he started talking to us. Instead of going on his own during the missions, he started watching our backs. Eventually, we became friends."

Not knowing what else to say, Rick shut up, and for a long twenty minutes, they drove in silence until the car stopped in front of a recently built apartment building.

Gray said, "Arrived."

Rick looked out of the window, not recognizing the street, then back at Gray, who searched his pockets a moment before tossing Rick a key. "You've got no place to stay, right? Tenth floor, apartment 306. You can stay there until you find another place, or it can permanently become yours. If you need a job, I could do with someone like you. Think about it."

One more time, Rick examined the posh interior of the car, Gray's expensive suit, and the tall building they parked by. His instincts kicked in, alerting him.

"Thanks, but no. I'll be out in a few days." Rick said, then got out. Watching the car depart, he fished the phone out and dialed Kuon. After the second ring, Kuon picked up. "Yes?"

"Kuon, I'm out of jail, and I've met your brother."

THREE MONTHS LATER. LAUSANNE, SWITZERLAND.

SITTING ON THE BOTTOM OF THE BOAT, Kuon rested his cheek over the edge of the board. It smelled of paint, moist wood, and mold. Even without seeing it, he could tell the boat was old, oared. His fingers ran over the rough surface, and he picked off a piece of old paint for no reason. It felt oddly satisfying, so he did it again.

"Do you want to paddle?" Gray asked, pushing the boat away from the shore.

Bending overboard, Kuon sunk his hand in the icy water and sucked in a lungful of sharp, fresh air. The cold temperature and increasing moisture promised a windy February, but that day was windless, and the winter sun licked his skin with warmth.

"Later."

Splash after splash, vibrating through the boat, resounded in Kuon's bones, creating a weird illusion of the boat being an extension of him. He felt everything. The slight incline to the left, as they took a smooth turn, the dropping speed, and how Gray lay on the oars.

Gray shuffled to the stern, then back to him.

"I fixed your fishing rod. Want to cast the line?" Gray asked, dropping a comforter over his shoulders.

"Nah… Don't wanna move. Maybe later."

"Whatever…" Something clanged by his side. Kuon wanted to remove the sunglasses and present his face to the sun. Feel its healing warmth over his eyes and lips. He didn't. Gray's reaction to his face had left him with a haunting feeling of déjà vu. He didn't need to see Gray's silvery eyes to know that a bitter mixture of pity and sympathy darkened them. He had already seen it many years ago.

"Do you remember how we went fishing with dad once?" Kuon lifted his head, listening to Gray's voice, saturated with nostalgia.

"We did?" Kuon asked, searching his memory but didn't find anything.

"Yeah. Dad told us to dig for worms, and we gathered them in mom's porcelain cup."

Kuon chuckled. "No, we didn't…"

"I tell you. She was so mad she even stepped out of her heels to catch us. Dad saved us from her fury." The boat rocked on small waves. "It was your first time fishing. You were so excited."

"Really?"

"That day, Dad was on fire. He pulled out so many fish, the bucket rattled with activity. When you realized what fishing was, and that all those fish would die, you started crying."

"I didn't!" Kuon protested, embarrassed for some reason.

"You so did. To make you stop, I helped you throw all the fish back into the river. Dad was livid. We were supposed to stay the night in a tent. Instead of the grilled fish for dinner, Dad served us sandwiches with worms to teach us a lesson. He said that we eat what we earn. I knew he wasn't serious, but you took the sandwich and threw it into the river. You called him a despot. Dad never took you fishing again, and you refused to eat fish ever since."

"I don't remember any of this," Kuon said through the laughter. "And I do eat fish. You lie!"

"I don't!" Gray chuckled.

We can have a normal conversation… Kuon thought, listening to Gray moving about the boat. The water splashed, then everything quieted again. *We used to be best friends when we were kids. We used to be a family, and no one understood me better than Gray. When did this change? Maybe, if we try, we can become a family again? I can meet Helen.*

He opened his mouth to ask Gray about it, but the phone chimed, then again and again. At first, Kuon ignored it, but the annoying signal kept repeating piquing his interest. The reluctant, slow way Gray answered the call made Kuon suspicious.

"Yes," Gray finally said. Kuon lifted his head, and his hearing sharpened. It was so quiet that he could hear the voice coming from the speaker. A voice that sounded like a breaking crust of bread. Kuon's teeth clenched. "I'm busy now. I'll call you back later. Just keep still."

"That was Rick, wasn't it?" Kuon asked as soon as Gray hung up. "Why the hell does he call you?"

"Huh, so it's true. If you lose one sense the others are enhanced. Now I'm curious…"

"Gray, why did Rick call you?" Kuon insisted.

"Relax, it's just a small return favor. Nothing important."

Even though Kuon couldn't see Gray's face, the air of irritation coming from him was clear. *A return favor?* A bad feeling crumpled his chest. "What kind of favor?"

"Kuon, I'm not Mother Theresa. My help isn't free. I got him out of jail, and now I need something back." Kuon scrambled to his feet, and the boat swayed. It tilted right, then left. Gray grabbed Kuon's shoulder, steadying him on his feet. "Careful, if you fall into the water I won't jump after."

"What the hell, Gray? That was your deal with me. Don't mix my friends into your shady shit!" Sinking his fingers in Gray's wrist, Kuon ordered, "Call him. Or better, give me your phone. NOW!"

Sounds of lapping water and rhythmical rocking of the boat filled a moment of hesitance. A slim smartphone landed on Kuon's palm.

"Why are you pissed?" Gray asked, recovering his usual, patronizing tone. "He's a big boy. I didn't force him. Just asked for a favor, and he said 'yes'."

"As if he could refuse. You're unbelievable… And here I thought that I can trust you, but the truth is, you always exploit people. You never let an opportunity slide. Just like before. Dial him!"

The light pressure applying to the phone informed Kuon that Gray complied. The tones cut the air, and Kuon lifted the phone to his ear. "Rick, It's me…"

"KUON, COME ON. I PROMISE I won't mess with your friends anymore." The conciliatory notes in Gray's voice did nothing to pacify Kuon. He kept twisting the Rubik's cube for blind people in his hands. Raised designs on the tiles tickled his finger pads, but instead of calming him, it infuriated him.

"I don't believe you." Kuon twisted the row and winced, as he realized the perfect side on the left was ruined. "Tsk…"

He put it aside and buried his face into his palms. So much anger and frustration built inside of him, that he didn't know if anything else remained in there.

"Come on, how long are you going to be mad? Nothing bad happened to your precious friend. Let's forget about it, okay?" When Kuon said nothing, Gray added, "You won't see me for the next two weeks."

That stirred a reaction. Kuon threw up his face, concerned. "Two weeks? Why so long? Gray, I'm sick of this place…"

"I know… Just a little longer, baby brother. They promised to start the scar therapy in a week." A cold hand ruffled his hair, and Kuon thought that Gray smoked too much, to the point where his vascular system failed to keep his limbs warm even indoors.

"They promised it a month ago…" Kuon slapped his hand away.

"I know, but… Hey, it was a good day. Let's not ruin it. I said I'm sorry. What else do you want?"

Kuon huffed, unable to let the topic go. He felt responsible. After all, he introduced Gray to Rick. "What kind of job did you assign him?"

"Nothing important. He just has to pick up a package at one point and drop it in another."

"Drugs?"

"No. Information."

"I hate you," Kuon growled, scooping the Rubik's cube again. The damn thing didn't want to solve, no matter how long he twisted it, and for that, he couldn't let it go.

"Whatever. I'm hungry. Want to eat out?"

"Finger food…" Kuon sighed, getting up. The thought that he would have to stay alone for another two weeks soured his mood.

CHAPTER 4

The next two months drowned in routine. Occasionally Gray stopped by, but Kuon spent most of the time alone, locked in his mind and memories. When the days merged into an eventless existence, Kuon's patience thinned out.

He tossed the headphones aside. His ears hurt, head splitting from listening. He wanted to work out to distract himself from the empty feeling in his chest the apathy caused, but his muscles still trembled from overuse.

Wavering, he picked up his phone; the prominent numbers on the big buttons tickled his finger pads. Using the speed dialing feature, he called. Gray replied after the second tone. "Kuon?"

"I'm tired of staying here. The doctors don't do anything anymore. They said the inflammation is gone and that I'm no longer at risk. I can be treated anywhere. I want to return to Vienna."

"It's gone, but your scars aren't. Your eyes have only healed enough to start more aggressive treatment. Anyway, what does it matter where you are? What would you do in Vienna?"

Kuon sighed, resting back on the sofa. His fingers ran over the smooth velvety texture of its upholstery. "I don't know... Meet someone? Talk to people? Didn't you want me to see Helen?"

"I did. But if Mom sees you like this, she'll cry. You are where you are because this clinic is the best. In a year, you will look as good as before. Leaving now would be stupid."

"Austrian clinics aren't bad."

Gray didn't reply, but a faint sigh reached Kuon from the phone.

"I'm bored from talking to the virtual assistant all day long." Kuon winced, realizing that he sounded like a kid moaning to his older brother, but couldn't stop. "I think she doesn't like me much, and... I can't say if she is joking or being slightly psychopathic. And the people here don't speak German. I'm tired of speaking English all the time."

"Okay, I got your problem. Don't sulk; I'll drop by in a few hours."

"HEY, BABY BROTHER, how are you doing?" Gray said from the doorway after entering Kuon's hotel suite.

Kuon turned the TV off and shrugged while fiddling with the remote control. "Did you talk with the doc?"

"Yes, I did." The male shoes rapped against the parquet flooring; Kuon's neck rotated following the sound. Gray circled the sofa, stopping behind his back, and his cold hands landed over Kuon's shoulders. A familiar mix of tobacco and menthol washed over Kuon, but it had some foreign hint in it as if mixed with thin, female perfume. Kuon wondered if Gray came to him after seeing a woman. "You're tense. Why do you refuse the massages?"

The side of Kuon's mouth jerked. Having no desire to show and explain his scars, Kuon lied, "I hate being touched."

The floral scent intensified, and a weird hunch that someone else was present in the room alarmed Kuon. He strained his ears and concentrated on the tactile sensations, trying to catch the small air oscillations with his skin.

"I see." Gray's hands rubbed his shoulders before kneading Kuon's sore muscles through his t-shirt. "Your doctor said you don't go to therapy sessions."

"I don't need a shrink. I'm fine." Kuon's shoulder jerked. "What I need is to get out of here. Can't I go back to a normal life, to the people I know? I want to do something to occupy my mind. I feel like I'm getting dumber every day. I need people, Gray. Real people, not medical workers who treat me like a nut case about to have a crisis."

"There are group sessions."

"People with PTSD? Thanks, but no thanks. I don't want to hear their stories or share mine."

"You never go to the workshop either."

"Are you for real? Do you expect me to take clay sculpting classes?" Kuon tried to get up, but the powerful hands, digging into his skin, pinned him in place.

"They're there for a reason. They help to keep you busy. The psychologist said that you're hostile and mercurial."

"Anyone would be if they're locked in four walls for five months." The sweet floral scent overpowered the tobacco one, making Kuon straighten his back and lean forward.

"Hmm, maybe you're right." Gray pressured the painful spots in his trapezius muscles. The sharp pain cut through his neck and spine as Gray kneaded deeper.

"Ouch!"

"You have knots. The next time a masseur comes, I expect you to accept the treatment."

"Is there anyone else here?" Kuon asked as the haunting feeling refused to abate, but Gray ignored him.

"When was the last time you had sex? Do you masturbate?"

"What? That's none of your business." Kuon clasped Gray's wrists, wrenching them away from his body, but the attempt failed as his muscles still trembled from working out earlier. "Let go!"

"Relax."

Something full and soft brushed against Kuon's knees before two hands slipped up his thighs, and someone settled between his legs.

"What the hell?" Instinctively, Kuon shrunk back, flattening his spine against the backrest. His hands struggled to unclasp the vice of Gray's arms. "Gray, let go of me!"

Gray didn't.

"You're frustrated, aren't you? No wonder. I bet it's been forever since you slept with a woman." Kuon's zipper vibrated against his groin, and hot breath washed over his abdomen.

"What do you think you are doing? It's not funny. Gray, stop it right now!"

"Just relax and enjoy. Consider it a gift," Gray murmured, pleased with himself. A female, amused hum warmed Kuon's pubis. A slim hand touched his abdomen and snuck up under his shirt and over his chest; another one tugged the waistband of his trunks down. His every cell rebelled; he released Gray's wrists to grab the woman's hands, but the icy fingers intercepted his forearms, forcing them up and back, behind his head. "Let Chloe help you relax. The world will be a brighter place after you cum, you'll see."

"Are you fucking for real?" Kuon asked incredulously and tried to get up. "Let me go! Fuck off, or I'll kick her!"

"You're overreacting."

"Am I? You brought me a whore!"

"Don't be rude. Chloe isn't a prostitute, she is an escort."

"It's the same!"

"No, she takes money for her company. She doesn't have to have sex. Anyway, we're all concerned, Kuon. The life you lead isn't healthy. The doctor said you only willingly go to the gym. You never socialize, never relax. You're tense, depressed, and clearly frustrated. That's why I'm here. That's why Chloe came." Gray's breath warmed Kuon's left cheek. His body tensed, and he sucked air in, as the soft hotness of a mouth engulfed his cock.

Blood slammed into Kuon's head, bringing back long-forgotten humiliation. His heart drummed against his ribs as the memories of Yugo's touch reincarnated in his mind. Vivid. Palpable. The mouth of a woman became Yugo's, and the steel of Gray's hands became the leather restraints that held him to the bed. Sinking a canine tooth into his bottom lip, Kuon tried to clear his head with pain.

"Ughm..." Kuon refused to admit that there were grains of truth in Gray's words. His body reacted even though he was pissed.

"That's it. Good boy," Gray murmured when Kuon's fingers crumpled the lapels of his jacket and slipped up to his neck. He didn't stop Kuon from cupping the back of his head and fisting his hair.

Shuddering under the flick of the tongue, Kuon swayed right before he faced his brother and crashed his forehead against Gray's. The powerful impact rang in his ears, and Gray's hands unclasped, releasing him. Pushing the woman aside, Kuon got up and zipped his jeans. "Get the fuck out and take your 'gift' with you."

"That was rude..." Gray wheezed, his husky voice drenching with pain.

"Go to hell."

"Stop being stubborn. I'm just trying to help."

"Help?" A burst of brief, sharp laughter scratched Kuon's throat. "How? By bringing me a hooker? You think that will solve my problems?"

"Chloe isn't a hooker. She is a high-class escort. She is smart and beautiful. She speaks four languages."

"Yet, she is here to sell herself."

"She is clean if that's what concerns you, and she kindly agreed to stay with you and keep you company for as long as it takes, so don't be rude and ungrateful!"

"Ungrateful?" Kuon repeated the word, tasting it on his tongue. "I'm out of here… Trusting you was a mistake."

"Out? Where? This is the best place for you right now. Where do you think you can possibly go?"

"Anywhere. Austrian clinics aren't bad. My insurance is intact, so is my disability pension. I can get treated anywhere. Rick will help me settle if I ask him."

"Rick… Go ahead, be a liability to your friend. You didn't cause him enough problems, did you?" Sarcasm poisoned Gray's voice. "You're acting like a spoiled kid."

"Lia…bility?" A single word punched the air out of his lungs. He opened his mouth to repeat the word, but couldn't.

"Well, aren't you? You skip Orientation and Mobility classes as well as Independent Living Skills. It means you can't wipe your own ass, and he would have to babysit you twenty-four/seven."

"Huh… Is that what you think? Thank you, Gray. I won't bother you anymore. I'm leaving."

"No, you are not."

"Liability…" Kuon shook his head, feeling bitter. "I never asked for your help. You were the one who showed up out of the blue. I don't need anything from you!"

"I'm your family. You are my responsibility."

"Responsibility? You and Helen… You never treated me like an adult. Always so overprotective and condescending. Back then, you turned yourself inside out to stop me from entering the police. Do you think I forgot? If not for your dad, I would never have made it!"

"Yeah? Maybe we were right, after all. Cheating on psychological tests didn't make you a good soldier, just like it didn't make you a good cop. Look where it brought you."

"I'm a good co… I was a good cop." Kuon swallowed the insult, but pre-fight tension settled in his shoulders and neck. "And I was a good soldier."

"Were you?" Something in the way Gray asked, made Kuon frown.

"Why do you say that?" he asked, teeth screeching with pressure. "I served my country well, and I saved lives. I put away a serial killer."

"You were lucky."

"Lucky?" Nails bit into his palms, Kuon huffed. "If you call luck a search for evidence, then police all over the world functions on pure luck. I found a witness when everyone else gave up. Yeah, maybe I didn't follow protocol, but he was arrested. I spent days and nights working that case and it paid off. I can't believe you called it luck. Take it back."

"I won't. With your psychological profile, you wouldn't even be on the force if Dad didn't train you to trick psychologists."

"It doesn't matter how I got accepted. I was a good cop with a greater record of arrests than many. You know what? Instead of Yugo's people, I should have concentrated on yours."

Gray laughed. "Don't be naïve, Kuon."

"What does that mean?"

"Nothing."

"I asked you a question, Gray!"

"You want to know? Fine. All those cargos the police seized were just crumbs from Yugo's table that he fed you. He used you!"

"Bullshit."

"We all do this. We call it 'taxes'. From time to time, we gotta let the police show results. So we occasionally give them a sacrificial goat along with a decent amount of goods. While we do that, the government lets us work. Everyone's happy."

"That can't be..." Kuon desisted in confusion.

"Yes, it can. If the government wanted Yugo or me arrested, we would be rotting in jail. Open your eyes. He used you. That cargo you seized, do you know how you got it? Do you think you did a great job? You were led to it. Yugo played you. He let you seize it. Except miscommunication happened, and instead of the 'taxes' you got the real goods."

"You lie..." The soft place under Kuon's tongue chilled, paralyzing his speech function, so he mouthed, "I don't believe you."

"It doesn't matter what you believe. It's true."

Gray's words unsettled and stirred every emotion he possessed. Everything he knew fragmented into small pieces as the information ricocheted against his skull, demolishing and rebuilding his past. *Was I played?*

He needed to think, but Gray's words hurt his mind and pride.

I can't believe this... The more he thought about it, the more he felt like falling into a deep rabbit hole, where everything was inside out. *If what Gray said is true, there was no reason for Yugo to kidnap me. If I was a part of the plan, why did he punish me? This doesn't make sense... And Rudolph...*

He remembered the talk he eavesdropped with great detail. *'Please, hand him over to me. With his body, he will be admired. And when he is worn out, I'll make sure he is gotten rid of quietly. You will not have any trouble.'* How persuasive Rudolph had been. Back then, Kuon believed him. *And here I wondered why he is so concerned about me. He just wanted Gray's money...*

And Yugo... He just wanted a toy to play with and break.

"Out..." he said.

"Kuon..." Gray's voice changed again, and Kuon wondered what kind of expression he wore right now because he heard fear in it.

"I don't want to see you ever again, Gray. I mean it. We're done."

I'm stupid for thinking that we could be a family again. Gray never respected things that were important to me. He only knows how to order me around, and how to make me feel useless, miserable. As if I don't have enough of it already...

"Don't overreact."

"Leave."

"Fine, I'll go. Don't be mad. I'll drop by next week."

After Gray left, it took Kuon about half an hour to calm down. When his fingers stopped trembling with rage, he picked up the phone and dialed Rick. Signal after signal, slashing through the air weakened his determination. Ready to hang up he found the 'cancel' button when Rick finally picked up the phone.

"Kuon? Ughm, what time is it?" His voice sounded groggy as if he'd just woken up, and guilt panged in Kuon's chest.

"Sorry, I didn't think. I'll call you later."

"No, wait. I'm awake now. Are you okay?"

"I am...?" Failing to convince himself, Kuon winced.

"It's three AM. Why aren't you sleeping? What happened?"

"Nothing much, but... Rick, I want to ask for a favor." Sighing, Kuon hesitated. Asking for a favour, even a small one, was harder than he imagined.

SITTING IN THE DARK, RICK KEPT STARING at the dead screen, fully awake. Kuon had sounded odd, disturbed, and every cell in Rick's body wanted, needed, to make sure he was fine, but it was too early to go to the airport. *Wasn't he with Gray? What on earth happened?*

Finding no answer, he unlocked the screen and found Gray's number. Still using the flat the man provided, Rick couldn't help feeling obligated toward him. Filling his lungs with air, he dialed. After a moment, the husky voice said, "Yes?"

"Kuon called. He's coming to Vienna," Rick said.

"Shit..." Gray cursed. Something rustled in the background before he cleared his throat. "Okay, listen to me, Richard. Kuon is pissed right now. Go pick him up, and don't let him leave your place. Eventually, he'll cool down, and I'll take him back. Until then, take care of him and keep me updated. I'll make sure your expenses are covered. And remember, no matter what he says, don't let him leave."

Gray hung up, but Rick kept staring at the screen, feeling slightly happy at the idea that Kuon would stay at his place, even if not for long.

THE ANNOYING RINGTONE PULLED Yugo out of his sleep. Weak light broke through the curtains, and he assumed it was still early morning. Having gone to bed after four AM, he didn't feel rested. Blowing out a gust of air, he picked up his cell phone and glanced at the screen.

'TOBIAS'.

He blinked into the darkness, collecting his thoughts, then accepted the call. "What?"

"I'm going to Kabul. Do you want souvenirs?"

Yugo wondered how Tobias always managed to annoy him with a single phrase. "Are you calling just to say this? I'm hanging up."

"Not only." Tobias snorted, sounding awake and in a good mood for such an early hour. "I'm taking the little shit with me. Thought you would want to know."

"Isn't it too early to take him to Ahmad? He already ruined your flat. Do you want him to ruin your deal?"

"Oh, I'm not taking him to Ahmad. I'm just going to show him around. Let's say to learn the business. How things… grow?"

"Don't get him killed. Is that all?"

"Yep." Mischief made its way into Tobias' voice, sparking alertness in Yugo's mind. "Oh, by the way, your puppy is back. He looks rather lost. Oh, wait… I'm wrong. Someone just found him."

"What?" Yugo sat up wide-awake, but Tobias had already hung up.

THE FLIGHT LEFT KUON with a shitty feeling of hopeless doom. Like an inanimate object, he was transferred from the hands of a taxi driver to the hands of airport personnel, then to a flight assistant and back to the airport personnel. Tensed and stressed, he had regretted his decision more than once, but he never turned back. Only when his back rested against the car seat and Rick drove away from the overwhelming airport noise, did he finally relax.

"Would you tell me what's going on? You call in the middle of the night, take the first flight, and arrive alone without any luggage. If you keep silent, my imagination will run wild." Rick said, trying to keep his voice up, cheerful, but Kuon knew him for too long to miss the concern.

"Sorry..." Kuon's weak reply drowned in the buzzing of the road. On his way to Vienna, he intended to ask for Rick's help. To freeload at his place for a couple of weeks until he found a small apartment to live in, but now Gray's words haunted him. A burden, a liability. He finally understood what Gray meant. Within those long seven months, constantly lonely, Kuon had never been alone. The nurses, the guards, then Gray and doctors, rehab workers. He never needed to cook, wash his clothes, or go grocery shopping. Everything had been delivered to his suite, ready to use. Suffocating in his shrunken, limited world, he never noticed those small things other people did for him. Now he faced the truth—he couldn't even use the bathroom on the plane without help. "It's nothing. I don't want to bother you. If you could just drop me to the nearest hotel, that would be..."

"You don't have to talk to me if you don't want to, but I won't leave you alone in a hotel. You'll stay at my place. It's big enough for two, and I have an extra bedroom no one ever used. It's not debatable."

"I don't' think it's a good idea..." Kuon sighed.

"Let me decide on that, okay?"

Kuon smirked, shaking his head. Rick had always been stubborn. Maybe that's why they eventually grew close. "Fine, but we are splitting the rent and bills."

HAPPINESS EXPANDED IN RICK'S CHEST, depriving him of oxygen. He couldn't remember being this happy in a long time. Even now, looking at the white bandages covering Kuon's eyes, new hope bloomed in his soul.

"Come on in," he breathed, leading Kuon by the hand into the vast apartment. He'd grown used to this place over the last few months and now was delighted that they would both call it home.

"Wanna know what our home looks like?" he said, nudging Kuon with his elbow. "Shall I be your guide?"

Kuon smiled, and Rick gave himself a mental high five.

"Then let me begin." He slid his thumb over Kuon's prominent knuckles. Giddy from touching Kuon's hand, he wondered how it would feel to tug him closer and merge their lips together. Swallowing the powerful impulse, he sidestepped and pressed Kuon's palm against the wall. "The walls are plain ivory, but the floor is polished walnut—so dark, it's almost black, except for the reddish hue."

Rick wanted to add 'just like your eyes,' but didn't. Kuon made a small step forward, and Rick's heart leaped to his throat. The faint smell of shower gel washed over him, messing with his mind. All his being screamed for him to lean closer and claim Kuon's lips with his. To stop the loss of control, he diverted his eyes.

"If you make five steps along this wall, you'll find a small padded stool. Wanna try finding it?"

"Sure...?" Kuon's voice lacked confidence, but his smile didn't vanish.

The feeling of loss hit Rick the same instant he released Kuon's hand. Stepping back, he froze, watching the younger man take a few uncertain steps. Kuon's knee hit the padded seat. He halted, then bent forward. His black shirt slipping up, revealed a stripe of skin on his lower back as Kuon explored the soft surface with both hands.

"What color is it?"

"Coffee..." Rick croaked and shook his head, trying to clear his mind. "If you go further, there is a sliding-door closet. Follow it, and in six steps you will end up in the living area."

Straightening up, Kuon slapped the mirrored door with his palm, leaving a few barely visible handprints behind. When he reached the end of the closet, Rick approached. Wrapping his fingers around Kuon's forearm, he waited for Kuon to get used to his touch.

"I moved the furniture to the walls, so it's easier for you to navigate and you don't bump into things. Except for the sofa, that's in the middle of the room, in front of the TV." Rick swallowed, unable to tear his gaze away from Kuon's chapped lips. Now, when Kuon couldn't see his face, there was no reason to seal his feelings behind friendly smiles and concealed glances. Kuon had already rejected him many months ago, but that didn't ruin their friendship, nor his hope that one day they'd become something more to each other.

"Rick, listen..." Kuon's low, barely audible voice broke the brief pause. "Are you sure this is a good idea? You know, you don't have to feel bad or obligated. I don't want to be a burden. I can manage."

Kuon dropped his chin and scratched his temple in a childish gesture.

I'm so fucked... Unable to control himself, Rick leaned forward but froze; his mouth an inch away from the side of Kuon's face. Kuon moved, and his warm breath brushed against Rick's lips. Squeezing his eyes, Rick steeled himself. His heart drummed so loud, he was sure Kuon heard it too.

"Just rely on me a little, would you?" he whispered, and Kuon tensed.

"Rick, you're too close." A heavy sigh, brushing against Rick's lips, worked like a slap. Dropping his hands, he pulled back. He knew what Kuon wanted to say. There would be an abrupt speech filled with stretched vowels, unfinished lines, and long pauses, then awkward silence and avoidance. They had been there before.

"Sorry." His voice—too low, too muffled—sounded unfamiliar to his own ears. "I didn't think."

"I..."

"I'm hungry. How about some steaks?" Rick prompted to change the subject. A weird expression crossed Kuon's face, but he nodded, and the tense line of his powerful shoulders relaxed.

If this continues, I'll have a heart attack before I'm thirty. Letting out a sigh, Rick pressed his palm to his aching chest where his heart slammed against his ribs.

CHAPTER 5

ONE WEEK LATER

The sun warmed Kuon's cheek and the plastic under his hand as he sat in the hospital waiting room. The bustling noise suffused the air, filled with the ringing laughter of romping children. His ass numbed from the long wait and the hard, uncomfortable plastic seat. The same numbness crept into his mind, diluted with the shreds of unintelligible child babbling and boring political talks of grownups.

Wandering somewhere in the depth of his thoughts, he listened for a little boy's mumbles as he swallowed word endings and stuttered now and then. He recounted to his mother how the other day his friend Frederic and the neighbor's cat, Wiener, had played Godzilla with sand buildings. Wiener, of course, had the best role and ruined the whole city. Fighting the smile, Kuon tilted his head to the side.

A cool hand cupped his cheek, caressing his skin with slow, circular motions. A gentle thumb brushed over his lips, outlined his chin. Kuon instinctively shrunk back. The hand twitched and disappeared, leaving behind the mixed scent of spicy fragrance and bitter tobacco.

BA-DUMP. Kuon's heart slammed against his ribs, then tripled its rate. He rushed to his feet and turned to the direction where he thought another person stood and stretched out his hand. His fingers wide apart, he chased after the slipping mirage. Inching forward, he swung his hand in the air but caught nothing.

"What are you doing?" The low voice that sounded like a breaking crust of bread reached his ears, followed by the deep throaty laughter, then a wide palm landed on his shoulder. The clean scent of mandarin and lavender washed over Kuon. "Catching a fly?"

This time the voice came from above, and Kuon instinctively lifted his face. He could feel the warmth coming from Rick's body with his skin. *Too close.* Subduing the first urge to step back, Kuon shrugged.

"Nothing… It must be my imagination. It's not possible," he mumbled, touching his cheek. "I guess I'm just nervous."

"Come on, the doc is waiting for you. Take my hand and be careful; the staircase is coming. Unless you want me to get a wheelchair?"

Kuon shook his head, hating the idea. When a huge palm weaved with his, the immense warmth coming from Rick engulfed Kuon, suffocating him. Pushing through the need to snatch his hand away, he clenched his teeth and leaned closer to Rick's shoulder so he could feel the balance of his body and orient better.

"Watch out, there're three steps down."

THE WORLD CRASHED IN FRONT of Yugo's eyes as he watched the man he didn't know leading Kuon down the corridor. He couldn't bring himself to blink, and soon his eyes burned from the dry air. Even when Kuon's frame disappeared on the lower level, he kept staring unable to look away.

"What happened to his eyes?" Yugo whispered and dropped his focus to his fingers, where the warmth of Kuon's skin still lingered.

Greg didn't reply, but Yugo felt his confused gaze at the back of his head.

"What the fuck is wrong with his eyes?" Yugo yelled, spun on his heels, and grabbed his subordinate by the collar of his baggy jacket. The pain and desperation shredded his self-control to pieces.

Greg hung his head, and Yugo released the collar.

"Go and find out who his doctor is. I want to talk to him."

"HE HAS A LIGHTER STAGE of the third-degree ocular burn. His corneas sustained serious thermal damage. Luckily, due to the short impact and the immediate medical attention, his crystalline lens and nerves are fine, and there is no sign of deep necrosis, but he still requires a keratoplasty."

The doctor's calm voice irritated Yugo's every nerve. "A what?"

"A cornea transplantation." The doctor circled the neat mahogany desk and lowered himself in a black office chair. His fingers clasped together as he leaned forward, resting his forearms on the smooth surface of the polished wood. His blue scrubs bulged on his arms with toned muscles. His wrinkled, speckled face was intelligent and lively, his eyes kind but attentive, as the silver on his temples brought him a strong sense of reliability.

"Then what are you waiting for? When will you operate?" Yugo's voice dripped with irritation. The urge to have a smoke ignited his blood, as his neurotic fingers fiddled with an unlit cigarette that exuded the sweet smell of tobacco leaves and vanilla.

"His healing process is going well. There is no inflammation, no necrosis, so we put him on medication and a waiting list. Thousands of people wait for transplantation, you know," the doctor explained. He took off his glasses and rubbed the red prints on the bridge of his nose left by the nose pads.

"How much?" Shaking the unpleasant feeling that bargaining always caused him, Yugo waited for the answer. Money ruled the world. This was the only truth—the truth he knew best. Money never let him down, had never done before, and it was not about to start now.

The doctor chuckled and shook his head. Yugo frowned. He didn't like feeling like an idiot. His hand twitched, then clenched in a fist.

The doctor's expression and his smile turned sympathetic.

"You don't understand, Herr Santell. His insurance can cover the costs, so money isn't a problem."

"Then what the hell is the problem?" Yugo's chest vibrated with annoyance. "Do your fucking job! Restore his vision."

Despite Yugo's tone, the doctor didn't lose his smile. The man put the glasses on. "Let me explain the process. Corneas, like any other organs, come from a donation from a recently deceased individual with no diseases. Organs go to people at the top of the list with the best compatibility. To ensure the highest success rate of the surgery and decrease rejection, we run a series of tests to make sure the HLA-DR and HLA-B genes match." The doctor smiled, his index finger drawing a phantom spiral in the air. "As I have already informed Herr Leiris, transplantation carries certain risks. It doesn't guarantee his vision will be fully restored or that his body wouldn't reject new corneas. But even if the corneas are the perfect match and he is at the top of the list, it's still too early. Only seven months have passed. To perform keratoplasty at least a year needs to pass after the trauma."

Yugo pushed the air through gritted teeth, rose from the chair, and approached the window. The bright sun blessed juicy grass and trees, filling the air with serenity. The pristine blue sky rolled over the horizon, and not a single cloud marred it. For some reason, the view made Yugo feel wrong. He crumpled a cigarette in his fist as a need to splash the blackness of his soul all over the landscape and destroy this beautiful day took over.

"How did this happen?" he twisted his lips, cringing from the weak sound of his voice.

"I don't know the details. All I know is that the thermal damage came from some kind of explosives." The doctor lifted his hands in dismay and granted Yugo with an apologetic smile. "Why don't you ask Herr Leiris about it? I have already overstepped my boundaries here."

As if I can do that... Yugo thought before coming up to the doctor and shaking his hand.

"KUON," RICK CALLED, after hearing his distressed groans, and turned the lights on. Rushing to the bed, he put his knee onto the mattress to scrutinize the distorted, pained features. The bandage was loosened and soaked in sweat, but it didn't fall off Kuon's eyes. "Wake up. It's just a dream."

Kuon's head rolled to the side as another painful moan broke from his pale lips. Brushing the wet hair away from Kuon's forehead, Rick rubbed his cheek.

"Come on, wake up."

"No!" Kuon shouted, jerking upright. Clashing his teeth in the air, he slapped his hands to his face, fumbling about his bandaged eyes. "I can't see."

"It's okay," Rick said, trying to keep his voice as calm as possible and not let the pain seep into his words. Seizing Kuon's forearms, he tore his hands off the bandage. "Don't rub your eyes, okay? It was just a nightmare. You're safe."

"No..." Rivers of sweat cascaded down Kuon's muscular torso. Reaching his trunks, they repainted the waistband into a darker shade of blue. Taking several deep breaths, Kuon pulled his hands out of Rick's grasp and wiped his sweaty forehead. His pulse, beating in the thick vein on his throat, slowed down, as he found the edge of the bed and placed his feet against the floor.

"I'm sorry, I woke you up," Kuon croaked and cleared his throat. Shaking his head, he rubbed his temple with the heel of his palm. Rick had learned this 'tell' of Kuon's confusion and embarrassment long ago. Covering his face with his palms, Kuon pushed another deep breath out and hunched forward.

Not sure what to do, Rick sat by his side, wrapped his arm around Kuon's waist, and tugged him closer until Kuon's forehead bumped against his shoulder.

"You don't have to go through this alone. Seven months aren't nearly enough to get used to constant darkness. Rely on me, talk to me. I'm here." Pulse spiking, Rick froze. When Kuon said nothing, he continued, "I will always be by your side. I can protect you; I can make you happy. Please, let me."

As soon as the words left his mouth, Rick's blood chilled in his veins. The sudden fear of rejection kicked him in his guts, and he glued his gaze to the wall, scared to see the painful twist of Kuon's mouth.

"Don't look down on me because I can't see. I still can kick your ass! I am not weak. I don't need your protection or pity." A hot, wet palm bumped against his chest as Kuon pushed back. Biting his bottom lip and clenching his fists, Kuon got up. "I need to wash my face."

Turning left, then right, Kuon froze, dropped his chin and his shoulders. Defiance trembling in his voice, when he mumbled, "I can't navigate well enough yet. I need your help. Please…"

Rick sighed. It'd been almost two years since he'd met Kuon. During this time, he'd made many wrong assumptions, many mistakes, but he'd learned how to handle Kuon's pride. When Kuon needed space, he stepped back and didn't pressure; when Kuon needed time, Rick tried to be as invisible as possible, leaving the younger man on his own. He understood that robbed of his vision, Kuon would have felt vulnerable as never before. Every time Kuon had to ask for assistance with simple tasks, distress bled through his features.

A few times, Rick watched Kuon struggle with food and tea preparation. He never interrupted. Standing by the wall, he'd never indicated his presence even though he knew it would inevitably result in a disaster and mental breakdown. Still, the fear of wounding Kuon's pride made Rick leave him alone to fight his way out of his emotional anguish. If Kuon knew how many times Rick witnessed his weakness, he would never stay by his side, would never again ask for his help. Rick knew it and therefore kept his mouth shut, allowing Kuon to pretend to be strong and save the remains of his pride.

Standing up, Rick clasped his fingers around Kuon's forearm. Leading the younger man out of the bedroom, where the only furniture was the bed and closet, he turned right and entered the gray-tiled bathroom. Bringing

Kuon to the vanity sink, he placed his palm over the edge.

"Do you want me to stay?" he carefully asked, cautious that his obtrusiveness would make Kuon angry. Especially sensitive and emotional at night, when nightmares took over, Kuon was often sharp and rude with his responses.

"No, I want to be alone," Kuon said, then cleared his throat, rubbing his temple with the heel of his palm. "Thank you."

AS SOON AS THE SOFT CLICK of a closing door reached his ears, Kuon let a breath out. Keeping his temper in check had never been so hard. Every time he failed to do something simple, a suffocating wave of bile rushed up to his throat. Ugly feelings boiled in his chest. He hated letting them out on Rick, but controlling them became harder and harder every day.

This is a bad idea... Living with Rick is a bad idea. His whole essence screamed it. *I'll only hurt him. I can never return his feelings. This is low, unfair, dishonest.*

Rick's guilt was the worst. The heavy, palpable, asphyxiating guilt that hung in the air every time Kuon undid his bandages. He didn't have to wear them anymore, but he couldn't stand the shift in the air every time he removed them.

Kuon's thoughts strayed as he leaned against the cold, tiled wall. He brought his hand to the place where the icy touch of the ghostly hand still lingered on his cheek from last morning. The sweet scent of vanilla and tobacco mixed with the woody fragrance of the spicy cologne was still vivid in his memory.

"I'm going crazy," he whispered. Sliding down to the floor, he tugged his knees to his chest. "I'm fucking hallucinating..."

CHAPTER 6

"**K**uon, let's get a puppy!" Rick could barely contain his excitement as he led Kuon to the bench.

"Isn't it enough that you have to deal with me?" Kuon laughed, showing a row of white teeth, and Rick's heart stopped beating for a second. Kuon barely ever laughed; even his smiles were thin-lipped and strained. Rick tilted his head, drinking in the moment. Now, absorbing the freshness of the spring, Kuon resembled a big dog unleashed after a long imprisonment. His chest rose and fell in deep breaths as his nostrils greedily chased after the flowery fragrance of blooming April.

A riot of colors turned the landscape of the city park into a surreal picture of a fairytale, and Rick's heart soared with guilt. He would have given anything for Kuon to see this rich-green grass and clear blue sky. The sun, so bright that Rick's eyes hurt from looking at the light parts of the discolored gravel covering the park paths. Birds chirped trying to compete with the piercing screams of children, as the whispering wind played with rich foliage and Kuon's dark brown hair.

"We could walk him together. When I'm not home, the puppy would keep you company. We could train him to bring things." Rick dreamed aloud. "Just imagine what you could do with a service dog."

He bit his tongue before he managed to stop himself, but Kuon didn't seem to notice his remark. Throwing his head back, he offered his bandaged face to the midday sultry sunrays. A lazy headshake gave the impression that this unsophisticated move drained him of all strength.

Rick chuckled, relaxing. His gaze slipped over the grass, jumping from one tree to another until it stumbled over a distant figure of a man. With every nerve coming to attention, Rick got up. The tension seized his shoulders as he remembered that he'd seen this man in the park before. He always watched Kuon. Just like now. A thought that Gray had sent him to watch over Kuon melted as his focus sharpened. No bodyguard would look at a client with such a weird expression.

"Kuon, are you thirsty? Or maybe you want an ice cream?" he asked, adding a fair amount of cheerfulness into his voice.

"I'm good." Kuon smiled, catching a brisk wind with his face.

"I'll be right back, okay? I'm thirsty." Unable to resist the urge, he ruffled Kuon's hair before facing the watching man. A white suit hugged the stranger's body as he leaned against the tree, a black shirt contrasting beneath. He stood about a hundred feet away, but there was no mistake—his eyes were fixated on Kuon.

Determination grew in Rick's heart with every step he took. He didn't like the frost in the man's gray eyes, or the unspoken confidence radiating from him. However, the stranger's physique favored Rick, as he stood a half-head taller and a few inches wider. Approaching the stranger, he flexed his shoulders and asked, "What do you want from him? Why are you stalking him?"

The man didn't react, as if he didn't hear the questions. Fetching a cigarette out of his chest pocket, he lit it. His eyelids dropped for a second before he turned to Rick and blew thick smoke into his face.

"That's none of your business." The honeyed, soft baritone rolled out of the thin lips as the stranger spoke.

Rick's chest vibrated with anger. The provocative insult hit his nerves. Any other time, he would hit the bastard, but that would draw Kuon's attention, and, maybe, the police. Fighting in a public place would mean leaving Kuon on his own. Rick couldn't do that. Clenching his fists, he spat the words out, "Everything about him is my business."

He shifted left, shielding Kuon from the man's field of vision with his chest. Satisfaction quickened his blood, as annoyance surfaced on the man's face. The gray eyes looked him up and down with such arrogance as if the stranger was two heads taller. Snorting, the man flicked the half-finished cigarette to Rick's chest, turned around, and strolled toward the parking lot. Blood slammed into Rick's head, he grabbed the man's elbow and forced him one hundred and eighty degrees.

"Don't fucking mess with me. I know your type; I've killed people like you with no regrets. I don't know what brought you here, but don't get close to him ever again."

The man smirked. His manicured fingers pulled a cigarette pack out of his chest pocket. Movements lazy and measured, he lit another cigarette and once again blew smoke into Rick's face.

"WHO THE HELL ARE YOU, DOG?" Yugo peered into the man's features, for the first time examining him. The crew-cut hairstyle screamed of the military; his muscular chest and arms bulged under the plain black t-shirt, and a dog tag hung around his neck. His chiseled jaw and wide cheekbones accented his hollow cheeks and a tall, straight nose that Yugo itched to break.

Yugo had zero intentions of facing Kuon today. As on all the days before, the need to see Kuon's face hit his guts without warning. Every day he kept telling himself that this would be the last time; that he would check up on Kuon and let him go as he'd decided two years ago. Every day he'd been breaking his promises, as whenever the need occurred, he would pick up his phone and give out instructions to track Kuon down.

"That's none of your business. Get lost."

Since the incident at the hospital, Yugo had never approached Kuon. He hadn't planned to resurface in his life, but the words of this arrogant bastard, who stuck to Kuon like a piece of toilet paper, kicked him out of his comfort zone.

Shouldering the man out of his way, Yugo strode toward Kuon, dropping the cigarette in his wake. With every step, his heart beat louder and faster. His mouth dried up, fingertips tingled, and he couldn't tear his gaze away from Kuon's upturned face. He froze in front of the bench, casting a shadow over Kuon's body. For a split second, he hesitated. Needles of doubt, piercing his mind, reanimated the memories of the pier and the black muzzle of the gun. A million 'what ifs' swirled in his head, but a single word, rolling out of Kuon's mouth, erased them all.

"Rick?"

Yugo squatted down. His hand caressed Kuon's face, exploring it. His vision sharpened, increasing the contrast. The roughness of Kuon's lips… the light stubble, scratching his fingertips… the gentle breath, tickling his palm. He squeezed his eyes, trying to control the overpowering mix of desires as his hands shook, fighting the need to slide lower and rip Kuon's clothes apart.

Summoning his will power, he pulled back.

"Y-Yugo?" Blood left Kuon's face.

Yugo's heart stopped beating.

THE BITTER SMELL OF VANILLA AND TOBACCO washed over Kuon as two strong hands wrapped around his torso, tugging him forward into an awkward embrace. Confusion washed over him as his cheek pressed to the padded shoulder of a suit. Thick fabric rubbed his skin, making him frown. Rick didn't wear suits, and it was too hot for one. The painfully-familiar woody and spicy fragrance washed over him, distressing his every cell.

Nooo… This is not happening.

Mouth too dry to swallow, he squeezed his hand between their chests and reached up. Smooth skin greeted his fingertips as he found the sharp edge of a cheekbone. Bringing his other hand to the person's face, he sucked a sharp breath in, trying to subdue the loud drumming of his heart. Hollow cheeks and thin lips… clean-shaven chin. Kuon had to open his mouth to ease his shallow breathing. His head spun as his fingers moved up, tangling in the slick, brushed-back hair.

That wasn't a hallucination. He came to the hospital.

"Yugo?" he mouthed because his voice failed him. Fingers shaking, he had to clench his fists to stop the tremor.

"I hope you aren't dating that gorilla. This will turn bloody otherwise." A low baritone abraded his ear. "I came for you. Come home with me."

No-o-o…

A sharp pain pierced Kuon's head. Pushing Yugo away, he sank his fingers into his hair as memories sledgehammered into his mind. For a moment, he felt like vomiting, but then anger lit up his blood, setting his eyes and chest on fire. For two years, he'd been doing his best to return to normal, to erase Yugo from his memory and dreams.

What for? For a single touch to wipe clean all his attempts to forget the bitter taste of Yugo's burning kisses. Rage bubbled in his throat as the minute of confusion and nostalgia passed. His mind cleared.

"Fucking bastard!" he growled. His hand formed a fist as he threw it forward in a crushing punch.

RICK DIDN'T KNOW WHAT TO DO. Events had escalated so fast that he wasn't sure if he had the right to interfere. He'd wanted to drag the man away from Kuon, but that would bring police attention, as people were already staring. Spending time in jail and dragging Kuon along didn't sound like a good plan. Leaving him in the park with no one around sounded even worse. When Kuon called the man's name, Rick's determination to stop the stranger from touching Kuon melted as confusion took over. The way the man looked at

Kuon didn't seem harmful in any way, so Rick couldn't say what exactly he was witnessing.

Could he be another member of Kuon's family?

When Kuon threw a punch forward, Rick blinked, wondering what was going on. But since Kuon didn't look in danger and the nose of the arrogant bastard burst with blood, he did nothing.

DESPITE THE TIGHT BANDAGE, wrapped around the blind eyes, Kuon's fist didn't miss its mark. The impact shattered Yugo's vision and destroyed his balance. Half-twisting his body, he tried to soften the landing. His elbow, crushing the grass, turned green. A coppery taste filled his mouth, and warmth dripped down his chin. Wiping his nose with his palm, he blinked through the muddy vision. Red drops, slipping through his fingers, splashed against his black shirt.

Wow, such passion... An idiotic smile invaded Yugo's face as he tried to stop the bleeding.

Kuon's lips twitched, as a thick red rushed up his neck, and disappeared under his bandage. Yugo grinned, watching emotions change on Kuon's face, from confusion to anger, and then to something else he couldn't identify. When Kuon rubbed his mouth with his forearm, Yugo said, "Yes. I am here."

A light headshake accompanied a painful twist of the weather-beaten lips before Kuon got to his feet and put his hand forward, stretching his fingers apart. He tilted his head to the side as if trying to navigate using his hearing only, then took a small step. The top of his tennis shoe hit Yugo's thigh. Clenching his fists, Kuon dropped to his knees. Yugo blinked, gawking at the fist rushing down toward him.

Black pain eclipsed the daylight. Yugo swallowed the blood and clung to the dimming white spot somewhere at the edge of his shattered consciousness.

"I hate you, bastard!" Kuon's voice trembled with emotions, and Yugo smiled.

"I know..." he barely managed. The tiny spot zoomed out, morphing into the spiraling sky. He stretched his hands to both sides. Trying to steady his sense of balance, he made no attempts to defend himself. Only now, lying on the grass under Kuon's weight, did he realize how much he'd feared that his appearance would trigger no emotions in Kuon. Now, seeing the storming rage on Kuon's face and hearing the familiar curse, he felt the tension bleeding out of his muscles.

Hope took root in his soul.

RICK'S MOOD DARKENED as he watched Kuon's face flip through emotions. His shoulders hunched forward. They shook as Kuon's fingers grabbed the collar of the man's shirt who sprawled on the ground. Kuon slouched forward until his forehead bumped against the stranger's chest.

Failing to understand the situation, Rick felt helpless. His whole being wanted to drag the man away from Kuon, but the lack of information and the friendzone kept him glued to the spot. Kuon wasn't in any danger, so he didn't have a reason to step in.

"You know?" Unlike Kuon's weak posture, his voice sounded strong, sharp even. It ringed with ice as emotions drained from his face. "You don't know shit, Yugo."

Kuon released the man's jacket and got to his feet, his lips twitching with contempt. The stranger scowled.

"Why did you come? Why now? Haven't you messed with my life enough already?" Chills rushed down Rick's spine as he listened to the emotionless, measured words. Kuon's lips stretched into a thin smile as he spoke in a distant tone he'd never heard before. "Two years have passed. What could you possibly want? Was I that good that you can't forget me?"

Dismal laughter broke out from Kuon's chest. Rick's heart froze.

"The brothels would serve you better than me. Why the fuck did you come?" When Yugo said nothing, Kuon smirked. "Oh, I see. You're bored again. You want a challenge, am I right? Look someplace else."

When the man didn't reply, Kuon yelled, "Why the fuck are you silent now? Say something!"

Rick couldn't bring himself to blink. With every word, the face of the man Kuon called Yugo darkened. The arrogance drained from his features, hardening them with determination. He got to his feet and stretched out his hand, as if wanting to touch Kuon's neck, but froze inches away, the inner fight twitching his facial muscles.

"Come home with me," Yugo said, but Kuon shook his head and lifted his palm in the air. "Kuon…"

"No. What the fuck do you want?"

"You." Kuon didn't react, and Yugo's cheek flinched. His voice quiet but firm when he added, "Return to me. All this time, I kept thinking about you. I can see that you couldn't forget me either. I'm glad because this time I want things to be different."

Yugo didn't ask, but demanded, as if he had the right to do so.

Kuon laughed. His head dropped back as his mouth parted.

"You haven't changed at all," he finally managed, trying to catch his breath.

Hunching forward, he pressed his palms against his knee; his face lost all signs of merriment as sympathy took over. He straightened up and reached forward with both hands in an attempt to touch Yugo's face. The man instantly accepted the gesture.

Rick frowned. He hated the moment of helplessness as he stood and watched Kuon's fingers fumble over Yugo's face.

"You aren't joking, are you? I can't feel a smile." Searching Yugo's face for another moment, Kuon dropped his palms. "You're really something. You know, for a second I felt curious. Only for a second. Go home, or Mio will cry again."

"You don't have to worry about Mio. He is taken care of."

"You miss the point. I don't give a fuck." Despite Kuon's exaggerated lack of care, his lopsided smile kept slipping. "You know, I don't even hate you. But if you keep annoying me, I might remember the things you've done to me. Back then, I didn't know how to kill. Now I do. Don't tempt me."

"I'll do what I want!" The mask of dispassion fell from Yugo's face, and Rick took a warning step forward. The sudden change of dynamic left him glancing between the men. He wanted to interfere, but couldn't decide if it was his place to step in. After all, he didn't know anything about Kuon's past and nothing about Yugo. Kuon hadn't told him about his family, the scars covering his body, or his nightmares. The friend zone he hung in anchored him to the spot and left him with the bitter taste of impotence.

"So you have no emotions for me? Then who the fuck just yelled, 'I hate you'? I believe you still have feelings to spare. Bad or good—I'll take them all. I wanted to leave you alone. I swear, Kuon, I did. I've been watching you for a while, hoping to see that you're happy, but you are not. You aren't happy with me, you aren't happy without me, so why the fuck should I leave you alone? You have nothing to give me? Fine. I have many things I want to give you. I came for you, and you will be mine again, whether you like it or not."

"What will you do, force me again? Go ahead. After all, you always take what you want…" Kuon dropped his chin and shook his head.

"Would it make things easier for you?" The calm, mundane tone Yugo used to pose his question chilled Rick's blood. "I will if that's what you need."

"You haven't changed at all," Kuon smirked; the corners of his mouth dropped. "Goodbye, Yugo. I hope I never see you again."

Kuon's words kicked Rick out of his confusion. He stepped forward, putting himself as a barrier between the two men. "Haven't you heard? Get lost."

"You don't believe me?" Yugo lit up a cigarette, ignoring Rick. "You will, Kuon. As you said, I always get what I want, no matter the cost. And don't forget what I told you. I will be the only man who ever touches you. If you know what's good for you and the people around you, don't ever forget it."

STRUCK WITH THE LIGHTNING of Yugo's words, Kuon stood in the middle of his darkness, listening to the distancing footsteps. Despite Yugo's selfish words, for the first time in two years, he felt warmth streaming through his veins.

He hasn't changed one bit. He thought, as happiness that Yugo still remembered him warmed his insides. *And I am an idiot. Why the fuck does it make me happy?*

"Kuon, who the hell is he?" Rick's words brushed against his cheek as huge palms landed on his shoulder.

Kuon lowered his head, trying to hide his expression. He didn't know what to say, so he just shook his head but the smile refused to leave his lips. "No one…"

"Kuon…" Confusion and pain twisted the sound of his name, as Rick urged him out of the park; at least that was what Kuon assumed.

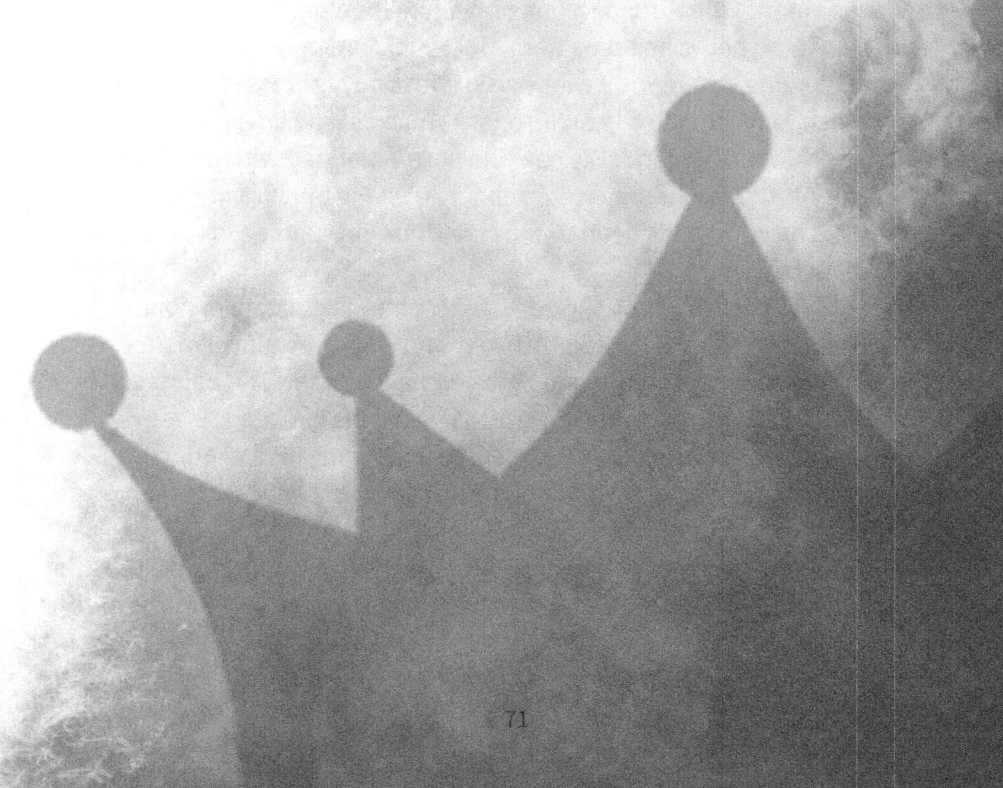

CHAPTER 7

The doctor's office greeted them with a cool blow of the air conditioner, faint medical smells, and resonant sound of their tennis shoes hitting the stone floor. Two padded chairs stood in front of the wide wooden desk. Grabbing the backrest of the nearest one, Rick tugged it closer and put Kuon's palm on top of it.

"Okay?" he asked. Kuon nodded, and Rick slumped on the next seat. Relaxing at first, he straightened up as his eyes met the mocking glance of gray eyes. Angry words rushed out of his lungs before he managed to stop them. "What the hell is he doing here, Doc? Kick him out!"

Lounging on the wide windowsill with one leg crossed over the other, Yugo stretched his thin lips in an arrogant smile as if he knew that the doctor would reject Rick's demand. His coal-black suit blended with his shirt so well that it was hard to say if they were separate. The toe of his shoe drew circles in the air as he cocked his head to the side, triumph sparked in his cold eyes.

"Yugo?"

Rick's cheek flinched when he heard something similar to hope tremble in Kuon's voice. Leaning forward with his whole body, the younger man searched the air with his nose, as if trying to catch a familiar scent. The bandaged head moved left, then right, and a deep vertical line cut his forehead.

"I always get what I want, remember?" Shifting his attention from Rick to Kuon, Yugo looked him up and down with an air of confidence of an owner. The corners of his mouth curled up, softening his expression.

Rick crossed his arms over his chest. The oily glances the man caressed Kuon with, made his blood boil, and he had to subdue the urge to smash Yugo's arrogant face against the windowsill. Wanting to spit out the bitter taste of powerlessness, Rick glanced at Kuon. The straight line of Kuon's back betrayed his tension. At that moment, Rick would have given anything to know what bothered him. For more than a year, he'd tried to get close to Kuon only to realize that he'd never managed to make even a tiny breach in his defenses. Kuon never talked about his life, never shared his feelings. Despite the dozens of questions Rick threw at him the other day, Kuon never replied. Hiding behind tight-lipped smiles, the younger man dodged every one with the same line, 'I don't want to talk about it. It's in the past.'

The doctor cleared his throat, drawing attention and breaking the heavy atmosphere. His face picked up a thoughtful expression.

"Herr Santell is here because he found a donor. Of course, if his presence bothers you, Herr Leiris, he will leave right away." Rick's attention rushed back to his friend; he wanted Kuon to object to Yugo's presence, but a light headshake destroyed his hopes.

"A d-donor?" Kuon stuttered; his neurotic fingers grabbed the hem of his tight khaki t-shirt. "I thought that it's too early for the surgery."

"Yes, indeed. We still have to wait for at least five months before we could proceed with the surgery, but it's always great to secure a donor at such an early stage. It's a brain dead patient, and the family agreed to sign the release. The first results came back positive. You have good compatibility with this donor, and the chances for the corneas to assimilate are solid. The donor will remain in the clinic until the date of the transplantation.

"Meanwhile, I'd like to run more tests and start the scar treatment therapy. Now, let's proceed with the check-up," the doctor finished in a warm, compassionate tone and with an open smile. His knotty fingers picked up an ivory ink pen then scribbled something on paper with wide, loopy handwriting. Putting the pen down, he entwined his fingers in front of himself and looked up, as if waiting for something. The plastic door at the other side of the office swished open, and a young, heavily built nurse, dressed in a blue uniform, entered. She threw a fleeting smile at the men before approaching Kuon. Her hand landed on his forearm, then sneaked under it.

"I'm nurse Schmidt; I'm going to check your vitals, okay? Follow me, please." Her melodic contralto sounded guttural as if it came from the depths of her chest. Kuon got up, wiped his palm against his t-shirt, before making a timid step after her. "Come, come."

Rick didn't blink, watching her lead Kuon to the three-section medical examination table. Adjusting the height, she helped Kuon hop on before reaching up to his eyes.

YUGO'S BREATH CAUGHT as he watched the nurse manipulate Kuon's bandages. Layer by layer, unwrapping, it revealed brownish, uneven skin. His lips pressed together, as his eyes fixed, unable to look away from the ugly burns covering Kuon's eyelids, short lashes, and eyebrows that hadn't fully grown back.

"Please, lie down and open your eyes for me. I'll give you some numbing drops, and then I will take your eye pressure. This time we can't use the 'air puff' test as it's not as accurate."

Kuon tensed. His shoulders dropped as he bit his lower lip, leaned back, and opened his eyes.

Yugo's heart halted, washing him in cold sweat. Bitterness flooded his mouth, making him want to spit. He gulped it down and shook his head, unable to process the blood-curdling image, then dropped his gaze.

Horrible... he thought as his masochistic gaze found its way back to Kuon's upper face. A sharp pain of loss clogged his heart as he watched the opaque milky surface clouding Kuon's, once dark, soulful eyes. The eyes he used to love were now dead, sparkless, empty.

He turned away, unable to look any longer. His lips twitched, fists clenched as he sucked the air through gritted teeth, but his emotions only unraveled further. Without granting Kuon another look, he jumped off the windowsill and left the doctor's office.

KUON'S LIPS TWITCHED as he tried to glue a smile on his face. His eyes burned, blood chilled in his veins stopping his heart and, for a moment, he was grateful for the eye-drops that rolled down his cheeks as they hid his confusion.

The situation dawned upon him. *Yugo left...* The hurried footfalls of the fancy shoes unmistakably belonged to him. When the door slammed, his hand flew up, stopping the nurse's hand in the air. *So what if he left? Why do I care?*

"It has to be done, Herr Leiris. Please, let me." A thin, flowery scent tickled his nose as she freed her hand. Kuon sunk his canine teeth deep in his lip, closing his eyes. Trying to control his emotions, he sucked a breath in and rested his back against the medical table.

Why did he leave? Was he disgusted to the point where he can't even look at me? Kuon tried to force a smile again, but his lips twitched, and the corners turned downwards. *I must look like fucking Freddy Krueger...*

ANGER FILLED RICK'S HEART as he watched Kuon's hands grip the sides of the examining table. The hatred toward Yugo expanded in his chest; taking up all the space, it suffocated him. He'd seen Kuon's face many times. Even though it wasn't glossy-red anymore, he still couldn't get used to the matte whiteness of his eyes and the brownish skin covering his eyelids, but that was a weak excuse for Yugo's behavior.

Fucking asshole! Getting to his feet, he cast a long glance at the white slash of Kuon's mouth. "I'll be right back."

Not waiting for a reply, he stormed out of the room. The blood boiled in his ears, demanding he kill, but as soon as his pupils fixed on Yugo, the urge lessened.

The man stood hunched forward with his elbows pressed against the beige wall, his eyes closed, face pale. Rick squinted.

"I have no idea who the fuck you are, but leave him alone. Last warning." Towering above the man, he added, "He was fine until you came. Now he is a wreck again. I don't care what you want and what kind of past you share. Leave. Him. Alone."

"How did this happen?" Yugo asked as if he hadn't heard a word Rick said. Despite the paleness, his voice came out steady and calm.

Rick scowled, wondering if he should explain anything to this arrogant bastard. There was no reason for him to talk, but the single thought of Yugo going to Kuon for answers settled his mind.

"Afghanistan. Six months after the election of the new president, Baha al Din Salah, and enforcement of his new Anti-Terrorism Reform, the terroristic group Al-Amin seized the school the youngest daughter of the president attended." Rick started, catching himself on a thought that he reported, rather than explained. "Almost three hundred people were taken hostage, but the demands of the terrorists weren't immediately met. On the third day of negotiation, we heard explosions, and soon everything caught on fire. We were thrown into the flames to save the kids who, by that time, due to the dehydration and heat, were barely able to stand. Those bastards were loaded with weapons and explosives. A lot of our people were killed as the rest of the suicide bombers detonated their bombs."

Rick rubbed his eyes with his fingers, as the revived memories drained him of strength.

"One of the buildings collapsed. Kuon, another guy, and I were assigned to seize a side building, which we knew was already empty. It was a poor strategic point and didn't overlook the gym where the kids were held. Kuon ignored the order and rushed to the gym. We had to follow. Our third was killed by a stray bullet."

"Why would they send you to an empty building?" Yugo scowled, and Rick explained.

"The commanding officers didn't like Kuon, but it wasn't only them. Barely anyone would work with him. They didn't want him anywhere close to the epicenter."

"Why?"

"Bad omen. Going on a mission with Kuon was equal to suicide. He often broke orders, which forced soldiers to face a moral dilemma—to break them too or to leave him with no backup."

"Why was such behavior tolerated?"

"No one knows. Anyway, in the fire, we lost sight of Kuon; when found, he had already taken off his gas mask and put it on a kid who couldn't breathe on his own. He handed the child to our third, then rushed back in, using his bandana to protect himself from the smoke. I covered him when we entered the gym. It was already on fire. A lot of ours was there too, getting wounded kids out. But in the mess, we missed that under the dead bodies, someone still lived. I was carrying two kids when Kuon shoved me aside. We tumbled down, and a shock wave hit me as the last explosives detonated. I can't remember much after."

Rick ran a palm over the healed burn on his left arm, ignoring the neurotic fumbling of a man looking for something in his pockets.

"When I came to my senses, Kuon tossed on the floor, pressing his hands to his eyes. He was wounded, and parts of his clothes were burned through, but he managed to extinguish the flames."

The tiny hairs all over his body bristled, as Rick remembered the crimson glossy skin surrounded Kuon's tightly squeezed eyes, the singed eyelashes and brows.

"His eyes were fucked…" Rick gritted his teeth, and the silence flooded his ears. Squatting down, Yugo lit up a cigarette. "So, you see, I'm serious about him, and I have zero intention of giving up. If you got the message, get lost. He deserves to be happy, but people like you don't understand things like this."

Rick peered into Yugo's eyes, expecting a reply.

YUGO BLEW OUT THE SMOKE, trying to calm his nerves. With every word Rick said, the realization of his indirect involvement in the events that left

Kuon blind dawned upon him.

The chain of events, formed in front of his eyes: the trucks, loaded with weapons crossing the desert; men dressed in knee-long, loose tops, and hanging pants, unloading boxes onto the withered ground; young men and women strapping the explosives to their vests. He could see Kuon's life as if he'd been there himself. The dirt and blood, the explosions and swishing bullets; the seizure of the school; Kuon, tossing on the ground covering his eyes with his palms. The more he thought of it, the more he realized how his political games had affected Kuon's life.

The memory of the matte eyes and creased, damaged skin surfaced in front of his eyes. He got up, flicked the cigarette out of the opened window with a shaky hand, then turned to Rick. His mood darkened as he decided what to do next.

"I've already freed him once, thinking it would be best for him. What did he do with his freedom? He went to Afghanistan and got himself blinded. There's no way I'll ever let him go again or hand him over to you." Watching the tanned, masculine face darken with hatred, Yugo kept going, aiming to destroy every hope Rick felt toward Kuon. "Don't be delusional. He'll never love you; he'll never be happy with you because he'll never forget me. I'll forever remain his first and his last man. So, go home, dog; he no longer requires your services."

Shoving Rick out of his way with his shoulder, Yugo strolled toward the doctor's office. His palm grabbed the door handle at the same moment iron fingers wrapped around his biceps and flipped him around.

Instincts kicking in, Yugo shifted right, avoiding the crushing fist aimed at his spleen. Back against the door, he bombarded Rick with a hail of fast short jabs to his torso, trying to win some space and deliver a knee-strike. His knuckles burned as he managed to side-step and finish the combo with a powerful kick to the middle of Rick's chest, throwing the bigger man to the opposite wall.

Despite the effort Yugo put into his attack, his opponent didn't lose his breath. Sliding his palm down his combat pants, Rick hooked his fingers into the top of his military boot. Metal glinting in his hand as he moved in for a counterattack.

THE HEAVY THUD FOLLOWED by rustling made Kuon strain his ears. Dropping the bandages on Kuon's knees, the nurse rushed away. He heard a click; hinges screeched as the door flew open. Gripping the edge of the medical table, Kuon hopped off but froze as the sounds of a fight intensified.

"Oh my god, a knife!" a female screamed. Kuon's heart dropped.

"A knife?" he whispered and, feeling his way with an open palm, followed the noise. Another rustle reached him from his left. *The doctor?*

Step, another one, swaying his hand in front of him, he sought the exit when Yugo's low, sinister laughter froze the blood in his veins. Fearing that Yugo might do something to Rick, Kuon rushed forward but stumbled and crashed against someone. A thin flowery scent slammed against his face as he realized this was the nurse. Bypassing her, he pushed her behind himself and into the doctor's office.

"What the hell?" he yelled so hard his throat burned, and the pressure jumped to his eyes. "What do you think you're doing? Get out of here, both of you!"

RICK STUMBLED BACK, flattening himself against the opposite wall. His eyes fixed, staring over Yugo's shoulder. Flicking his knife between his fingers, he tucked it behind his back.

Yugo turned around. Standing in the doorframe, Kuon stared ahead with unseeing eyes. His bandages were off, and the scarred skin only intensified the whiteness of his open eyes. The nurse, standing behind him fumbled over her pockets, then fished out a phone.

"Put the phone away," Yugo said, dropping his voice. Switching his attention to the woman, he invested all the warning he could muster into his glare.

Kuon spun around. "**Schwester** Schmidt," he prompted, draping his arm around her shoulder, "they will leave NOW." Yugo cringed at the accented word. "Let's not bring unnecessary attention to this minor episode. Nothing happened, right?"

Kuon shifted, then turned the nurse toward himself, putting her back to the men. Yugo's aggression, caused by the heavy adrenaline flow, died out as a blinding smile split Kuon's face. Even with the ugly scars and dead eyes, Kuon still attracted him. During the past two years, Yugo had gone through many lovers. All of them were gorgeous, intelligent, almost perfect. Still, none of them managed to pique his interest enough to linger in his life. Only now, when every cell of his body demanded he get closer to Kuon, did he realize how painfully-insufferable a distance of a few feet could be. Watching the familiar tilt of Kuon's head and the fluid movements of his shoulders, Yugo remembered to the smallest detail every night they had spent together.

With a slight shake of her blonde head, the nurse heaved a sigh, "Of course. Please, don't worry, Herr Leiris."

MINE. MINE. MINE. Yugo's heart demanded he take and possess what belonged to him by the right of the strongest. Unable to resist the gravity pull, he stepped forward but halted when Kuon's tired voice cut the air. "Yugo, don't come anymore."

Yugo's teeth crackled as the rejection hit hard. Anger, waking up, fired his chest but he clenched his fists, choking his wounded pride.

The doctor, who stood behind Kuon, pierced Yugo with a warning glare but didn't voice his dissatisfaction. Conveying his disapproval with a headshake, he retreated into his office.

With his arm still draped around the wide shoulder of **Schwester** Schmidt, Kuon added, "Rick, you leave, too. I'll catch a taxi when I'm done."

The closing door shut Yugo off from Kuon's world. Conflicted, cut out, he felt weird. A part of him understood that Kuon was angry, so he didn't want to irritate him even more. But no one has ever told him what to do. He stepped toward the doctor's office, intending to enter and reclaim his right to do as he pleased, when Rick grumbled out, "He told you to leave. If you go in there now, they will call security, and we'll both be blacklisted."

"Get lost, dog," Yugo said, but instead of leaving, Rick flexed his shoulders and moved forward.

Annoying... Yugo thought. Mentally preparing for the fight, he wondered if he should shrug off the jacket, as it restricted his movements. He spun on his heels the same moment the door flew open, and **Schwester** Schmidt secured it with a stopper. Granting both men with a cautious glance, she returned to the doctor's office. When she reappeared, she pushed a wheelchair in front of her. Fresh bandages wrapped around his eyes, Kuon tilted his head, hands gripping the armrests. Face etching with concentration, he tilted his head as if trying to feel their presence. Never acknowledging the two men, the nurse rolled the wheelchair down the corridor, then turned the corner taking Kuon away with her.

The loss hit harder than rejection. For some reason, Yugo wasn't ready to let Kuon go. The need to mark his territory corroded his blood. Without sparing Rick a glance, he moved after the nurse.

Taking the turn, Yugo smirked, watching the woman hurry into the elevator. Her palm slapped the button a few times. She swallowed and clutched the handle grips, knuckles bleaching white. The doors started to close when Yugo slammed his fist against the elevator 'call' button.

"Don't be so tense, **Schwester** Schmidt, I don't bite," he said, entering.

Suppressing a smile, he turned toward the elevator panel, pressed the 'door close' button, when Rick stormed into the cabin. "We're all civilized people, aren't we? The third floor?"

Kuon's mouth opened, as if he wanted to say something, but closed the next moment.

"Yes," she said in a tiny voice, then cleared her throat.

Yugo hummed, turned around, and leaned against the cold wall. His attention automatically fixed on Kuon, studying the small changes in his appearance. He'd matured. His jawline had sharpened as stubble speckled his cheeks and chin. Yugo's gaze moved lower, scrutinizing Kuon's ripped chest and shoulders hugged by a tight military t-shirt. The itch to remove his clothes and examine every little change in his body settled in Yugo's fingertips.

A tiny **DING** notified them of their arrival. The elevator stopped, and the door swished open. Stepping aside, Yugo let the nurse roll the wheelchair out of the elevator and down the corridor.

"Would you mind giving us a minute?" Twisting his neck, Kuon faced the nurse and hit her with another blinding smile. Yugo hated it. Painfully fake, it looked so unnatural as if made of sharp glass.

"I'm not sure it's a good idea, Herr Leiris."

"It'll be fine, I promise."

"Fine… You have fifteen minutes. If they don't leave after, I will call the police." She rolled the chair to the window that overlooked the small park. "You aren't allowed to move without the wheelchair and supervision, Herr Leiris. If you need anything, please call. I'll be around."

The nurse gave a glare to Rick and Yugo before leaving.

AS SOON AS THE FOOTFALLS died out, Kuon's shoulders slumped. Anger bubbled in his throat, shuffling his thoughts. In a habitual movement, he palmed his eyes, fingers brushing against the rough bandage. So familiar, yet so alien, he wanted to tear it off his face, but the feel of the tender, uneven skin around his eyes was even worse.

"What do you think you are doing?" His blood seethed with rage as his voice came out low and menacing. When no one answered him, he lost his temper. "I asked, what the fuck was that? Do you even understand where you are? It's a fucking hospital!"

His voice bordering on a yell. Running his fingers through his hair, he tried to control himself, then the realization hit him.

"You know what?" He couldn't suppress a thin, evil smile. "On the other thought, be my guests. Why don't you kill each other right now? The morgue is nearby; you will save the paramedics from racing to the scene."

WATCHING KUON'S SPIRIT breaking through the emotionless shell, a weird satisfaction filling Yugo's chest. The same as two years ago, the need to stir Kuon's reactions possessed him. The same delight tingled under his skin, as he noticed a trembling vein on Kuon's neck, and his helpless fingers, clenching and unclenching as if this simple movement helped Kuon to contain his anger. Yugo basked in delight, knowing he was the reason for Kuon's distress. When Kuon crumpled his shirt, the urge to get closer and grab his hand overwhelmed him. The desire to muffle his fast and torn speech with a kiss and feel Kuon's angry words vibrate against his tongue messed with his mind. He wanted, needed, to be the only person on Earth who could stir Kuon's emotions.

"Sorry..." Rick offered.

Yugo flinched. He'd forgotten about the man's presence.

Rick approached the wheelchair, squatted in front of Kuon. His fingers covered Kuon's palm. Yugo wanted to pull a gun and shoot the bastard, who dared to touch what belonged to him. The screeching sound of his gritted teeth filled his ears as Kuon didn't immediately pull back. His blood boiled, chest tightened, and his pride bled out with darkness. He wanted to step forward and break Kuon's arm, so it would never again touch anyone else, but him.

Yugo shifted his attention to Rick. His dropped gaze and flushing cheeks and ears gave him an apologetic look, but Yugo remembered the direct, warning gaze of his black, piercing eyes. *Annoying...*

"You should both leave," Kuon said, folding his arms over his chest. "If you don't, I will be the one calling the police."

"Kuon!" Rick's voice brimmed with pitiful, pleading notes. His fingers twitched when he raised his hand, wanting to touch Kuon's face, but dropped it.

Pathetic... Yugo smirked.

Turning his face toward Rick, Kuon kept going, "I don't need your help, your pity, or your so-called protection. What I needed was your support, but you're unable to give it to me."

Stretching out his hand, Kuon froze with his palm up. "The knife."

"Kuon, don't be silly..." Rick tried to reason.

"The knife. Now!" Kuon repeated; the sides of his face sharpened with tension.

Yugo's smile widened, as Rick fished the knife from behind his back and placed it on Kuon's palm. Putting it aside, Kuon outstretched his hand again.

"Yugo, your gun."

"Phht…" Yugo couldn't help snorting. "Forget about it."

"Fine, but the next time I see you, I'll get a restraining order."

"It won't hold," Yugo laughed.

"I'll make sure it will."

Yugo's shoulders tensed, as he wondered if Kuon was bluffing. Either way, testing Kuon's limits wasn't a part of his plan. Not yet, anyway.

"Fine." Squinting, he stepped forward, pulled out his gun, and unloaded it before placing it on Kuon's palm. His fingers lingered over Kuon's for a long second, before retreating.

"Now, get out. Both of you," Kuon said in an uncompromising voice. "I don't want to see you here anymore."

Watching the floor, Rick shifted from leg to leg, rubbed the back of his head with his palm, then shuffled away. Right before leaving he paused and granted Kuon with a long, pleading look. "I'll wait outside. Please call me when you're done."

For a long second, Yugo considered if he should respect Kuon's wish and let him win this time, but it was impossible. He'd stayed away for two years; he couldn't tolerate another day. Cutting the distance, he caressed Kuon's cheek with his fingers but dropped his hand before the younger man could slap it away.

"I'll see you tomorrow," Yugo promised.

Kuon huffed but didn't say anything else.

Fuck my life, so freaking cute… Yugo tugged a pack of cigarettes out of his chest pocket while strolling to the elevator.

"You won't see him tomorrow, no matter what," Rick warned, tagging along.

Twizzling the unlit cigarette between his index and middle fingers, Yugo lifted a brow. Upon reaching the elevator, he granted Rick a long considering look. "Listen up, dog, crawl into the darkest hole you can find and don't reflect the light. My kindness isn't limitless. The only reason you're still breathing is that Kuon most likely won't forgive me if I kill you. You see, I'm trying hard to play nice." Yugo smiled, shrugging. "But don't mistake my kindness for weakness. Don't tempt me. I'd rather Kuon think that he has a choice. Keep irritating me, and I might lose my temper. Kuon might disappear in the middle of the day, and so many bad things can happen to you. Let's say, you fall from the stairs and break a leg or maybe your spine. Life is so unpredictable."

Yugo turned and pressed the call button. Rick took the stairs.

WEAKNESS CREPT INTO Kuon's heart as silence thickened. A tiny regret for chasing Rick away twitched in his chest. He hated being alone. Robbed of his vision, he felt as if he'd been thrown back into that white, empty room, except everything was black now. Despite that, he wasn't in a hurry to call for the nurse.

Why did Yugo come? The thought wormed its way into his mind. *What does he want now?*

Shallow memories surfaced in front of his eyes. The memories he wasn't sure he remembered anymore. The warmth of Yugo's body… the caresses of his hands… the bitter-sweet taste of his kisses. Kuon shook his head, trying to get rid of the weird longing for something that was never real.

Shaking his head, he called, "Nurse!"

CHAPTER 8

Slamming the rear passenger door closed, Yugo propped his elbow against the window and rested his chin on his fist. The casual touch, when Rick covered Kuon's fingers with his, painted his world red. The more Yugo thought about it, the more he wanted to break every bone in the man's body.

Kuon didn't pull back... This thought irritated him even more when Yugo realized that if he did the same, Kuon would shake off his touch the next instant.

"I want to know more about this Rick," he ordered, throwing a glance up to the rearview mirror. Greg's reflection gave a short nod, but the deep-seated eyes remained locked with his for a long moment, so Yugo asked, "What?"

"Why not just kill him?" Greg shrugged, starting the engine.

"Are you an idiot? What do you think I'm trying to do here? If I kill him, Kuon would instantly connect the dots. And then what? If I wanted to force him, I would have done it already. He is blind. Keeping him in check would be easy now..." The fleeting memory of dark eyes and cheeky smile surfaced and diffused in front of his eyes. "No, killing him won't solve my problem. I want Kuon to choose me, to want me. If he doesn't, then... then I will consider my options."

"**THIS IS WHERE YOU LIVE, HUH?**" Yugo said, entering Rick's apartment the next day. The cheap, plain décor didn't catch his attention, but Kuon's scowl did. "What's with this face? Didn't I say I'll come?"

"Yeah, and I told you not to bother." Kuon slammed the door closed after him. "What do you want?"

"My gun, for starters, and coffee would be nice."

"Then make it yourself," Kuon muttered, inching his way to the living room. Reaching the sofa, he perched on the armrest and folded his arms over his chest.

Yugo didn't move while examining Kuon's expression with excessive attention. His sharp replies and defensive posture resembled a cornered animal. Yugo wondered if Kuon was scared because there was no one to protect him. Rick had left thirty minutes ago, and Yugo didn't expect him anytime soon as the 'tail' he put on the man never called back. Was Kuon worried that he couldn't fight back blind?

Approaching the kitchen counter, he made sure to make as much noise as possible, so Kuon would always know his location. His brain worked on full capacity, choosing strategy and behavior. Breaking a beast was easy, but what about gaining his trust and acceptance? *Should I tame him? Slowly, inevitably?*

Yugo smiled, deciding on the tactic. Kuon tensed as he approached. His hands dropped to his knees in stone hard fists.

"You don't have to be so defensive," Yugo said, gliding the nail of his index finger down Kuon's cheek. "I won't do anything."

Kuon lifted his chin in a defiant gesture that also broke the skin contact. His Adam's apple worked, but no words left his mouth.

"Fine... I'll see you tomorrow." Yugo didn't want to leave. It felt like a defeat, but somewhere deep down he knew that short, unobtrusive visits would bring more results than long, pushy ones. Making Kuon used to him, look forward to his short visits might work just fine to remind Kuon who he belonged to.

On his way to the door, Yugo grabbed the spare keys from the small stand that stood by the door.

THE CALENDAR EXHALED DAYS, flipping by. Kuon felt the change with his skin, with his ears, with his heart. In an attempt to familiarize himself with his surroundings, he'd knocked into the furniture so many times that his toes swelled. Concerned, Rick had suggested that he wear tennis shoes around the apartment. Hearing the apprehension in his friend's voice, Kuon once again realized how much he had changed and how every little thing riled him up now. Trying to be grateful, he'd nodded, and wore his tennis shoes all the time. Soon enough, he could navigate through the rooms without bumping into furniture.

During that time, Kuon barely left the apartment. Busy with his work on a construction site, Rick had been constantly out. Loneliness, darkness, and the up-to-the-maximum-volume TV filled his days. The regret at declining Rick's proposal to get a dog slowly grew. The wet nose of a friendly creature nuzzling his palm would ease his loneliness, or so he thought.

If anyone asked Kuon what day it was, he would shrug, as days merged into dull, gray nothingness, where even scar therapy treatments were an entertainment.

Gray called a few times, but since Kuon never took his calls the attempts eventually stopped. Kuon didn't regret cutting the man off. The word 'liability' still rang in his ears, agitating and unsettling him whenever he remembered it.

Yugo came every day, but kept visits short. If Kuon was in a good mood, he stayed longer, but he never went further than touching Kuon's face, and even then he instantly let go.

Kuon grew used to his visits. He kept his grumpy attitude because he wasn't sure how to behave around Yugo, but he had to admit that he didn't hate his presence. More than that, he looked forward to it, and the low sound of his voice.

The summer filled Kuon's blood with excitement and anxiety. August was approaching—inevitably, irreversibly. And August brewed fear. What if the surgery didn't go well? What if this darkness was permanent? What if he wouldn't be able to see the sun, blue sky, even Yugo's annoying face ever again?

Whenever those thoughts appeared, Kuon chased them away with severe workouts. But that day, his body was stiff, and even a small movement left him with no energy. Lying on the sofa, he clicked through the channels, but the constant adverts, cartoons, and soap operas turned his brain to mush.

Getting up, he turned off the TV and shuffled to the kitchen counter. Fingers found the edge, slid over the cool, stone-like surface before grabbing the kettle. With a habitual movement, he pressed the button. The kettle click reminded him of a gun being cocked. His mind trailed to sleepless nights he'd spent under the unfamiliar starry sky. Bullets hitting the ground fed him with dust. The heavy odor of camel dung in the air had been as intense as the gagging stench of human urine. Painful moans of wounded people grew so familiar, they didn't bother him anymore, becoming a constant accompaniment of the death march of pattering bullets. In the sleepless nights, fear ghosted through the trenches. It made the smell unbearable. Someone cried, someone prayed. Kuon had stared at the sky, looking for familiar stars.

The water boiling pulled him out of his lethargy. He reached up and grabbed the nearest mug from the shelf, then placed it on the counter. Finding the can of instant coffee and a spoon, he poured some powder into the mug. Concentration seizing his chest, he kept his hand over the rim, grabbed the kettle, and placed the spout on the rim, close to his fingers, before he tilted it. The sound of running water reached his ears. Kuon breathed out, listening for the change in tone that indicated the mug had filled.

SHRIIIILLLLL! The chime of the doorbell demolished his focus, and his hand caught on fire. The mug slipped from his fingers and crashed against the floor, splashing hot water all over his naked legs.

"Damn it!" he cursed, as the sharp pain inflamed his skin. Heart slamming against his ribcage, he jumped back, and more water splashed around. Panic flared. His foot slipped on the wet floor when he tried to return the kettle on the counter. The shrill repeated, syringing anger into his system. His hand jerked, and he hit something with the kettle. Another smash shredded his nerves, and something powdery stuck to his burned leg.

"Fuck!" Rage and helplessness flooding his system, he pushed the air out of his lungs when the sound of the doorbell repeated. It maddened him. The inability to complete a simple task poisoned his blood, making him feel impotent, powerless.

Throwing the kettle to the counter, he propped his arms against the wet surface, breathing in and out. Trying to calm down, he searched his mind for where Rick kept a broom but found nothing. For some reason, he couldn't let the mess be. Ignoring and walking away from it would mean a defeat. It would also mean that Gray had been right, and Kuon was a liability to everyone. There was no way he would prove Gray right.

If I can't even make coffee, what am I good for?

Ignoring the annoying repetitive chime that drilled through his skull, Kuon squatted down. Pressing the edge of his palm against the floor, he inched it to the epicenter of the disaster, scooping the muddy water and the shards of the smashed mug. When the chimes stopped, Kuon let out another calming breath, but his phone started ringing instead. Jerking from the sound, sharp pain stabbed through the heel of his palm.

The last dam that repressed his electrified emotions broke, flooding his being with black fury. Growling with desperation, he slammed his fist against the cupboard, succumbing to the aggressive outburst. Adrenaline high in his blood, he didn't feel any pain, just the impact radiating to his elbow.

WHEN KUON DIDN'T OPEN THE DOOR and ignored his call, Yugo felt a pang of alertness in his chest. Fishing the copy of the keys he'd made from the ones he'd borrowed from Rick's apartment, he opened the door, only to be greeted with loud breaking sounds. Darting to the kitchen, he froze.

Water, shards of glass, and coffee powder littered the floor. Rage bared Kuon's teeth. He stormed through the kitchen, knocking objects off the counter—the kettle, then a microwave. His blind hand found a cupboard door, and he tried to break it from its hinges. His skin was mottled, t-shirt and shorts soaking wet, and his hands bleeding. Without thinking, Yugo grabbed Kuon from behind, but a rear elbow strike to his cheekbone caught him off guard and loosened his hold.

"Stop it!" Yugo growled, flinching back. Kuon spun; his teeth glinted with spite. Wordlessly, he moved toward the intruder, shoulders flexing with every step, then a hail of blows pounced upon Yugo. "Enough!"

"How did you get in?" Kuon growled, his voice so hoarse, it was barely recognizable. "Get out!"

Blocking the blind strikes, Yugo stepped back.

"Kuon, stop it. I'm not going to fight you," he tried to reason—in vain.

"How the fuck did you get in?"

Step by step, Yugo retreated under the inexhaustible volley of short jabs, until his shoulderblades bumped against the wall.

"Would you stop?" he groaned, losing his patience. He ducked under Kuon's arm, and spinning the younger man around, shoved his back to the wall. Fingers clasping around the wrists, he pinned them above Kuon's head. His knee spread Kuon's thighs as he pressed himself against his chest to prevent any attempts at resistance.

His heart drummed, matching the fast pulse on Kuon's throat. The heat Kuon's solid frame exuded seared Yugo's skin. The proximity messed with his head. He ogled the body in front of him, drinking in the trickles of sweat that skidded down the sides of Kuon's throat. His harsh, heavy breathing rocketed back and forth from his gaping mouth.

This is a bad idea... Yugo thought, wanting to taste the saltiness of Kuon's upper lip. He wondered if Kuon's kisses were the same as he remembered, rough yet questioning, uncertain. *This is such a bad idea.*

Despite the thought, he leaned forward and sealed the angry mouth with a kiss.

A surprised gasp accompanied the raged grimace as sharp teeth sunk into Yugo's bottom lip. Despite the pain, Yugo leaned into the kiss. Sinking his fingers into the tender places of Kuon's inner wrists, he listened for the maddening thuds of his pulse. His bottom lip broke under Kuon's teeth, and blood trickled down his chin. Swallowing the metallic taste, he made a timid attempt to deepen the kiss. Sharp, angry huffs tickled his tongue. Kuon's body jerked once, then again, and a shudder ran through his body, changing the dynamic. With the same passion Kuon had attacked a moment ago, he kissed him back.

A bloody tongue ran over Yugo's bottom lip; Kuon leaned forward, freeing his hands. Teeth clashing, he yanked Yugo's jacket off.

Light and darkness shuffling suffused everything with a haze of lust. Yugo sunk his palms under the waistband of Kuon's shorts, found the smooth, hard globes of his ass. Licking and nibbling at Kuon's lips, he peeled the shorts down along with the underwear at the same moment as Kuon's fingers tangled in the front of his shirt. Something hard poked his groin, and Yugo smiled against the kiss.

In the silence filled with panting, Yugo tore the belt out of the loops, unzipped his pants, and freed his heavy dick. His length brushed against Kuon's slick with precum cock. Grabbing Kuon's hand, he wrapped the blind fingers around their dripping desires. Kuon shuddered, and his slack mouth skidded against Yugo's cheek.

"No cumming yet," Yugo warned.

Imprinting Kuon into his skin, he sunk his teeth into the sweat-drenching neck as his fingers slipped into the crack and found Kuon's entrance. With the small, circling motions, he probed the softness of Kuon's anus. His other hand slid down Kuon's thigh toward the knee, before Yugo yanked it up and wrapped it around his hip.

"Hold onto me," he breathed into Kuon's neck.

Dry and hot, Kuon's entrance resisted the intrusion. Tearing his fingers away from Kuon's ass, Yugo licked them wet, before shoving them back into the crack. His head, toes, and fingertips buzzed, as all the blood he possessed concentrated in his groin. The first knuckle thrust its way through the tight ring of Kuon's inner muscles, making the younger man hiss and bite his own lip.

"Shit. So fucking tight..." Yugo hissed. "I won't be able to enter like this. Relax."

Kuon shook his head, blood beading around his canine tooth.

"Can't…"

Yugo gave up. With a flat lick, he collected the ruby drops of Kuon's blood, as his fingers dug deeper into the passage, searching for the prostate. The heat and pulsing of Kuon's insides messed with his self-control, making his every muscle tremble with urgency. Kuon's wet t-shirt impeded his probing. Yanking it up with his free hand, he brought the hem to Kuon's mouth.

"Bite." Kuon did. Yugo wrapped his hand around Kuon's palm. The precum coated his fingers, he increased the rhythm. His thoughts messy, he leaned upon Kuon, imprinting the younger man into the wall. His hips moved in the torn music of their disjointed panting, and soon enough, soft, suppressed groans filled his ears.

"That's it…" Yugo whispered. "Cum for me."

Kuon's fingers sunk under his shirt and clawed at his flank, as he shuddered, teeth unclenched, releasing the hem of the t-shirt. The blindfolded head fell backward, revealing the perfect line of his jaw. Without thinking, Yugo sunk his teeth into the side of Kuon's face as a violent discharge shot through his body.

"HOW DID YOU ENTER?" KUON ASKED, sitting on the cold floor on his bare ass. Still feeling Yugo's finger inside him, he squirmed but didn't get up. His heart drummed but not with anger—with embarrassment. The orgasm had flushed the anxiety and rage out of his system, but as the afterglow dissolved, the ability to think rationally returned.

What have I done? For the first time, he appreciated his blindness because he wasn't sure he would be able to tolerate the glowing triumph in Yugo's eyes he knew was there. *What am I going to do now?*

"I have a key," Yugo said in a neutral voice as if it was something natural.

"Where did you get it?"

"Well, I stole it."

"Now you are a thief?" Kuon knew he should be mad, but he wasn't. At least not at Yugo. His reactions concerned him. He'd tried to forget Yugo for too long to fall into his trap again. *This is so messed up. Why did I do this? Because I'm lonely and haven't had sex in ages?*

Kuon worked his mouth left and right. He had been pent up before, and Gray brought him a prostitute, yet he'd never wanted her. *Why?*

Yugo chuckled and sat by his side, distracting him from his thoughts. His cold fingers found Kuon's hand and turned it palm up. "You're bleeding. And you need a shower. Let me wash you."

"No," the reply left Kuon's lips too fast.

"You don't have to be so shy. There is nothing I haven't seen already."

"I'm not being shy. Yugo, what happened just now was…" He wanted to say a mistake, but his tongue refused to move. "It doesn't mean anything. It changes nothing."

"Okay." A smile sounded in Yugo's voice as the man rested his head on Kuon's shoulder.

"I'm serious. It doesn't mean anything," Kuon repeated, pulling away from him.

"I got it. It means nothing," Yugo echoed in a voice that made it clear the message wasn't delivered. Without the support Kuon's shoulder provided, Yugo's body tilted and his head ended up on Kuon's thighs.

Kuon sighed. Shoving Yugo off himself, he said, "I'm going to shower. Please, leave before I'm out."

SITTING ON THE SOFA WITH FRESH BANDAGES wrapped around his eyes, Kuon exuded the minty smell of shower gel and a murderous aura. His black sweatpants matched his t-shirt, and Yugo caught himself thinking that he already missed his own smell on Kuon's skin. Even if Kuon denied any meaning to the activity, Yugo counted it as a win. At least, he knew Kuon still desired him. With the smile never leaving his face, he secured the bandage at Kuon's wrist.

"What are you still doing here? Didn't I ask you to leave?" Kuon growled.

"Treating your wounds." The sharp words didn't affect Yugo as he rolled the leg of Kuon's sweatpants up, revealing the reddened skin on his shin. Kneeling on the floor in front of the sofa, Yugo grabbed the aloe gel and squeezed some on his palm, before smearing it all over Kuon's leg. "You can thank me later for cleaning the mess you made. By the way, the kettle and microwave are fucked."

"Shit…" Kuon cursed, grimacing.

"Does it happen often?"

Kuon shrugged. Hands stopping, Yugo looked up.

"Kuon, move in with me. I can help you."

"Help me? How?" Kuon got to his feet, anger spotting his face with red. Failing to process the instant change in the attitude, Yugo listened to the rushed tirade. "By fucking me and throwing me away? I want nothing from you! Stop acting all kind! I know the real you. What happened today was a mistake. It means nothing, as it didn't have to be you. It could have been anyone! It was just an impulse, nothing else."

"So you'd spread your legs for anyone? This is what you're saying?" Yugo hissed, getting to his feet. A rush of blood slammed to his head. His hand flew into the air, ready to hit the disrespectful mouth, but he wavered and instead clasped around Kuon's jaw, nails sinking into the hinges. Kuon paled, his fingers caught Yugo's wrist, attempting to break the grip. A venomous knot of emotions stung his organs, and Yugo added, "You're driving me insane. Why do you make me mad all the time? Why do you say things that make me want to hurt you? Do you enjoy testing my limits? Could it really be anyone?"

Silence flooded the room. Kuon's Adam's apple jumped. "Let go…"

"Watch what you say, Kuon. If anyone is fine for you, maybe I shouldn't be so considerate." Yugo released his jaw, then stomped out of the apartment.

SLUMPING BACK TO THE SOFA Kuon sighed, his head spinning from the events.

He was furious. I thought he would hit me. He rubbed his hurting jaw. *Why did he even come? Why did I kiss him, touch him… What an idiot. On top of that, I ruined Rick's kitchen… Fuck.*

Kuon rushed to his feet and probed his way to the kitchen. His palms fumbled over the counter. Everything was clean as if no disaster ever happened; only the broken kettle and microwave gave evidence otherwise.

"How am I going to explain this? Maybe I am a…liability," Kuon breathed into the idle air. "Maybe Gray is right, after all."

CHAPTER 9

Rick never mentioned the broken things. He never asked what happened to Kuon's hands and the kitchen, but the next day, new devices were installed on the kitchen counter, aggravating Kuon's guilt.

Yugo had stopped coming, but every time Kuon had to use the kettle or microwave he couldn't help but remember the searing kisses, the impatient, ardent touches, and his own cruel words that he'd come to regret.

When August came, and with it the date of his pre-surgery check-up, Kuon became sure Yugo would never resurface in his life again, but the thought didn't make him happy.

THE NOISES OF THE ACTIVE HOSPITAL life grew louder with every step of the nurse as they left the elevator. When they passed the crowded waiting room, the echo picked up the footfalls of the nurse again. The wheelchair inclined as they took the left turn and halted.

"I'll be right back, Herr Leiris." A small hand landed on Kuon's shoulder and gave it a reassuring squeeze.

He nodded, listening as the footsteps retreated. The white noise of distant voices lulled Kuon as the morning drowsiness intensified, but the sharp slamming of the door kicked him out of the falling slumber.

"Why are we being pushed back again, Dr. Klor? We have been waiting for over two years. How much longer do we wait? She can't see, do you understand? It's the second time!" The anguish in the woman's voice alerted Kuon. "Do you have kids, Dr. Klor? She's only six. She's scared of the dark! Do you understand what two years in the dark means for a six-year-old? She can't be left alone, even for a moment. Do you understand?"

"Frau Brunner..." The tiredness in the doctor's voice was almost palpable. "I'm sorry. We do what we can here. As I've told you, Nelly is at high risk of transplant rejection. It's better if we wait."

"You just don't want to take responsibility," she prompted.

"Frau Brunner, with every year immunosuppressants and steroids develop and become more effective. She will have a better chance of successful corneal engraftment if we wait. Even with the most effective anti-inflammatory preparation, I can't estimate her chances higher than fifty-three percent. Your insurance company refuses to approve the transplantation until she has at least sixty-five. Now, please, excuse me."

Kuon dropped his chin, feeling like an intruder. The heavy steps that he assumed belonged to the doctor faded, but the sobbing remained close by. A few times he opened his mouth to ask if the woman needed anything, or if he could help, but the questions died, as he realized how stupid they were. He couldn't even help himself, let alone offer assistance to others.

Helplessness—sticky and cold—glued his lips together. The need to be useful throbbed in his chest, reanimating in his mind all the reasons why he'd become a police officer, and his need to be strong, to protect those who faced evil in their lives. He hung his head, trying to return to the emotional numbness of a moment ago.

"Are you okay?" the woman asked, sniffling. "Do you need help?"

That's right... I'm the one who needs help, he thought, but said, "I'm okay."

"Say... how is it, not being able to see?" Her voice, soft yet throaty, trembled with emotions. "Very scary?"

He frowned, shrugged, but for some reason, told the truth, "Yes."

"My daughter... she is only six. She..." Her choppy speech stopped as abruptly as it started. A shaky breath tore from her lips. "I'm a photographer. I keep a lot of chemicals at home."

No, stop... He didn't want to know how a life of a little child had changed due to her mother's carelessness. How the mother felt guilty for having aided in the loss of her kid's sight. He already knew how the story ended, and he was powerless to change it. He wasn't a doctor. He wasn't an insurance worker. There was no reason for him to hear the details. He didn't know the woman; he didn't know the girl. It wasn't his problem and, buried with his own, he didn't want it to be. Yet, with every word, the woman kept involving him.

"I didn't lock the darkroom. Nelly always loved to play with lens filters. She loved looking through them at the sky, watching colors change. She must have tried to reach them but knocked the developer off a shelf. Everything got spilled on her beautiful face, her eyes." She started crying again, and for several long minutes, Kuon sat in the darkness all alone, not knowing what to do. "It's been more than two years already. At first, they said they needed the burns to heal, then they tried meds, but her vision didn't return. She is only six, and she is scared of the dark. I am so tired. I can't leave her side for a moment, without her crying. I can't work anymore. I have no one to leave her with. I had some money saved, but it's running out. And today they pushed her back again. Now she is five thousand something on the list. It's a joke!"

Without vision, Kuon's imagination developed, providing him with elusive visuals. For the last year, his life involved constant dependence on other people, where he couldn't even prepare food without asking for assistance.

But I'm an adult. I'm strong. I can deal with it. Can a six-year-old kid deal with the constant darkness?

He wanted to say that he was sorry, but his tongue stuck to his palate. For the last two years, this woman must have heard those words so often, that by now they most likely rubbed her the wrong way.

"I'm sorry for telling you all this." She blew her nose. The strength that seeped into her voice informed him she had managed to collect herself. She sucked in a deep breath and added, "You have your own problems."

He opened his mouth to say that everything would be okay when the heavy footsteps of the doctor returned. The door creaked open, and another set of light footfalls approached as the high-pitched voice of the nurse reached him from his right. "Herr Leiris, your turn."

"I hope…" he managed, the motion of his wheelchair being rolled away vibrating in the soles of his feet and his fingers. He twisted around toward the place where he thought the woman was but couldn't find words. "It's gonna be…"

The door slammed closed before he finished, and he hoped that the story the woman had told him would remain behind the doors, somewhere in the corridor.

It didn't.

'How is it, not being able to see? Very scary?' The question she'd asked haunted him, reanimating the events that left him blind. He remembered the first day after the terroristic act and how desperately he'd wanted to remove

the bandages to check if he could see anything at all, but the sedatives kept his limbs glued to the bed. He remembered the doctor removing the bandages for the first time, but only gray nothingness greeted him.

To keep his eyelids immobilized and speed the healing process, they had kept the bandages on. There was no need for them anymore, but he kept bandaging his upper face because the slick skin around his eyes terrified him. He was a grown man, yet he was frightened of his potential blind future. What would he do if the doctors couldn't restore his vision? Would he have to learn how to read Braille books and use a stick to feel the way in front of him? Would he have to rely on others for the rest of his life? Only the thought of him being a burden turned his spine into a spire of ice.

I am scared, and I'm an adult. How does this child feel being robbed of her vision?

"How are you feeling?" Dr. Klor's too cheerful voice was uncomfortably loud for Kuon's ears. "Are you ready for the surgery?"

"How am I feeling?" Kuon repeated the question. He searched for the answer within but found nothing. Instead, he started talking. His voice came out calm and even when he spoke about the war and death, people who served with him, and kids who were professional murderers by the age of ten. He wasn't sure for how long he talked, or why he was speaking at all. Despite the busy schedule, the doctor didn't stop him. When he ran out of words, he realized what he wanted, so he shrugged and prompted a single request that drowned in the death-like silence. Unsure what to add, Kuon rubbed his temple.

"Herr Leiris..." the heavy sigh broke the silence. When the doctor continued, his voice was quiet, yet firm. "Your surgery is scheduled for tomorrow. Do you even understand what you asked for?"

"I do," Kuon interrupted. "Just run the tests."

"Sleep on it. We will talk tomorrow," the doctor said, before the wheelchair moved again, bringing him into the black, devastating silence of the hospital room.

"WHAT DO YOU MEAN HE LEFT?" Yugo slammed his palms against the smooth surface of the polished wood as he towered above the doctor. "He has surgery today."

"He asked me to check the compatibility between the donor and another patient of mine. They're a good match, so he abandoned the corneas in favor of a little girl. I have a signed agreement." The doctor pushed a paper toward him.

"You gotta be fucking kidding me!" With another slam of his palm, Yugo forced the doctor's attention from the sheet of paper back to himself. "I fucking paid for those corneas. Cancel it!"

"You should settle this issue with Herr Leiris." The doctor's voice didn't waver.

Black rage clouded Yugo's soul. Fists and jaw clenched, cracking with tension. "Where is he?"

He wasn't sure what he would do once he faced Kuon, but one thing he knew—it would hurt.

"The nurse took him to the park. His friend was here ten minutes ago. If they didn't leave…" Yugo wasn't listening. Pushing the door open, he rushed down the corridor and toward the automatic doors that led outside.

KUON'S HAIR SPARKED WITH RED under the bright sun. The end of his loose bandage hung untucked and wrapped around his neck, but he didn't seem to notice it. He sat on the narrow bench in the middle of the park, as Rick, squatting in front of him, buried his face in his hands.

"What the hell have you done?" Yugo growled, storming toward them. He had to stop a few feet away so the urge to punch Kuon wouldn't overpower him. "Do you know how hard it was to get those corneas legally?"

Kuon's face lit up, his lips twitched with laughter as he faced the sky, basking in the sun.

"If you're talking about money, I'll pay you back as soon as I can. Now consider it as charity and payback to society for all those innocent lives you've ruined. You don't pay taxes, do you?"

"Fuck the money! Why the hell did you do that?" The splashing, uncontrollable anger curdled Yugo's blood. His gaze fell at the end of the unwrapped bandage, and he vividly imagined how sweet it would feel to tie it around Kuon's neck and watch him choke.

Kuon shrugged, dropped his chin, then lifted his face toward Yugo, as if he could see him. "She is scared of the dark."

"What?" Yugo frowned. The meaning of the words eluded him, but

Kuon's serious tone, seeping under his skin, subdued his blood-thirst.

"She is only six, and she is scared of the dark," Kuon repeated as if it was something obvious and only Yugo didn't understand it.

Rick's head jerked up, and Yugo instantly detested the eyes full of puppy loyalty. Rick's wide palm landed on the top of Kuon's, and Yugo clenched his teeth. He grew sick of this waiting game. All of his nature demanded he take what was his. To ignore Kuon's stupid whims. To take him back where he belonged, where he didn't have a choice to do stupid things. To shut him away from everyone, from everything. He took a step to the bench, wishing to do so, when a white dandelion seed, swirling in the air, landed on top of Kuon's head. Ice speared his chest; Yugo halted. He watched the seed tremble in the wind then tear away, just like a fluffy snowflake. Yugo blinked the memory off, his voice lost the sharpness, when he asked, "What about you?"

"I am scared too…" Kuon whispered. Darkness swallowed Yugo's soul. His chest clenched with the need to destroy, to kill.

"Idiot." A single word left his lips; he turned around and stormed toward the parking lot before the wish to hurt Kuon overwhelmed him.

"YOU DON'T HAVE TO DO this every time, you know? I can manage…" Kuon said, listening for the running water. The humidity changed as a hot wave washed over his face. The sound changed as well, and Kuon realized that Rick had adjusted the temperature.

"What if you slip?" Rick's voice reached him from his left.

"I won't."

"Like the other time?"

"I only fell once. Since then, I've grown used to this place. I'll be fine," Kuon promised. His hands found the top button of his shirt as he started undressing.

"Come on, let me help." Kuon flinched when unwelcomed fingers fumbled over his shirt, unbuttoning it. Stepping back, Kuon slapped Rick's hands away.

"Stop it!" Kuon sounded sharper than he intended but could do nothing about it. Every time Rick helped him with a simple task, he felt worthless. At some point, his agitated feelings produced paranoia, making him guess if Rick even thought of him as an equal. "I can undress myself!"

"I know you can," Rick easily agreed, trying to avoid the confrontation. The rustle, coming from Kuon's right, suggested that the man had taken his usual spot on the floor.

A habitual nasty aftertaste flooded Kuon's mouth. It appeared every time he couldn't keep his temper on the leash and accept Rick's help. Somewhere deep down, he understood that it was only his hypertrophied pride and built up complexes, but still, he failed to suppress them.

When the last piece of clothing dropped to the floor, he stretched out his arm. Spreading his fingers and feeling the air, he moved into the sound of running water.

"Kuon..." A worried voice came from his right.

"I'll manage."

"At least remove the bandage..." Rick rushed to his feet, or so Kuon thought, according to the rustle.

"I said, I'm fine," Kuon snapped, for some reason remembering Yugo and his first reaction to his appearance. Even without seeing his cold, gray eyes he'd imagined disgust lurking behind them. Jerking his shoulder in rejection, Kuon added, "I'll do it later..."

Step after step, he inched forward until his palm touched cold, slippery glass. Sliding his hand along, he found the edge, then lifted his foot to step over the shower curb he knew was there. He'd hit his toes against it way too many times already. Hot needles of water prickled his shoulders, washing away his tiredness. Cracking his neck, he pressed his palms against the tile wall and dipped his head, enjoying the powerful streams massaging his upper back. His bandages grew heavy and loosened, as water rushed down his face.

SITTING ON THE FLOOR, Rick watched Kuon lean his forearms against the wall. Never whitened, raised scars crisscrossed his strong yet powerless back. Every time Rick saw them, he fought back a desire to wrap his arms around Kuon's torso and press the man into his chest. His fingers burned with a need to trace every red line someone else had left as if he could erase them from Kuon's skin and memory.

'Who left them? Who did it to you?' Many times Rick had asked those questions. Kuon had never answered, but that didn't stop Rick from wondering.

A blind hand explored the wall and found the shower gel dispenser that stood on a small corner shelf. Pressing the pump, Kuon collected some chartreuse liquid into his palm, rubbed it over his neck. Soaping up, the foam rushed down his spine, then over his round buttocks. Rick's pulse quickened as immense heat washed over him. Swallowing, he dropped his gaze to the floor.

Thank god he can't see me... he thought, feeling a growing pressure in his jeans. To mute his arousal, he forced his thoughts away from Kuon's ass, and they inevitably trailed back to his scars and Yugo. The way the man behaved and carried himself reeked of money, gunpowder, and blood.

No doubt, he's Kuon's first... Rick thought as he remembered the words Yugo had said in the park months ago. *'I will be the only man who ever touches you. If you know what's good for you and the people around you, don't ever forget it.'* The thought stung. No matter how hard he tried, he couldn't imagine Kuon dating such a man. He didn't know Yugo well, but what he had seen left a bad aftertaste in his mouth. *Why the fuck did he resurface again?*

As soon as he opened his mouth to ask Kuon about Yugo, another memory wormed its way into his mind; the memory he had forgotten due to the anger and adrenaline overflow. *'What will you do, force me again? Go ahead. After all, you always take what you want...'* Rick's gaze shot up to Kuon's back, his mind connecting the dots.

"Who did this to you?" he asked. Kuon's hands froze over his chest.

"Did what?" Despite the casual tone, alertness squared Kuon's shoulders.

"Those scars on your back, is it belting? Flogging?"

"It doesn't matter. Let it go." Kuon faced Rick as if he could see him. Determination hardened his jawline.

"It matters to me. Did he do that?"

Kuon turned to the wall, water muffling his words. "It's none of your business."

Something snapped in Rick's head, flooding it with a roaring sound. He got up. Without undressing, he stepped into the shower cubicle. Denim, turning wet, clung to his skin, so did his shirt.

"He did, didn't he?" A palm, connecting with Kuon's back, pressed the younger man into the wall. "And you smile like an idiot every time he comes to see you. Did you enjoy it or what? Maybe you're just too shy to ask for what you need? Do you want someone to be rough with you, to hurt you? Is this why I'm not good enough for you? Are you a masochist, Kuon?"

"RICK!" A WARNING VIBRATED in Kuon's throat as the wide chest imprinted into his back. The heat, coming from the other man, raised every hair on Kuon's body to attention. He heard the fast drumming of Rick's heart with his skin as something hard pressed against his ass. "What the hell are you doing?

Back off!"

Trying to win some space, Kuon pressed his palms against the slick wall and pushed away. He spun as Rick's fingers seized his hips, tugged him closer.

"I love you." The words startled Kuon. With his forearms against Rick's chest, Kuon froze; Rick's fingers didn't. Foaming up, they drifted toward his butt crack. "I can make you happy. I'll do whatever you want. I can be anything you need."

Kuon opened his mouth to tell the man to leave when a rough kiss was forced upon him. Biting down onto Rick's lip, Kuon pulled back and threw his fist forward. The meaty, wet sound reached his ears as the vibration from the impact rushed up to his shoulder. A heavy **THUD** and a splash followed.

Panting, Kuon turned toward the wall and rested his forehead against the tile.

What a fucking mess... Kuon remembered all the times Yugo raped him before his thoughts switched to Gray and the hooker he'd brought him. *Is it something about me that makes people think they can do force themselves on me?*

The sound of rushing water condensed the silence, making words meaningless. His lips twitched, formed a painful grin, and he smashed his fist against the wall, seeking pain as a distraction from his powerlessness. The longer he stood, listening to his own breathing, throbbing pain in his knuckles, and the running water, the more betrayal tainted his soul.

"He might have done a lot of things..." Kuon's voice, barely above a whisper, sounded unfamiliar to his own ears. Too low, too robotic, it lacked emotions and strength. "But he never lied to me."

"Kuon..."

"You did." The pain in his chest worsened with every second as his thoughts jumped about his skull. He couldn't believe that Rick had taken advantage of his weakness and betrayed his trust. "I'll move out tomorrow."

"Why can't you give me a chance?" The splash and a slapping sound forced Kuon to face the noise and protect his back by pressing it against the wall. Rick's voice trembled, when he asked, "Do you love that asshole? What does he have that I don't? Why can't it be me?"

Kuon shook his head. "Love? What are you talking about? I don't."

"You lie. He is the only one you smile at. I try so fucking hard to stir a small emotion, but he only has to show up to make you grin." Rick's breath washed over his wet cheek. Kuon recoiled.

If Rick decides to use force, I won't be able to stop him. Ice filled his veins. For the first time, Kuon felt insecure in Rick's presence.

"You never smile at me like that."

"Like what? I don't know what you think you see, but you are mistaken," Kuon said, dropping his chin. "Love? For love, you have to respect a person, trust them. I don't trust him, and I certainly don't love him. I'm not even sure if there is anything good in him at all. You're wrong. I don't have feelings for him."

It's complicated. I don't want him to see me defeated. I am just glad he still remembers me. Maybe I'm a little happy to know that he cares.

Something, buzzing at the back of his mind, whispered *'weakness'*, so he said no more.

The pause stretched. When Kuon shifted, wanting to get out of the shower, Rick broke the silence.

"When you look into the future, what do you see?"

Kuon stiffened when Rick's shoulder touched his, but instantly relaxed as he realized that the man took the wall by his side.

"You staying alone for the rest of your life? What kind of life do you want to have? Is there anyone by your side? Do you see him?"

Kuon bit his bottom lip as Yugo's face bled through the darkness, then fell apart into a kaleidoscope of fragmented memories: the war, police operations, the white room, guns, and drugs. He shook his head, refusing to think about it.

"I see you." The simple words stopped Kuon's heart. "I pray that one day you notice me and realize that in the whole world I only look at you. That I would be enough. Even if we are both sixty-something, and there is no dark hair on our heads, I think I will still love you."

"This isn't fair." Kuon's guts knotted, and icy, sticky anguish oppressed his heart. "You can't say things like that."

"Why? I'm being honest. Let me into your life, and I'll be by your side no matter what. I'll never walk away even if things are too complicated. I won't betray you."

Kuon shook his head, as weakness overtook his heart. Rick's words stirred a weird longing in his soul. *Maybe I should move on. Maybe I can leave everything behind and start anew? Maybe, if I let him love me, I will develop feelings for him. Just like with Yugo.*

Kuon breathed, dropping his chin. "Let me think."

Rick didn't move, but Kuon felt the instant change in the air so clearly as if he could see the happiness and hope lighting up Rick's black eyes.

CHAPTER 10

A few days passed, but nothing changed. Kuon couldn't give Rick a reply, as whenever he looked into the future, all he saw was his past. He wanted things he could no longer have, and those thoughts drowned him faster than a sinking anchor ever could. He feared them. He avoided them. He ran away from them. To escape thinking, he turned to training. The more he worked out, the lighter his head became.

Wearing his tennis shoes and sport shorts, Kuon stood with his back pressed against the wall. The remote control in his hand, he waited—neurotic and impatient. As soon as the door closed behind Rick's back, Kuon turned the volume up, picked a music channel, and dropping to the floor, started counting push-ups.

Energy streamed through his veins, firing up every cell. His muscles sang, blood boiled, and habitual, white lightness, saturating, pushed every thought out of his head. Working out had often been boring. Without Rick's support, Kuon didn't risk heavy-lifting and only worked with simple exercises using his body weight. But even with the limited set of exercises, Kuon still managed to reach that endorphin high where nothing bothered him. He'd also found a way to cope with his unsettled emotions. Whenever alone, Kuon poured out his built-up frustration into the punching bag that Rick had bolted to the ceiling. After wrapping his hands, he could punch the bag for hours. By the time Rick got home, Kuon had always been so exhausted that there was no aggression left in his body.

Today he craved the whiteness more than ever. Rick's words still swirled in his head, forcing him to think about his future and face the fact that he had no idea how to move on. Sometimes the weakness in his heart grew stronger. At moments like this, he wondered if Yugo had a place in his future, but no matter how hard he tried to imagine such a relationship in his life, he simply couldn't. It looked like only physical attraction connected them. Kuon didn't belong in Yugo's world any more than Yugo belonged in his.

Do I smile like an idiot every time he comes? So embarrassing... Rick is right. I should let the past go. I should tell Yugo not to visit anymore, or I can never move on. Why do I even think about him? Why did I touch him, kiss him? It doesn't make any sense.

Strike after strike Kuon desperately thrashed the heavy sand-filled bag. Trying to kill the suffocating, dark emotions, he didn't notice the endless shrill of the doorbell through the loud music. The rhythm lost, he turned the TV off. Silence flooded his ears, sending a chill down his spine. He hated silence. In his darkest fears, the hell he would definitely go to didn't consist of torture and physical pain. It was filled with eternal silence and darkness; maddening non-existence where he would slowly forget the faces of the people he loved and even his own name. Shifting from one foot to the other, he wondered if he'd hallucinated the doorbell when the shrieking repeated.

Who could that be? Kuon wondered, throwing the remote control to the sofa. *Did Rick forget the key? Or maybe the music was too loud, and the neighbors are angry? Maybe Yugo?*

One foot in front of the other, he stretched out his hand and counted steps. When the texture under his foot changed to soft and bouncy rag, his palm touched the wooden door. The lock rattled, he pulled the door open.

Silence greeted him, as a small draft chilled his sweat. He waited, but no one spoke, and he wondered if it had been a prank. Scowling, he wanted to close the door, when a quiet female voice greeted him. "Hi."

Familiar notes in her timbre made him strain his ears. Wondering where he had met her, he said, "Hi."

No reply. Kuon hated awkward silence, so before the pause stretched further, he said with a smile, "Sorry, I have a bad memory for faces. Would you remind me where we have met?"

A chuckle reached his ears. The sound let him confirm her height—she stood at least a head shorter than him. He dropped his chin, wishing she would say something else, so he could identify her.

"We met in the hospital." Her soft yet throaty voice stirred the memory.

"Oh..." he managed, remembering the crying woman and her story.

"I'm sorry I came like this. I should have called, but something told me you wouldn't open the door if I did. May I come in?"

Kuon didn't move, realizing where this situation headed.

"I'm sorry; I'm busy right now." He tried to close the door, but something resisted him. Fearing to hurt the woman if he pushed harder, he heaved a sigh. "Listen, whatever you have to say, I'm not interested."

"Have you eaten? I brought pizza. It's going to get cold," she paused, then added, "Please, let me in." When he didn't reply, she repeated, "Please?"

Fuck... He stepped aside, letting the woman in. *I'll so regret it.*

The floral scent washed over him as she passed by. He closed the door.

"Do you live alone?" she asked, and Kuon wondered if she examined his apartment for signs of a woman's presence.

"No. I live with a friend due to the circumstances." Slapping the wall with his palm, he moved toward the living room, turned right, and grabbed the backrest of the sofa. Sitting down, he said, "Please, make yourself comfortable."

"Thank you." A soft rustle reached him from his left, and he cocked his head, listening.

"I wasn't sure what you drink, so I only brought ice tea."

Hating the small talk, Kuon said nothing.

"I didn't mean to impose," she said with an audible sigh. "I came to thank you. I thought that maybe you're curious about the destiny of your corneas. If I were you, I would be wondering if my sacrifice was for nothing."

Kuon folded his arms over his chest. His jaw clenched. Her words hit their mark. He had wondered about it more than once but wasn't ready to admit it.

"I didn't mean it like that." She hastened to correct herself. "I just wanted to say that there is no sign of rejection so far. The doctors keep saying that nothing is written in stone, but I'm hopeful. If we're lucky, her vision would soon restore."

Voice brimming with hope, she kept talking about her daughter, and for a moment, Kuon wondered what was her agenda. She didn't have to come.

"Who gave you my address?" Kuon interrupted her speech.

A long pause stretched in time, draining air from the room. Suffocating, he blew out a breath, ran his fingers through his hair, then got up. "Listen…"

"Doctor Klor." Reluctance vibrated in her voice when she confessed. "Please don't get mad. He couldn't tell me 'no'."

"Why? What could you possibly want?" Kuon asked, facing the direction her voice came from.

"I wanted to ask you, why did you do this? You didn't have to…"

"I don't know. Now, please leave," Kuon said, hoping his dry reply would repel the woman, and she would get the message. He had no desire to talk about his fears and insecurities, not with her anyway. He moved to the door to see her out when thin arms wrapped around his neck. A light kiss brushed against his cheek, then the woman pulled away. Kuon froze, not fully understanding what had happened.

"Thank you." Her sweet breath touched his neck. "My name is Kristina. I'll visit again."

Her hand touched his, and he instinctively squeezed her palm, feeling its size and imagining her composition. Bony, soft, and frail, her long fingers suggested small, delicate build.

Squeezing his hand one more time, she let go, and the light steps distanced. The door closed and everything quieted.

"What the hell was that…?" Kuon mumbled, feeling dumb.

FOR MANY DAYS, EVERY CELL in Yugo's body reeled, before he'd finally managed to calm down. The insulting words Kuon had thrown his way after their moment of intimacy demolished his self-control, making him see red. He wanted to kill Kuon on the spot, but something stopped him. He couldn't say if it was the familiar twist of Kuon's lips, his shaking fingers, or the thickening smell of fear. Maybe all together. Many times, Yugo had wanted to visit Kuon, but a mere memory made him see red again. The canceled surgery magnified his growing irritation.

The itch to see Kuon's face and his splitting smile eventually brought Yugo to Rick's apartment, but whenever he did, the wish to hurt Kuon returned, making his visits short and silent.

THOUGH KUON'S RELATIONSHIP WITH RICK never developed, the atmosphere changed. Sticky, suffocating suspense hung in the air, and Kuon was glad they didn't spend much time together anymore.

Rick's behavior gradually altered. He didn't press Kuon for a reply, but his body betrayed his anticipation. Every evening, when Kuon was listening to audiobooks, he would lay on the sofa, resting his head on Kuon's lap. This subservient attitude, when Rick agreed to everything he said, weighed on Kuon. He understood that he had to give Rick a reply, but he didn't have it. Searching his soul for answers, he didn't know what he could offer. He didn't have a foreseeable future, he couldn't share his past, and his present was limited, boring. Even his sex drive barely existed anymore. He had nothing to offer Rick, and that didn't feel fair.

Kristina became a frequent visitor. Feeling awkward at first, Kuon slowly grew used to her visits, and soon started anticipating them. Listening to her voice, he couldn't help remembering how his life had been before Yugo. The fleeting kisses she greeted him with, reanimated in his mind the warmth of a woman's body. Her frail build and thin limbs stirred his protective instincts. Thinking back, he realized how easy dating a woman had been. With a woman, he had always known where he stood and what his role had been. He hadn't doubted himself or his future, trying to picture it all together. With a woman, he hadn't questioned his manliness or needed to crush his pride.

Sometimes, Yugo stopped by. His visits were always short. They confused Kuon, made him uneasy. Yugo barely talked, never forced physical contact, and Kuon couldn't help thinking that the man wasn't over the cruel words he'd said after their moment of intimacy. Still, whenever Yugo came, Kuon felt his burning gaze, drenched with lust and shameless carnivorous hunger. It made Kuon feel naked, exposed from the inside out, and there was no escape from Yugo's eyes. Kuon had to summon the shreds of his willpower to glue a mask of dispassion over his face.

Whenever Yugo looked at him this way, Kuon remembered the touch of his cool fingers and his bitter-sweet kisses. Afraid that his voice would betray his thoughts, Kuon kept silent, but that didn't seem to bother Yugo… until today.

Rick left before dawn. Alone, Kuon yawned, wondering if he should sleep longer to take up some more time when the loud shrill of the doorbell abraded his sleepy nerves. Making his way to the corridor, he opened the door. The pressure, applied from the other side, forced Kuon to retreat as someone entered. The mix of spicy, woody fragrance and bitter tobacco hit his face. He didn't argue against the intrusion. There was no point, as Yugo wouldn't leave anyway.

"Why are you here?" choking the first sparks of excitement, Kuon grumbled, then slammed the door closed. His pride didn't let him admit that Rick was right and he indeed grinned like an idiot every time Yugo visited. Not wanting to think about it, he shuffled to the kitchen and put the kettle on. Sleeping wasn't an option anymore, but coffee still was.

"Get dressed." Yugo's uncompromising voice made Kuon fold his arms over his naked chest. "Come on, let's take a ride."

"I'm not going anywhere with you." Kuon blew out a fake, irritated breath; his heart picked up a faster pace.

"Don't be unreasonable." Kuon lifted a brow, wondering if it was concern that vibrated in Yugo's voice. "When was the last time you went out?"

"Who cares? I'm blind. I don't care where I am."

"You're wasting my time. It wasn't easy to clear my schedule, so you have a choice. Either you go with me, or I stay here all day, but I'm spending the day with you." Lost for words, Kuon listened for heavy steps to cross the room. The sofa creaked under Yugo's weight. "Wanna watch a movie?"

"Haaa…" Pressing his hands against the kitchen counter, Kuon wondered what Yugo's agenda was. The thought of spending a whole day in a closed place together frayed his nerves.

No matter what his motivation is, nothing good will come of it. If he stays, who knows what might happen… If I go… Ugh, why do I have a feeling that I'll regret either choice? Confused, he rubbed his temple, refusing to look at the man.

"I won't do anything if that is what you're worried about," Yugo said.

"Why should I trust you?" The words left Kuon's mouth before he managed to stop them.

"If I wanted to kidnap you, I would have done it already." The smile in Yugo's voice made Kuon believe him.

Facing the window, he wondered if the sun shone brightly today. He missed the wind on his skin. The temptation to say 'yes' bubbled in every cell. Rick didn't have the time to walk with him anymore, and sitting in the apartment, locked away in his head, was torture.

"So, what will it be?"

Wavering for a moment, Kuon nodded. "I'll get dressed."

"WHERE ARE WE GOING?" Kuon asked, squirming in the seat.

"Where do you want to go?" Yugo started the engine and turned the wheel, steering the car out of the underground parking.

"I don't care. It's the same everywhere." Kuon shrugged. "Are you driving alone? Where are your goons?"

"Why? Could it be that you're worried about me?" Yugo smirked, peering into Kuon's features. So close, yet so far. He could press the door lock button, lean forward, and force a kiss upon him. Feel the familiar resistance, maybe have a small fight before Kuon's pride let him accept another man and submit. He was about to erase the distance between them when Kuon lowered the backrest.

"Yeah, right." Tugging the hood on, Kuon snuggled in his black hoodie. "I just don't want to be in the same car with you when you get attacked."

Disappointed, Yugo shifted his gaze back to the road. "Don't worry, it's bulletproof."

THE CAR VIBRATED as Yugo kept driving. At first, the silence didn't bother Kuon, but sometimes he felt Yugo's long, searing gazes over his face. His anxiety grew as the silence stretched.

To distract himself, he concentrated on the road and his sensations, but after yet another turn, he lost his sense of direction. The warmth on his cheek intensified with every minute. He tried to picture the landscape. How the old buildings fused into one long gray wall because Yugo seemed to have sped up. How colorful spots splashed now and then, coming from floral dresses of passing women and the summer umbrellas of cafes.

Yugo's clothes rustled every time he moved. This low noise calmed Kuon. His mind slowed, sticky thoughts blurred, and he couldn't concentrate on them anymore. His limbs weighed, so did his head. Everything became distant as the colorful dreams carried his mind away.

The gentle lurch of the car coming to a stop pulled Kuon out of sleep. Stirring, he lifted his hand and, shoving his index finger under the bandages, scratched the corner of his eye. "Where are we?"

"Nowhere," Yugo replied. His deep, velvety voice wrapped around Kuon, making him feel secure.

"Why did we stop?" Kuon tried to shake off the illusion of security. Yugo wasn't safe, he'd never been safe, but he had taken all Kuon's attention, had made the world recede. Kuon missed it, just a little.

"No reason. You can sleep if you want to." Heat flooded Kuon's chest. The familiar feeling of Yugo's gaze roaming over his body seared his cheeks.

"It's creepy when you stare like that," Kuon said, but instantly regretted his words, as Yugo inched closer.

"How do you know how I look at you?" Yugo's breath tickled Kuon's lips. Swallowing, Kuon lifted his hand, found Yugo's face, and pushed the man back.

"You're too close." He expected resistance, but to his surprise, Yugo laughed and pulled back.

"Can you see anything at all?" The sound of a lighter being stroked reached Kuon's ears. Yugo opened the window, and the buzzing of a summer field rushed inside, bringing along the flowery scent and sweet smoke.

"Not really," Kuon confessed. "Light and dark, but mostly gray nothingness."

"Get out." Yugo's rough order confused Kuon; his lips numbed, but he obeyed.

THE ENTIRE TRIP Yugo had watched Kuon, noticing every little detail. How Kuon lifted his face, catching the sun, how he froze every time Yugo spoke, and those small, barely visible movements of his head when Kuon listened to him move. The more he watched, the more he understood how significantly Kuon's world had shrunk.

He wondered why he hadn't noticed it sooner. Kuon had always tried to appear confident, independent. His movements were short and precise, as he didn't move more than he had to, but sometimes when Kuon thought Yugo wasn't watching, a lonely expression crept upon his face. *Just like now.*

The longing had settled in Yugo's chest as they stood in the middle of the road, surrounded by fields, under the unbearable, scorching sun; the ghosts of the mountains hovering far away, near the horizon. He wished Kuon could explore this immense space, and the high golden oats.

Noticing the corners of Kuon's mouth droop, Yugo added, "Take the wheel."

"What?"

"I want you to drive."

"Are you insane?" Kuon laughed. "I'm blind."

"It's an empty road. We have been here for twenty minutes, and no cars have passed." Yugo took a step toward Kuon, getting drunk on the idea. Adrenaline, fear, and excitement could shake Kuon out of this miserable state; he was sure about it.

Short neurotic laughter broke out from Kuon's mouth as he recoiled. Yugo licked his lips, wanting to taste his uncertain, but genuine smile.

"Come on, trust me. You can do that. I've got you."

"N-no... We can hurt someone." Kuon shook his head. "Or we'll crash.

It's a stupid idea."

"Chicken," Yugo laughed. "Then I'll tie my eyes, and the GPS will direct me. Hop in."

"What?" Kuon yelled, and Yugo laughed.

"I'm curious how you feel things. I'm going to try driving blindfolded."

"No."

"Fine. You can stay here and wait for me to return and pick you up, that is, if I don't crash, of course. Or you can go with me."

"There is no way you leave me in the middle of nowhere. Please, don't do this. Yugo, it's dangerous."

Kuon's serious voice let Yugo know that he'd already won. "Then you drive."

"FUCK! FUCK! FUCK!" Kuon gripped the wheel, regretting the decision with every fiber of his soul. "We will so crash. I'm not paying for the repair, just for the record."

"You're doing fine," Yugo chuckled, and Kuon knew that the man enjoyed his agitated state. "Take a twenty-degree left turn in ten feet."

"Shit..." Kuon switched the gear to first, released the clutch, then slowly turned the wheel. His heart drumming, palms wet. Sweat trickled down his nape, but he didn't dare to tear his hands away from the wheel to wipe it.

"Nice!" Excitement and pride filled Yugo's voice, making Kuon feel drunk; the control, yet the complete lack of control, spiked his senses. "The road is clear. There are fifteen hundred feet of asphalt, speed up."

"No."

"Speed up, Kuon." The threat made its way into Yugo's voice. His hot palm landed on top of Kuon's, ready to switch the gear.

"No."

"I know you want to. Do it." Yugo's voice, wrapping around him, erased his common sense. Yugo's trust exhilarated him.

Kuon licked his lips with his dry tongue; currents of sweat streamed down his spine under the hoodie. His heart going insane as he pressed the gas pedal. "I will so regret it."

"You won't," Yugo chuckled. Guiding his hand, he switched to second, then third gear. "I've got you."

Kuon's dry tongue scratched the roof of his mouth. Adrenaline flowed in his veins, and Yugo's hand, covering his, did something to his head. He felt intoxicated with his heightened emotions. His fears evaporated, only the blissful feeling of freedom and the wind kissing his face remained. No fears, no doubt, no loneliness, just Yugo's voice guiding him through the darkness. He pressed the gas pedal harder.

KUON'S TRUST MESSED WITH YUGO'S self-control. The way Kuon followed his voice, the way he caught his every word, made Yugo feel giddy, drunk, high. Yugo wasn't sure where to look—the empty road or Kuon's teeth that nibbled at his bottom lip. The veins popped at the top of his neck drew Yugo's attention.

"Yugo?" Kuon's nervous voice called for him after a minute of silence, seeking reassurance.

I'm so fucked. Yugo closed his eyes. After all this time, he finally realized that deep inside, Kuon trusted him. Every time Yugo visited Kuon, he looked for signs of rejection, but they had always been contradictive. If Kuon hated his presence, he could have fought him, tried to kick him out of his apartment. Kuon never did. His half-assed opposition only fired up Yugo's desire. Just like that time when they had been intimate. Yugo had questioned if it was fear or Kuon's stubborn way to let him into his life again. But he didn't have answers, not until now.

He leaned closer, wanting to kiss the glistening side of Kuon's face when something yellow flickered at the corner of his vision. Roaming through the oat, the tractor jumped out of the field and onto the road.

Grabbing the wheel, Yugo yelled, "KUON, WATCH OUT!"

BEEP BEEP! KUON FLINCHED as adrenaline lit him up. Yugo grabbed the wheel and pulled left, switching the gear to second. Without thinking, Kuon hit the break. He felt the car coasting, vibrating before it bumped against something and stilled.

"What are you, blind?" The angry male voice kicked the remains of euphoria out of Kuon's system. His heart thrumming in his throat, he pushed the door open and got out. Tremors settling into his fingertips, he opened his mouth to ease his breathing.

"Kuon," Yugo approached.

"How could I fucking let you get me involved in something like this…" Kuon laughed, incredulous. "I must be out of my mind. Why do I always let you have your way?"

"Kuon…" Apology rippled through Yugo's voice as his palm landed on Kuon's shoulder.

"Save it." Shifting left, Kuon slapped the hand away.

The buzzing of the field grew louder as the pause stretched.
"Get in the car," Yugo said, his voice dry.

CHAPTER 11

Time slowed, stretched, and distorted. Kuon didn't know where they were, nor how much time had passed since the accident as neither of them spoke. Sitting on the grass in the middle of nowhere, he tried to ground his jumpy thoughts as the events looped in his head. He wasn't sure if he was mad with Yugo or with himself, or if he was even mad or disappointed. He couldn't believe he'd gotten carried away with Yugo's insane idea but, for a moment, he'd had fun. He'd felt alive.

It felt good... The corroding thought stained his mind. Submerged in Yugo's voice, he'd felt safe as if nothing wrong could happen as long as he followed Yugo's orders. The part of him questioned if it was the afterglow of Stockholm syndrome, or if it was his own reaction, but he couldn't be certain of either. *I enjoyed it.*

Having the control, yet not having the control or responsibilities; letting himself drown in the adrenaline overflow felt amazing, and Kuon caught himself on the thought that he already missed the pulsing blood in his fingertips and the sound of Yugo's voice.

I'm the worst. Fisting the grass, Kuon rested his forehead against his bent knees. *Whenever I'm with him, my morality bends and twists. Am I this shallow?*

"Stop thinking about it," Yugo's voice came from the ground, and Kuon wondered when he'd laid down. "Nothing happened."

"We could have killed someone." Kuon barely heard himself speak. Yugo hummed. A fleeting movement washed Kuon in a faint smell of cigarettes as Yugo ruffled his hair with his wide palm.

"We didn't, so stop thinking about it."

Kuon's heel dug into the soil. Seeing no point in this conversation, he changed the topic. "Where are we? I thought we were going back…"

The crystal-clear air, rich with oxygen, didn't taste like anything around the city. A brisk wind, sneaking under his clothes, chilled his sweat. Tugging the hoodie off, Kuon tossed it on the grass by his side, leaving him in only the wet t-shirt. The blazing sun instantly warmed his exposed skin.

"It's a small farm not far from Wilhelmsburg, Lower Austria."

"What are we doing here?" Kuon strained his ears. Birds chirped, the wind played with grass, and something wooden creaked in the distance.

"Nothing," Yugo replied, then added in a weird tone, "I haven't been here for ages, but nothing's changed."

Kuon had never heard such deep notes in Yugo's voice before.

"For ages..?" Kuon frowned, realizing that despite the year that he'd spent with Yugo, he barely knew anything about him. He'd never asked Yugo about his past or his future. Now, when he thought about it, he didn't even know the simple things. All he knew was his bad character and demanding touch. "Where are we?"

"This was my family safe house for generations. We used to come here to lick our wounds."

"A family safe house? Yugo, you have a family?" The air shifted as soon as Kuon asked. Heavy and solid, the question walled up between them erasing the easiness.

"No. Only Mio." Yugo got up. "I'm hungry. Don't move, I'll bring something."

DROPPING TO HIS KNEES ON THE GRASS Yugo placed a paper bag by his side, shoved a cup into Kuon's hand before pouring some milk in. "They don't have anything fancy, but everything is fresh."

"What's this?" Kuon craned his neck as the sun kissed the side of his throat.

"Milk." Yugo's gaze stuck on Kuon's face. Even with bandages wrapped around his eyes and the horrible attitude, Kuon still attracted him. Many times Yugo had questioned what it was about Kuon that didn't let him walk away, but he couldn't find the answer. Though handsome, Kuon hadn't been the most gorgeous man Yugo had fucked, and now, covered with all those scars, Yugo wasn't sure if Kuon could be called attractive at all. Stubborn and willful, Kuon had irritated the hell out of him every time they met. *Then why the fuck do I want him so bad?*

"It's sweet," Kuon said, taking a sip. A few drops remained on his upper lip as he put the cup down and smiled. The urge to taste the sweetness of the milk from Kuon's lips grew stronger; Yugo turned away and looked up. Watching the sky, he tried to imagine Kuon's life during the past few years. Barracks, shitty food, narrow, uncomfortable bunks, gunshots in the middle of the night. He wanted to ask why Kuon went to Afghanistan when he had his freedom back. Why Kuon never used the money he gave him.

He didn't, staying silent.

Obviously, Yugo knew what would be best for Kuon better than Kuon knew himself. Forcing him would be easy now; he just had to take him home and control his every action; limit Kuon's world to his bedroom and the sounds of his voice. Embrace him every night until Kuon gave up resisting. This way, Kuon wouldn't be able to do stupid things, things that endangered his life. He would have a warm bed, good food, the best medical attention, and Yugo's arms holding him every night. Wouldn't that be better?

A wry smile twisted his lips as he looked at Kuon. *Why the fuck don't I do it?* Yugo couldn't say.

Shoving his hand into the paper bag, he fished out the still-warm loaf of bread. Breaking it, he handed half to Kuon, then offered him some cheese. "Eat."

The lowering sun glazed empty fields with orange as they ate in silence.

WARM LIPS TOUCHED THE BACK of Kuon's palm. Startled, he dropped the unfinished bread, then fisted the grass under his hand. He didn't hear Yugo move, and for a second, he felt disoriented. The warm tongue licked between his fingers before hot lips moved up. Nibbling a trail along his forearm, they brushed over his shoulder before nuzzling his neck.

"What are you doing?" Kuon breathed, unable to move. His heart halted when a warm tongue grazed his cheek. The smell of mown grass washed over him when the tongue lapped over his face again, and someone tugged at his bandage. "No, Yugo, stop!"

The bandage loosened, and something tepid and sticky dribbled down his face.

"Ugh! That's gross!" Kuon threw his palms up and fumbled over something warm, soft, velvety. That didn't feel like Yugo. A quiet, suppressed laughter reached him from his right, messing with his inner compass even more. Looking for the explanation, Kuon called, "Yugo?"

"Not quite..." The laughter grew louder. Listening to the merry, rollicking sounds, Kuon couldn't help wondering what the hell was chewing on his bandage if Yugo sat by his other side? Fumbling up the soft texture, he found ears and pointy horns.

"What the..?"

"Relax, it's just a cow." Yugo couldn't stop laughing. "It came to ask for bread."

"A cow?" Releasing the horn, he found the ear and scratched behind it. The short, coarse fur tickled his palm. Kuon chuckled as the cow rubbed its muzzle against his face. It felt funny but smelled off, and Kuon pushed it back. "What color is it?"

"Black and white. She likes you," Yugo mused, as the cow muzzled Kuon's neck. Nibbling on his shirt, it started chewing on his hair.

"Oh, god. No, please, don't do this…"

Yugo burst out laughing again, and Kuon pleaded, "Not funny! Help me get this thing away!" Kuon scrunched up his face as panic started taking over. His bandages soaked in saliva, threatening to come undone any moment. "Please, Yugo, get it off. I don't have spare ones, and the saliva…"

The laughter died. Yugo jumped to his feet, and his knee brushed over Kuon's arm as the man stepped over his torso. The tug on the bandage grew stronger, and soon the slobbered end slapped against the side of his face.

"Gross…" Kuon mumbled, wiping his face, trying to deal with the sticky bandage.

The leg retreated, instead, Yugo's palm wrapped around his biceps. "Get up. Let's go into the house. You can wash up there."

Kuon got onto his feet, his chest bumping against Yugo's arm.

"Kuon…" Yugo paused, and Kuon's insides spasmed. He wasn't sure what he was waiting for, but for some reason, his body tensed. "I wanted to kiss you, but fuck, you reek of cow spit."

"Fuck off!" Hitting Yugo's chest with his fist, Kuon stepped back. "I need to wash up."

SITTING IN THE CAR, Kuon rubbed his cheek with the sleeve of his hoodie. Even after he'd spent twenty minutes in the bathroom, he still felt dirty. He wanted to take a shower and hide in the safety the bandages provided. Without them, he felt naked, exposed, vulnerable. The memory of Yugo's first reaction to his eyes added to his anxiety. He wanted to go home, to hide from the bright sun and Yugo's attention.

"Kuon…" The low, raspy baritone broke the silence. "Stay here with me."

"Not funny."

"We don't have to go back. Not today, anyway." The touch of Yugo's fingers abraded the top of his palm. Kuon lowered his chin. "There is only a handful of people here. You don't have to feel self-conscious. I told you, it's my place. It's well maintained."

Imagination, spiraling out of control, provided Kuon with pictures. He imagined the coming evening, spent together in the same room. How Yugo would be studying his face with a mix of pity and disgust in his eyes.

If I stay, what would happen?

Yugo's fingers resting on the top of his palm and the low notes in his voice were all the answers he needed. There would be sex and awkward moments where Yugo wouldn't know where to look so the view of Kuon's face wouldn't ruin his erection. His caresses wouldn't be demanding; they would be soothing, exuding sympathy.

A rush of insecurity made Kuon snatch his hand away and grab the drawstring of his hoodie. Biting his bottom lip, Kuon gave a slight headshake. "No."

"Why?"

KUON DIDN'T REPLY. A long few minutes passed before Yugo broke the stretched pause, his nerves tight, ringing with pressure. "Tell me about the woman."

Kuon snorted. "There is nothing to tell."

"Are you fucking her?"

"No."

"Do you want to?" Yugo plucked out the lighter, flipped it around his fingers.

"Would you stop? I barely know her. She's just grateful and feels obligated." Kuon cringed.

"You don't know her, yet you gave your corneas to her kid? Are you fucking with me?" Yugo leaned into Kuon.

"Stop!" Kuon said. "You see things that aren't there."

"Do I? You gave up on your vision as a favor for her daughter. What should I think? Are you related?"

"No."

"Why did you give them away, Kuon?"

"Yugo, stop!" Biting his lips closed, he turned toward the window, nails scraping down the glass as if he wanted to escape.

"Tell me, or I will take the girl and run a DNA test."

"I told you, there is nothing to tell! I was fucking scared, okay?" Kuon yelled, throwing a swift, unseeing glance to Yugo. Sucking the air through his teeth, he clenched and unclenched his fists. His voice dropped when he continued, "Are you happy now? Is this what you wanted to know?"

"Scared of what? Of seeing again?" Yugo's mind reeled. He couldn't understand what Kuon meant. "You want to stay blind?"

"You won't understand." Both palms flew in the air, then dropped to his knees as Kuon failed to come up with the answer. "I don't want to talk about it, okay? I'm not ready."

"It's okay. Take your time. We can stay here as long as it takes." Plucking a cigarette out of his chest pocket, Yugo lit up; swirling smoke rose from his fingertips. Nicotine soothed his nerves, taking the edge off.

"Why are you doing this? Let it go." Kuon gulped.

"No. I need to know. What are you scared of, Kuon?"

"That's none of your business."

"I'm making it my business." Warning reverberated in his voice. Grabbing the collar of Kuon's hoodie, Yugo hauled him closer. Kuon squeezed his eyes, but the pink and brown eyelids and the short lashes were enough for Yugo's skin to prickle. "Tell me."

"What right do you have to ask me anything at all? Who the fuck do you think you are?"

"I have every fucking right," Yugo pressed through gritted teeth. "You belong to me!"

"You haven't changed one bit." Bitterness dulled Kuon's voice.

Yugo released his collar. "Tell me."

A pause stretched. A few times Kuon opened his lips, then bit them closed, and small furrows notched his chin.

"Everything," he finally confessed; his dead eyes staring through the landscape. "Every morning I wake up but don't immediately open my eyes because I hope that the last months were just a bad dream. I am scared to see nothing. I wear the bandages because this way I can linger in the illusion that once I remove them, I will be able to see again. I don't use a stick, because it would make things real. You can't possibly understand, but I realized that I have never been truly scared in my life, until now."

Yugo couldn't blink, couldn't look away from the weak, unfamiliar grimace on Kuon's face. The cigarette smoldered and burned his fingers; he threw it out of the window.

"Every day I wonder, what if... things go wrong? What if my body rejects the corneas? What if I can never see again? What if I am stuck in this nothingness for the rest of my life?" Kuon's eyes closed; his chin dropped.

"So you decided to give up before trying." Yugo's cheek flinched, contempt rattling in his voice. Kuon's lips quivered, his face blanched, so did his knuckles as he fisted his hoodie.

"I told you, you won't understand." he mouthed. "Drive me home."

"Oh, I do understand," Yugo replied, clutching the wheel. The desire to slap Kuon grew with every second. "When is your next appointment?"

"Why? What do you want, Yugo? Why do you keep coming? Two years ago, in the hospital, you said you didn't need me anymore. Why do you care now?" Kuon didn't open his eyes, didn't lift his chin. "What is it? Pity? Guilt? Whatever it is, please spare me. I don't want it."

"Do I look like a person who does things out of pity or guilt?" Kuon kept silent, but a small flinch of his chin replied better than words. "I let you go because you almost blew your fucking brains out. You ask what I want? I came to collect what belongs to me!"

"You're horrible." Kuon's voice trembled. "You're just bored, you selfish bastard. The situation amuses you. My current state excites your twisted imagination. Such a wide scope for your superficial kindness, right? The control gives you a thrill. You enjoy pushing my limits like you did today. And you enjoy watching me follow because I..." Kuon stumbled, frowned, and didn't finish. "What do you want, Yugo? Did you go so broke that you don't have enough money for pretty toys anymore? Why did you find me after all this time? Why can't you just leave me alone?"

"Because I want you." Yugo breathed, unsure if this was the truth anymore. He had never seen Kuon like this before. Kuon had never been this open, weak, miserable. This wasn't fun. This was painful. Yugo's chest ached, longing for something, and he didn't know how to alleviate this pain.

"What can you possibly want with me? Who is blind here?" Kuon spun; a mad grin reigning over his face. Dead eyes peered into Yugo's face, sending a wave of dread down his spine. Kuon's mouth twisted; his voice broke when he added, "Don't you see? What's there to want?"

The white eyes glistened. Kuon licked his lips, swallowed, then turned away.

"Kuon..."

"No..." Kuon shook his head, refusing to look at Yugo. "I want to go back."

"Fine…" Yugo breathed and started the car.

KUON'S EYES BURNED, his throat closed up, and air failed to fill his lungs. He couldn't believe he'd had a breakdown in front of Yugo. All this time, he'd done his best to show the man that he had been fine, that nothing could break him.

Why today? How pathetic. The more he thought about it, the harder his chest ached. He opened his lips to ease the breathing, but the sour saliva flooding his mouth forced him to swallow every other second.

When the car stopped, and the engine died, Kuon tugged at the handle. Yugo's door slammed the same moment Kuon's feet touched the ground. It smelled like wet concrete and gas. He instantly recognized the underground parking lot. Iron fingers seized his elbow, demanding he follow. He didn't argue. The elevator chimed, doors opened, and they went inside.

"You can enjoy your freedom for the rest of your life." Yugo's quiet voice doubled Kuon's pulse. "You can be alone all you want. I won't force you into anything, but if you fuck someone, that person dies."

"You are ridiculous!" Kuon huffed. "You aren't serious, are you?"

"Reject the corneas again, and you lose your freedom. Is that clear?"

"Fuck you, Yugo," Kuon grounded out. "Why don't you go to hell? I never want to see you again."

"Well, that's not a problem for a while, is it? You're doing great achieving it."

Kuon's teeth ground together when he didn't find anything to say.

"Don't forget what I said. I'll be back." The doors opened, and Yugo pushed Kuon out of the elevator. "I believe you can manage from here."

Kuon heard the button being pressed and the doors slid closed.

CHAPTER 12

Yugo started visiting more often. He brought music and audio described movies. He didn't ask questions anymore, but Kuon felt the heavy silence floating between them concealed by small talk.

Rick rarely stayed home. Leaving early in the morning, he returned late at night, reeking of sweat and dust. Sometimes Kuon thought that he also smelled blood and gunpowder, but he chased that thought away, writing it off to his imagination. After all, why would a construction site smell of gun powder, unless they were doing demolitions? Rick never said anything about it. Their time together shrunk to early breakfasts and late-night snacks, accompanied by brief talks. Many times, Kuon wanted to tell Rick about Kristina, but explaining was harder than keeping silence. Feeling guilty for not giving Rick a reply, he feared that Rick might misunderstand his relationship with Kristina.

Kristina's visits grew more frequent too. She talked a lot, to the point where Kuon didn't have to engage in her monologues about life, Nelly, movies, and books. She never let a pause hang, so whenever she was around time flew by. Growing familiar, Kuon started going outside with her, and then they'd spend hours in a park, enjoying the sun and fresh air. It felt easy. Natural.

"Nelly will be discharged tomorrow. I'd love to introduce you two," Kristina said, as she led Kuon back to the apartment building.

"Sure." Kuon smiled. Kristina talked about Nelly so often that it felt as if he'd known the girl for ages, even though he'd never heard her voice or seen her face.

She halted and spun. The atmosphere around her shifted, became strained, uneasy, vulnerable. The floral smell grew stronger as hot, intermittent breathing touched Kuon's mouth. Thin fingers slid up his neck, and her lips pressed to his.

Kuon froze, unable to move. Every nerve tightened in attention, listening for the familiar, yet fresh sensation. The warmth, softness, and compliance of the female body rang with submission, soaring his pride. Her frail form lined perfectly against his, and at this moment he thought, *this is what the stability of family life feels like*. But as soon as the thought occurred, gray, cold eyes bled through the darkness. Peering through his soul, they stopped his heart and demanded he push the woman away. His chest constricted, and Kuon pulled back, terminating the kiss.

Yugo's single touch makes me nervous, yet her kisses didn't even speed up my pulse. The softness of her lips still lingered over his, when he rubbed his temple in confusion. *I'm weird. Isn't this more natural? Shouldn't I be elated?*

Not knowing what to say, but needing to say something, he asked, "Wait... Aren't you married?"

"You weren't listening," she accused in a low voice. "I've told you, I was widowed four years ago."

"You did? Sorry..." His thoughts scattered as an unspoken question hung in the air. Wishing to escape the situation, or delay dealing with it, he said, "Let's talk inside."

"IS THAT SO..." YUGO BREATHED, watching the kiss linger. He couldn't see Kuon's face, but he didn't need to see his expression to recognize the hand gesture. The same gesture that often followed their kisses.

Worn asphalt, absorbing the sun, exuded heat, but despite the high temperature, Yugo felt chilly. He couldn't blink, staring at the thin arm wound around Kuon's wide back through the miasma streaming up from the overheated ground. The blonde woman, dressed in a light blue sundress that matched her eyes, led Kuon away.

When the couple disappeared behind the front door of the apartment building, something swelled and pulsed in the pit of his stomach.

"Well, then..." he managed. "This is on you, Kuon. I hope you're ready for the consequences."

Getting into the car, he shot a glance in the rear-view mirror. Greg's black eyes feasted on his expression. "Check the girl's DNA. Compare it to Kuon's."

"The girl is easy, Boss. She is in the hospital," Greg shrugged before he paused. "How do I get Kuon's samples? Do you want me to approach him?"

"No. Check the garbage for used bandages. There have to be traces."

"Yes, Boss."

His gaze shifted to the gray apartment building that looked more like a concrete box than someone's home. The pulsing in his stomach became violent. Like a hot abscess, it throbbed and itched, needing to be cut open and cleaned.

When the eternity passed and the car didn't move, Yugo asked, "What?"

"Mio called." When Yugo ignored, Greg added, "He wants to meet you."

"Send him to Tobias." Searching the windows, Yugo wondered if he would be able to see Kuon in one of them.

"I did. He said he'll drop by anyway, and that you can't avoid him this time, because he won't leave until you talk to him."

"When?"

"I believe he's already waiting."

Pushing his hand through his hair, Yugo closed his eyes and rested his head against the backrest. "Drive."

SITTING ON THE SOFA, KUON LISTENED for the light movements of the woman. Kristina didn't talk, and Kuon didn't rush to break the oppressive silence.

KATANG.

"Coffee," she said. Kuon strained his ears, listening for the spot where the cup hit the table. Guiding his palm alongside the cool glass of the coffee table, he found the corner then, placing his palm on the edge, moved it toward the place from where the sound had come. The hot, ceramic cup touched his palm. Finding the handle, he lifted it to his lips. His senses spiked when the aromatic drink slipped down his throat. During the last few months, Kuon had knocked over so many cups of tea and coffee that he didn't risk returning the cup to the table anymore, even though it burned his palms.

She sat by his side; her naked leg brushed against his knee. His skin prickled under her inquisitive gaze.

"Did I rush things?" When Kuon didn't reply, she continued, "I've never seen a female presence around the apartment, and you've never talked about anyone, so I assumed..."

Kuon tried to find the right words, fruitlessly. "I'm sorry. I do like you..."

"But?" Her tone went up, and Kuon realized that she wouldn't give up on the topic without a proper answer.

"There is someone." He lifted his free palm in a give up gesture, then added, "It's complicated."

"Complicated..." Kristina repeated in a thoughtful voice as if tasting the word on her tongue. "Where is she, if you don't mind me asking? Why isn't she with you?"

Sinking into silence, Kuon didn't know what to say. He'd never liked talking about his personal life, convinced that things like sex, love, and affection belonged to privacy. The thought of admitting that it wasn't a woman made him feel awkward, embarrassed, and completely self-conscious. *Funny... I keep thinking about Yugo, yet I can't even admit he is a man. Aren't I a hypocrite?*

"It's..." Kuon stumbled.

"Complicated," she finished for him.

"Yeah..."

She got up, gathered the cups, and moved away. The water hit the sink bottom, then the screech of a sponge rubbing against the cup reached his ears.

"You know..." The metallic clang interrupted her, and he realized that she'd put the cups on the dish drying rack. "I'll bring Nelly tomorrow if that's okay?"

LEANING AGAINST THE WALL, Yugo folded his arms over his chest the same moment that Mio's slender form disappeared underwater. The faint smell of chlorine, ever-present in the poolroom, mixing with humidity, crawled under his skin, making him feel warm, uncomfortable. Bright sun, streaming through the windows, glinted off the surface, creating the effect of shallow water. Without a splash, Mio's face surfaced; shimmering cascades streamed down his pale cheeks. Azure eyes opened, blinked off the water, and linked with his.

"Yugo..." Mio's lips formed a silent word. His chin went to his chest, as he looked at Yugo from under his light eyelashes. With a few swift strokes, Mio crossed the pool, grabbed the edge, and pulled himself out of the water.

Yugo's eyes wandered over his naked frame. Though still thin, Mio didn't look anorexic anymore. His arms and legs, gaining muscles, had lost the painfully-broken look. Shoulders rounded, and his skin picked up a healthy glow.

Ungluing from the wall, Yugo took a few casual steps forward, picked up a towel from the white leather bench, and turned toward his nephew. Mio's chin trembled, eyes glistened, lips twisted in a painful grimace, he threw himself into Yugo's arms.

"I missed you…" Mio's voice broke. "I missed you! Why do you never meet me? Do you hate me now?"

Cold wetness engulfed Yugo's chest as Mio imprinted his drenched frame into Yugo's suit. Pushing out a sigh Yugo smirked, his determination to keep Mio away fading with every second. After ruffling Mio's wet, flaxen hair, he draped the towel around his shoulders, then replied, "Of course not."

"Then why haven't you met me for a month?" Hot breath brushed against Yugo's neck; Mio raised his eyes. "Please, let me stay with you. I'll do anything, please. I want to get back to… us."

The hope shimmered behind azure eyes.

"You look good," Yugo said, noticing a thickening layer of muscles under the almost transparent, pale skin on Mio's chest. The veins under his eyes were still visible, but the bloody-red circles had disappeared. "You've gained more weight since last month."

"Please, don't brush me off."

"What do you want to hear? You already know the answer," Yugo said, the back of his hand wiped the water off Mio's cheek. "I want you to stay with Tobias a little longer before you find your own place. He does a great job caring for you. Your latest blood tests are great; the best in the last ten years."

Mio bit his red bottom lip and gave an abrupt headshake. "He hates me… he looks down on me." His face lost the color, and Yugo realized that Mio wasn't playing. "He despises me."

"Does he hurt you?"

"No…"

"So what's the problem? Make him respect you. You have spent two years with him. If during this time you failed to gain his loyalty, what worth do you have for the S-Syndicate?"

"I hate the S-Syndicate! I hate it!" Mio screamed into his face, sending fire down Yugo's veins. Mio's small fist slammed against his chest in a powerless fury. "You don't give a shit about me. All you care about is your fucking business!"

"Well…" Yugo clenched his teeth. "Too bad you have nothing else. This is your legacy. But if you hate it, you're always welcome to walk away.

Go ahead; find yourself a decent job that pays a thousand euro a month. I'll watch you trying to survive on this, or do you think I'll always pay your bills?"

"It was supposed to be only a year!" Mio hissed; his eyes narrowed.

"And you were supposed to behave. Instead, you keep this childish attitude and cause Tobias problems with the police. If you're unhappy with how things are, earn your keep and move the fuck out! No one will stop you."

Mio's upper lip drew up. Yugo heaved a sigh. Palm slamming against Mio's chest, he pushed him back and into the pool. A splash caught his polished shoes when Mio's frame disappeared underwater; only the white towel remained floating. When an angry face resurfaced, Yugo said, "Grow up. If you want people to treat you seriously, gain their respect."

The plump mouth opened to say something, so Yugo warned, "Watch it."

Gnashing his teeth, Mio punched the water.

"Calm down and meet me in my office. I want an update on your progress." Turning around, Yugo threw over his shoulder. "You too, Tobias."

"Oh, you noticed," the man smirked, stepping out from the corner. Cracking his neck, he granted Mio with a derisive glance. "If you're done ratting me out, little shit, why don't you try crying? Maybe Yugo will take pity on you." His pale eyes squinted, then he added in a sharp, spiteful tone, "Man up."

"AREN'T YOU OVERDOING IT?" Yugo asked, watching Tobias take the guest chair. His black shirt looked clean, ironed. Yugo squinted, wondering if he'd finally gotten a decent lover. "Don't degrade him."

"I'm just giving him motivation."

"Motivation to do what, kill you? He hates you."

"It's Mio. He hates everyone, except you." Tobias grinned. "He is fine, and there is no better motivation than hatred, don't you think? Look where it got you."

"How is he doing?"

"Fine. He behaves. He tried to hack into my computer again." Tobias' grin widened. Yugo arched a brow, feeling somewhat disappointed. "But I changed the encryption. He was so close, and the last moment the system threw him out. You should have seen his face. It was priceless. Oh, wait. I have the footage from the security cameras."

"Not interested. How did he do in Kabul?" Approaching the desk, Yugo sat on the edge of it, facing Tobias.

"Fine, I guess. He doesn't show much interest, but he isn't completely useless." Tobias yawned without covering his mouth, and Yugo diverted his eyes, not willing to contemplate his pharynx. "His observation skills are great. He accompanied me to the military base to check the written-off helicopters, and he managed to get a better price than I did."

"So he is good with bargaining," Yugo summarized.

"I'd say so. His hacking skills are getting better too. My security system failed to detect him. If I hadn't hacked into his PC first, I wouldn't have known about him trying."

"Where do you think it's best to use him?" Yugo picked up a silver pen, aimlessly flipped it around his fingers.

"He'd do great in politics, but he has zero interest in it. He likes guns, though. He isn't bad with them either. I'm about to try him in extortion and torture. He is a twisted little shit, I'm sure…"

"No torture and stop calling him little shit. He is still my nephew," Yugo interrupted. "What would you do if he develops a taste for it? I don't want him to explore his sadistic tendencies and pour his complexes into his prey. Nothing good would come of it. Keep him 'clean'. No 'dirty' work."

The door opened without a knock, and Mio entered. His still wet hair was slicked back; a white suit hugged his lean body. Approaching the desk, Mio slumped into the chair next to Tobias and threw an ankle over his knee. The overpowering smell of cologne flooded the room, and Yugo wondered if he should send him to wash up again.

"You're free to go, Tobias."

"I'd rather stay. I'm curious what this little… my protégé has to say." Tobias stretched the vowels, giving Mio a curious glance.

Tossing the pen onto the desk, Yugo got up. "Thank you for coming, Tobias. Please, leave us. Unless you're so obsessed with Mio that you can't part for a moment? Is there anything I should know?"

"Good one," Tobias laughed, got up, and turning to Mio, added, "I'll see you at home. Grab dinner on your way. Your cooking sucks."

When the door closed behind Tobias, Yugo directed his attention to his nephew. "You failed. Again."

"I hate him!"

"I don't care," Yugo said, circling Mio's chair. Standing behind him, he placed his hands on Mio's shoulders. Fingers crawling up, they clasped around the thin neck. "I need a result, Mio."

"Whenever I get close the encryption changes, and I have to start all over again. What am I supposed to do?" Mio said. "I think his encryption automatically changes every few hours, or I don't know how he detects me. He doesn't trust me enough to leave me home alone for longer than an hour."

Yugo leaned forward. His breath stirred soft curls of Mio's hair when he whispered, "Because he knows!"

"H-how?" Mio frowned.

"Figure it out," Yugo said. Letting go of his neck, he returned to the desk. "Break into his computer. I want a copy of his hard drive before he upgrades his defense again."

"Why do you think I can even do this?" Mio pressed his lips together, throwing a glare at Yugo. "Every month, he offers a reward to hackers if they can break in. Why don't you hire someone better?"

"You can't do it?" Yugo hummed, adding a fair amount of disappointment into his voice. "If you can't gain Tobias' loyalty, or hack his computer, what's your value, Mio? What can you do?" When Mio didn't answer, Yugo sighed. "Go back to Rudolph. I bet he would be able to find something suitable for your abilities. Maybe you can manage one of his whore-houses; how does that sound?"

Jumping to his feet, Mio gnashed his teeth. Drilling Yugo with a cold glare, he said, "You're so fucking cruel. All my life, I've just wanted you to look at me."

Yugo smiled with his lips only. "You lost your privileges and my trust when you went against me. Now you have to earn them again. Bring me a copy of the hard drive. Don't call until you have it."

Mio's eyes stayed linked with Yugo's for another second before he stormed out of the office.

"That's the spirit," Yugo said to himself, a smile spreading over his face.

"SO?" YUGO ASKED AS SOON as Greg entered his office the next morning. The bright sun filtering through the blinds threw sharp, horizontal lines over the floor and Greg's black baggy suit.

Yugo's impatience reached its crest, his fingers bombarding the polished surface of the desk with taps. He wasn't sure what he would do if the results matched, but he needed to know anyway. Thinking and overthinking, he couldn't find a cure for the hot abscess that grew larger in his stomach with every passing hour.

"Not related," Greg said. His military boots clanked against the floor when he approached the desk and offered Yugo a wide, flat envelope.

"Not related, huh…" Without looking inside, Yugo grabbed the envelope and tossed it on the desk. "Were they familiar before?"

"Don't think so, Boss. The doctor said that the woman begged him for Kuon's name and address. It looks like they just met a few weeks ago. So, what do we do?"

Yugo didn't reply. Scratching his chest through his starched shirt, he tried to ease the burning itch, but it only grew stronger. "Only just met, huh?"

He remembered the kiss and how her slender body pressed against Kuon's solid frame. Getting up from his chair, he grabbed his jacket from the backrest. "I'll let you know."

NELLY TURNED OUT TO BE a lively and open girl. Kuon instantly found himself attracted to her inexhaustible energy. Running around him and Kristina in circles, she kept bragging about how brave she had been, and that she almost hadn't cried even when she was scared and didn't see anything.

Her vision hadn't been completely restored yet, and she mentioned that everything was still blurry and distorted, but at least it wasn't dark and scary. Her buoyancy and spirit, so characteristic of young kids, did something to Kuon within hours. Talking to her, he felt the darkness draining from his soul, taking his fears away.

In the park, they played blind-man's buff, but he was the only one catching. When he managed to snag one of the girls, they giggled and squealed in delight. Kristina yielded more often than Nelly, and Kuon noticed that she had a great body—toned, slim.

Kuon caught himself thinking that he could get used to the constant attention, family warmth, and care. With Kristina, Kuon could see a future. A stable life, a decent job, kids. She could give him something of his own— his flesh and blood. That thought visited his head more often with every passing day, but at the same time, it stirred a deep longing in his soul. Every evening, falling asleep, Kuon listened to the silent apartment and wondered why Yugo hadn't come for yet another day. Since his last visit, almost a week had passed.

YUGO'S VISION PULSED IN SYNC WITH the abscess bubbling in his stomach. With his back against a tree, he watched Kuon catch the woman and laugh; a brilliant smile brightening his face. Giggling, she didn't recoil but wrapped her arms around his torso, swirling him, disorienting him. The motion and the wind, playing with her yellow dress, revealed her long, slim legs.

The longer she held Kuon, the darker the bright, sunny day became. The birds chirped, but Yugo didn't hear them anymore. He didn't see the dusty leaves, begging for the rain to come. He didn't see the happy smiles of the passersby. Monochrome, dark, the world lay gloomy in front of him, as the pulsing in his chest became unbearable.

His eyes burned, but he couldn't tear his gaze away, absorbing Kuon's happy expressions and the flirty behavior of the woman. Soaking through his skin, it fed his abscess.

"We should go, Boss," Greg said as he leaned on the other side of the tree.

Yugo didn't move. The woman rose to her toes and kissed Kuon's cheek. The little girl with the unruly mop of platinum hair grabbed Kuon's knee and tried to tug him somewhere.

"Come on, Boss," Greg tried again, his voice full of sympathy. "Gustavo is waiting."

Bending forward, Kuon lifted the girl in the air and twirled her around. Yugo's chest constricted as the abscess vibrated, expanded, and burst, marring his soul with sticky, burning jealousy and hatred. Kuon didn't belong to them. Kuon belonged to him. Him only.

Unblinking, Yugo said, "Kill the woman. Make it look like an accident."

THE CAR STOOD IDLE. The climate control was off, and the air heated, making Yugo sweat under his jacket; the smell of leather hung heavy in the compartment.

"Will you drive already? Didn't you say Gustavo is waiting?" Yugo said; annoyance bounced in his chest, unsettling him even more. When Greg said nothing, and still didn't turn on the engine, Yugo asked, "What's your fucking problem?"

"Kuon looks happy, Boss." Greg twisted in the driver's seat, looking over his shoulder.

"When the fuck did you buy immortality? Or is this a suicide attempt?" Unable to believe his ears, Yugo squinted. Greg shrugged.

"I'm just saying that he looks happy. Didn't you want that?" He turned back, hiding behind the wide driver's seat. A muscle on Yugo's face jerked. *Yeah... That was before he let me touch him.* "Boss, what do you think will happen if you kill her?"

"You talk too much. Drive already."

Greg didn't. He rummaged in the pockets of his jacket before passing a square piece of paper to Yugo.

"What's this?" Yugo asked, snatching it out of his fingers. Glossy and monochrome, it looked like a glitch on black and white TV.

"An ultrasound picture. My wife is pregnant." Greg's wide smile reflected in the mirror. "It's a girl."

Taking another look at the picture, Yugo tried to understand what it showed, but everything looked like white noise. "Congratulations. You're fired."

Suffocating, he opened the window. The wind, breaking into the car, chilled the wet skin on his nape.

"You're going to be a godfather." Greg's grin grew wider.

"Aren't I already? Drive."

"Her godfather."

"Are you fucking trying to win me over?" Yugo frowned, head tilting to the side. Greg grinned, but Yugo's anger subdued. "What the fuck is your agenda?"

"We chose the name. Wanna hear?"

"No," Yugo said, glancing at the date the scan was taken. "You motherfucker... It's from last week! When did you intend to tell me?"

Ignoring him, Greg finished, "It's Milana." Pride rang in his voice as his smile turned dreamy.

"I know what you're doing," Yugo said, passing the photo back. "I won't change my mind. The woman dies."

"It won't make you happy, Boss."

"You can't know that."

"I do. You do too. It won't end well."

"Let me get this right. She took what didn't belong to her. She is about to take from me again, and you want me to sit back and watch? Are you out of your mind?" Yugo asked, incredulous, then added, imprinting the order into his words, "Solve my problem. Kill the woman. Make it look like an accident. You can spare the girl."

"There's got to be another way. If you kill her, Kuon will never forgive you."

"There is no other way. I gave him my word. Now, shut the fuck up and drive," Yugo ordered, his mood even darker than before.

"Okay," Greg said and started the car.

THREE DAYS PASSED, BUT YUGO'S darkness didn't disperse. It condensed, magnified, until only pitch-black hatred remained. Greg did everything to procrastinate the order until Yugo's patience ran out. Sitting in the car, he watched the woman with a child enter the apartment building, wondering what Kuon saw in her. She was beautiful but Kuon couldn't possibly know that. For some reason, Yugo refused to believe that Kuon could pick the first woman who crossed his life. He didn't look that desperate. Even if Kuon wanted to have fun, why would he pick someone with a child?

Is it the way she talks? The way she laughs? Something in her words? What kind of woman she is? Smart? Dumb? What is he seeking? What does she have to pique his interest?

Unable to find the answer, he asked, "Why is she still alive?" Greg didn't answer. "You don't intend to do it, do you?"

"Boss..." The pleading notes in Greg's voice made him cringe.

"Fine." Yugo stepped out of the well-conditioned car into the afternoon sultriness.

"Boss, wait. Where are you going? Don't do this!" Greg called from the driver's seat, then got out. Yugo didn't stop.

"Stay in the car. If you follow me, I'll shoot you in the leg." Striding toward the entrance, he yanked the front door open and entered the building.

Darkness blinded him as a misty smell washed over. Eyes accustoming, he made out steps. Following the weak light, trickling from above, he went upstairs. Four flights later, he froze in front of the cheap, shabby door.

KNOCK-KNOCK.

Yugo wasn't sure why he came, but when the lock unlatched and the door opened, he pushed it with his shoulder and entered. Taking a step back, the woman yelped in surprise. Slamming the door closed, he studied the place.

Women's shoes lined up by the left wall, small children sandals taking half the space completed the second row. The ivory paint on the walls begged for refreshment, but the dozens of framed photographs on the wall had no dust on them. Yugo took a closer look: the woman hugging a smiling man, the woman with her daughter, all of them together in an aquarium, and many more.

Focus back to the woman, he squinted, eyeing her up and down. Fingers crumpling the hem of her summer dress with a flowery print, she peered up at him with alert eyes, but no obvious fear. Regret for not asking Greg to check her background washed over. Indicating the man on the nearest photo, he asked, "Who is that?"

"Who are you? What do you want?" she finally found her voice.

Yugo cocked his head, searching for fear in her timbre and features, but only the paleness betrayed her agitated state. Using the chance for close-up scrutiny, he examined her small face with a button nose, sprinkled with light freckles, bright blue eyes decorated with long lashes and dark, thick brows, and matte, colorless lips pressed together.

"Answer me," Yugo pressed, bumping the knuckles of his index and middle fingers against the picture.

"I'm calling the police," she warned, grabbing her phone from the small white stand behind her.

"Oh, be my guest." He smiled, never intending to stop her. "No one will come while I'm here."

Still holding the phone, she didn't dial the number, and Yugo wondered why she believed him.

"Did you swallow your tongue? Maybe the girl will tell me. Where is she?"

"My husband." Her cheek flinched as she replied.

So you have a husband. What a slut... Yugo smirked. "Where is he?"

"Died four years ago. What do you need?"

His gaze caught her bare feet and painted in pale pink toenails. Not taking his shoes off, Yugo strolled past her into the small, light kitchen. She followed. It smelled like fried bell-pepper and meat. Rough beige fabric covered the table, two chairs stood by. Slumping on one of them, he stretched his legs. "Sit."

Grabbing the back of the other chair, she complied.

"I've seen you before," she said, burning him with her unblinking stare.

"Where is the girl?"

She didn't flinch but squinted, scrutinizing him. "You were in the park. Many times. You always stare."

"Where is the girl?"

"Next room." No fear bled through her features, and Yugo wondered if she was so dumb that she wasn't scared. "What do you want?"

Yugo didn't listen. His gaze slid over the clean but old gas stove with nearly burned through rings, jumped to the fluffy, transparent curtains, and a line of plants on the windowsill. An old doll sat in the corner, dressed in a pink dress. The windows were clean as if have been just washed. On his left, above the table, a handful of child doodles hung in no particular order, small colorful pins holding them to a corkboard. Some of the drawings were so old, the corners curled forward and the paper had turned yellow. In colorful crayons, a woman and child figures were barely recognizable. Both had yellow ray lines sticking out from their heads.

"Who are you?"

"Shut up," Yugo said, examining the pictures. Each one was dated in neat, small handwriting, and he realized that most of them were from two years ago. Only two were fresh. One of the recent ones had a blue sky, sun, and a fluffy cloud with a rainbow sticking out of it. Another one was much messier. It had trees, knee-high grass, and three human figures. A child, a woman, and a man. The man's face was hatched with white horizontal lines at the place where his eyes should have been. Yugo swallowed, his throat tight.

Getting to his feet, he approached the window.

"Mom?" A tiny voice made him face the entrance. A girl in a blue dress held a piece of paper in her hands. Her curious, questioning gaze directed at him.

"Go to your room," the woman said.

"No. Stay," Yugo ordered in a tone that didn't leave room for disobedience. The woman shot him a glare, starting to get nervous.

For a few long minutes, he examined the girl. With blue eyes and a mop of platinum hair, she looked like a miniature copy of her mother. He approached. Squatting down, he peered into her eyes, noticing serrated stitching around the irises. "What's your name?"

"Nelly."

"What's this, Nelly?" he pointed to the piece of paper.

"A gift," the girl said, showing him the image. It resembled the last one he saw. The blind man, the woman, and the child, except the colors had changed.

"For whom?"

"For Kuon. This is me," her index finger poked the drawing, then moved about. "This is Mommy and Kuon. I'll give this to him tomorrow."

"Don't be stupid, he is blind," Yugo said, feeling irritated.

"You are stupid," the girl retorted, frowning. "Not forever. When he can see again, he will look at it and be happy. And we will go to the aquarium, and look at all the fish there. Even sharks."

Pressing her drawing to her tummy, she gave Yugo the evil eye and stomped to her mother. He got up.

"So it's about Kuon," the woman said, patting the girl's head. Getting to her feet, she approached the stove and put the kettle on. "Tea or coffee?"

Yugo scowled, watching the girl climb onto the now empty chair. Putting the paper on the table, she fished crayons out of her pocket and started doodling on the other side of the sheet.

Watching the girl draw, Yugo didn't move. The kettle whistled, and the woman turned it off.

"Tea or coffee?" she repeated her question, but Yugo didn't want to acknowledge her presence. She was no one. She wasn't important. He didn't even care to remember her name, so he didn't have to answer her questions. Soon she would disappear the same way she appeared—quietly, unnoticed.

A coffee cup appeared in front of his face the same moment the girl showed him her drawing.

"See? This is Kuon. He can see now," she said proudly and with an open challenge.

"Why are his eyes closed?" Yugo asked, staring at the picture. The bandage was off, and the crescents of Kuon's eyes had long ray lines coming out of them.

"Because..." she got confused and snatched the drawing back. "I don't know what color they are, okay?"

"Brown," Yugo whispered. Without looking back, he left the apartment.

ON THE WAY BACK, YUGO didn't utter a word. From the moment he left the woman's apartment, he couldn't stop thinking about Kuon's eyes. Soulful, sultry, yet challenging and honest, they never failed to excite him. The girl's eyes and the deep-seated challenge that looked so much like Kuon's shuttered his resolution. They made him want to see that tenacious, questioning look in Kuon's eyes again. To watch Kuon's pupils dilate with lust and bleed into his dark brown irises. To feel that burning, confronting gaze that stabbed through his soul, disarming him.

"Boss... Do I need to call for a cleaning crew?" The careful words sounded dull and flat.

Yugo smirked, rubbed his brow. For some reason, he felt stupid but no longer angry. "Relax, Gandhi, I did nothing."

In an automatic mode, he left the car and entered his mansion. Going upstairs, he stopped as his feet landed on the last step. Turning around, he faced Greg.

"Find another donor. I don't care how much it costs or how legal it is. I want him to see again."

"Yes, Boss."

CHAPTER 13

"**K**uon, we've got a donor. Please come over. We need to start the treatment today." The familiar rustle of Dr. Klor coming through the phone stirred the forgotten fear in Kuon's chest. Dropping his hand, he turned toward the kitchen counter where Rick was preparing breakfast.

"Rick, they've got … a donor."

"GOT IT, DOC. I'LL BE THERE," Yugo said, strolling down the corridor toward his office. He grabbed the doorknob and tugged it when the realization that the door wasn't closed hit him. Hand on his holster, he peered in.

A slender frame, dressed in white, spun around, and Mio's pale face greeted him with a mix of surprise and alertness.

"You scared me." Full lips stretched in a fake smile as Mio brought his hand to his chest. Yugo squinted, searching the desk where Mio's hand had been pressed against the scattered papers only a moment ago.

"What are you doing here?" Yugo asked, sparing him a glance. Approaching the desk, he grabbed his phone and scanned the papers. Balance sheets, dossiers, faxes—all of this was unimportant until Yugo's eyes caught the thin envelope with a laboratory stamp. *Did he look inside?* Yugo turned to his nephew. "Didn't I tell you to call before you come?"

Mio frowned; his transparent skin bleached.

"Yugo…" Mio croaked and licked his lips. A weird expression written on his face. "I…"

"Where are your bodyguards?"

"I came alone."

"Haven't we talked about that?"

"But Yugo…" His hand dove into his pocket, making it bulge as he glanced around. "I need to talk to you. It's about Tobias…"

"Greg, drive him home," Yugo ordered, his attention jumping from Mio to the bulky man standing in the doorway, then back to Mio. "If you ever drive without a security team, I will send you away for good. Anyway, what do you want? Did you bring me the hard drive?"

Mio's eyes frosted over, his full, sinful lips disappeared into a thin line, as his hand left his pocket.

"No…"

"Mio, if you have problems with Tobias, solve them with him. Grow up." Yugo glanced back at the desk, seeking signs that the envelope had been opened.

"But…"

"Go!"

"Fine…" Mio's barely audible whisper brimmed with hatred. Giving Yugo a long stare from under his colorless eyebrows, he stomped out of the office.

When his lean figure disappeared from his field of vision, Yugo said in a low voice. "Greg… When the hospital room is assigned to Kuon, put a guard to it."

"Got it."

SITTING ON A MEDICAL BED IN A HOSPITAL ROOM, Kuon crumpled the linens in his fists. The fabric crunched under his fingers. During the last three days, he'd undergone all kinds of checkups and now waited for his surgery.

His phone vibrated, and the familiar music Kristina put as her ringtone filled the air. His hand flinched, ready to reply, but he stopped it the last moment. He'd been intending to accept her calls or ring her back for three days but hadn't. All the check-ups and his crowding thoughts had been overwhelming, and Rick was constantly around. The idea of explaining to Rick about Kristina spiked his anxiety.

The music died, and through the darkness, slithery worms of fear made their way back into his head. A million 'what ifs' circled in his mind, and Kuon regretted letting Rick go home to snatch some things. Trying to chase them away, he fumbled for the remote control. Music and relief flooded the room as soon as he pressed the button. Listening to the drumming, he relaxed his shoulders and sucked in a deep breath, calming his nerves.

The door opened with a barely audible screech; Kuon turned the TV off. The familiar scent of the woody and spicy cologne and tobacco touched his face.

"Yugo?" Kuon's heart sped up. It'd been almost two weeks since Yugo visited. Many times Kuon wanted to call him, but he'd realized that he didn't know Yugo's number. Asking Rick to search his phone for the incoming calls didn't feel appropriate.

Kuon licked his lips. He wanted to ask where he'd been and if he was okay. Why hadn't he come? But the words refused to form.

"You're like a service dog," Yugo chuckled. He approached, and the warmth of his skin washed over Kuon's cheek. For a second, he anticipated the touch, but Yugo stepped back. "It's for you."

Was it my imagination? Kuon thought. When something landed on his lap, he frowned, "What's this?"

"Contraband." A smile in Yugo's voice made Kuon lift a brow. Feeling the warm box with his fingers, Kuon opened it, and the scent of cinnamon baked goods washed over him.

"You aren't supposed to bring food here... You know that I can't eat before the surgery, right?" Kuon said, unable to stop his smile. For some reason, this small gesture made him happy.

"Arrest me."

"I really should!" Kuon chuckled but instantly lost his smile. Since yesterday morning, he hadn't been able to eat. Whenever he took a bite it stuck in his throat, making him feel sick. Putting the box aside, Kuon heaved a sigh, the lump in his throat that had disappeared for a moment, formed again.

"Kuon..." Yugo's voice sounded weird, and Kuon strained his ears.

"What?"

"You aren't going to do anything stupid again, are you?"

Kuon touched his face, wondering if confusion was written all over it. "Of course not."

"You'll be fine. Just don't fuck this up, okay? Doc said your prognosis is high because of the compatibility." Kuon frowned. Yugo acted odd. Listening to the emotions coming from the man, Kuon couldn't help wondering what was going on. Then Yugo added in a familiar, demanding tone, "Don't fuck this up, or I'll be pissed."

Hearing Yugo moving away, Kuon asked before he managed to stop himself, "Where are you going?"

The steps halted.

"Why?" Yugo's voice dropped to a lower tune. "Could it be that you miss me? Want me to stay and hold your hand?"

"Phht, as if. Go away. Next time bring me coffee. It's shitty here." Forcing out a short laugh, Kuon bit his lip. That wasn't what he wanted to say. The darkness thickened whenever he was alone, and now, more than ever, he needed a distraction. He wanted to sense someone's presence by his side, to hear someone speak, even if it was nonsense. To know that he wasn't alone, that there was someone who would chase the darkness away. Kuon clenched his fist as the words refused to form.

Yugo waited for a long moment before he said, "Got it."

TAKING A SEAT ON THE WINDOWSILL, Yugo watched the doctor fold his arms on the desk.

"There is nothing to worry about, Herr Santell. I've already explained to Herr Leiris this morning that the trauma of this surgery is minimal. It can be performed on an awake patient, but to ensure the complete immobility of the eye, it's better if the patient is asleep. After the surgery, he can go home and have his first check-up tomorrow."

"So, you will sedate him..." Yugo frowned, "...and send him home groggy?"

"No, we will provide him with a room for a couple of hours to come around. Usually, it's more than enough. As I said, everything is under control."

The thought of Kuon, weak with drugs, going home with Rick painted his vision red. Before his imagination ran wild, he prompted, "If he has to return tomorrow, can't he stay overnight?"

"I assure you, there is no need for this. He won't require any medical assistance until tomorrow."

"Still, I'd like him to stay. Please, arrange a room."

"As you wish, Herr Santell." The doctor spread his arms, as if running out of arguments.

"How soon will his vision return?"

"It can take up to two weeks before the fog is gone. The sharpness and the quality won't be good for several months at least and will keep jumping before finally stabilizing. In a year, maybe a year and a half, we will talk about the additional LASIC correction if necessary. For now, he should rest and avoid doing anything reckless. No heavy lifting, no strenuous exercise, nothing that will apply pressure to his head and neck."

"Can he have sex?" Yugo asked, and the corners of the doctor's mouth twitched.

"Yes, he can. But, as I said, nothing that would put his neck in an uncomfortable, strained position. Corneas don't have any blood vessels, so engraftment will take time. Any pressure in the eye can stretch the corneas or stitches and slow down the healing process. We have already taken an additional risk by treating both eyes at the same time. We have to be extremely careful." The doctor stood up and threw a glance at the clock above the door. "Now excuse me, Herr Santell. I have to get ready."

THE QUIET TICKING OF THE CLOCK drummed in Yugo's head, making him anxious. Rick sat a few seats away with his elbows propped against his knees and his face buried in his palms. Choosing the seat nearest to the operating room, he behaved like an animal trying to establish its territory. Yugo didn't care, but he hated waiting. His restless fingers trifled with unlit cigarettes, disemboweling sweet-smelling tobacco to the floor. When the pack was almost exhausted, and the tiles around his feet were strewn with ground tobacco, the door to the operating room opened, and the doctor stepped out.

Yugo rushed to his feet, so did Rick.

"Now-now... What's with the long faces? He is fine, just resting," the doctor said, smiling at the men. "Everything went well."

"Thanks, Doc!" Face wreathed in a smile, Rick grabbed the doctor's hand and gave it a passionate shake.

Idiot. Of course, it went well. Klor is the best in the country. Yugo thought, giving Rick a hard stare. He was in that state of mind and spirit where every little thing irritated, and now the happy face of Kuon's guardian dog stirred his hatred.

"He will be available for visiting tomorrow." Having no intention of leaving, Yugo frowned and shoved his hands into his pants pockets. The doctor, as if reading his mind, placed his palm on his shoulder and guided him toward the elevator. "Tomorrow, Herr Santell."

When outside, Yugo lit up a smoke and leaned against the wall. Rick didn't stop, didn't look back, as if Yugo didn't exist. Giving the wide back a long stare, Yugo lifted his gaze to the dark, cloudy sky. Ever since he'd left the woman's flat, he couldn't stop thinking about Kuon, the little girl, and her stupid doodles. On her pictures, Kuon was laughing. In the park, playing with the woman and her daughter, Kuon had been laughing too. *Always.*

Clouds rushed over the sky, chased away by the strong wind. Following west, they darkened and thickened, throwing the world into stuffy, pre-thunderstorm heat.

Watching the sullen sky, Yugo realized that there were only a couple of times when Kuon laughed with him and very few times when Kuon gave him a genuine smile. More than ever, he wanted to hear Kuon laugh now. He tried to recall the sound but failed. Instead, another memory flooded his head: Kuon's white eyes, surrounded by the damaged skin, peering through his soul. The accusing words echoed in his ears, 'Why did you find me after all this time? Why can't you just leave me alone?'

Bitterness filled his mouth. Cringing, Yugo flicked the unfinished cigarette away. The atmosphere, condensing, lay heavy on his shoulders, as the last shreds of the pink and golden sunset disappeared behind the boiling sky. Asphyxiating, Yugo loosened his black tie, undid the top button of his shirt, but that didn't alleviate the crushing pressure that compressed his chest. The first drop hit his face, then another landed on the back of his palm.

The wish to see Kuon overwhelmed, instilling the weird idea that if he didn't do it right away, he would suffocate. Spinning on his heel, he entered the hospital and nearly bumped into the departing doctor. Dressed in an old t-shirt and ripped jeans, Klor slowed his steps, frowning.

"It's getting late, Herr Santell. He is asleep. Didn't you want him to stay overnight? To make him comfortable, we gave him mild sedatives. I don't recommend taking him home today. Wait until tomorrow."

"I can't, Doc. I have to see him now," Yugo said, strolling to the elevator.

Approaching Kuon's room, he slapped the security guy's shoulder. "You can take a break for an hour. If I need you, I'll call."

BLUE FLASHED BEHIND THE WINDOW. Breaking into the room through the vertical blinds, it illuminated the floor, linens, and Kuon's ashen face. Sitting on the bed by Kuon's side, Yugo listened to his soft, rhythmic breathing, whispers of the night, and the beeping of the heart monitor.

The longer he watched Kuon sleep, the louder the annoying tiny voice of the girl rung in his head. *'When he can see again, he will look at it and be happy. And we will go to the aquarium, and look at all the fish there. Even sharks.'*

"Happy, huh?" Yugo breathed. "Do you need kids and fish for this?"

A bright flash broke the bustling murkiness, followed by a peal of thunder. Heavy rain bombarded the window as if asking to let it into the room. The suffocating feeling exacerbated as another flash washed Kuon's face in neon blue, giving it a ghostly impression. Reaching out, Yugo touched Kuon's cold cheek just to make sure he was real and the image wouldn't melt in front of his eyes.

Letting you go was a mistake. Darkness, seeping from the outside, soaked his being. *As soon as I did, annoying flies swirled around you. And you… you let them. You gave them hope when you already belong to me, or did you forget? You did, didn't you? Almost two years, huh? I guess your memory is only that long. You've never missed me. You never called for me. The only expressions you show me are annoyance and anger. But you smile at that woman. And tomorrow you will return to another man's house. Nothing changes, huh. Just like before, you try to slip out of my grasp.* Jealousy, syringing into his blood, erased his humanity. The wish to clasp his hands around Kuon's neck and squeeze as hard as he could poisoned him. *You forgot that your life is in my hands. I granted your freedom, but I can take it back.* Hand, skidding down the side of Kuon's cheek, closed around his neck. Fingers, sinking into the flesh, found the tight vein. Yugo tilted his head, listening with his fingertips for the beat that matched the tiny beeping of the heart monitor.

I shouldn't have given you a choice. I should have killed that Rick to set an example. I should have gotten rid of that woman and the kid, so you would never look at anyone else ever again. I should have forced you back to me. What's happiness, anyway? The freedom to make stupid decisions? To go to Afghanistan and get mutilated there? Or run away from your fears and cover it with noble reasons? If so, then happiness is overrated. The thunder boomed in the distance. *I should break you this time. Make you crave my touch, my presence. Instill the fear of loneliness in your mind. Make you mine, whatever the cost, even if you hate me. Robbed of options, you will eventually settle like you did before. You will look at me again. Free or chained, you will be mine. Mine alone.*

The vein under his fingers swelled and vibrated, beckoning him. Leaning closer, he pressed his mouth to its thickness, and Kuon's pulse quivered on his lips. Trailing up, he licked Kuon's rough chin; the one day bristle scratched his tongue. The familiar smell of Kuon's skin tickled his senses. Leaning his left arm against the linens, Yugo caressed Kuon's cheek with his free hand, then outlined his jaw. Heart pounding in his throat, he pressed his mouth to the rough lips. Warm and dry, they didn't respond, but easily opened to his tongue.

Kuon stirred, moaned. The beeping of the heart monitor sped up, and blood flooded Yugo's head.

I should make you mine... He deepened the kiss, licking Kuon's tongue and the insides of his mouth. Weak hands pressed against his shoulders and pushed him away, but Yugo forced himself upon the resisting body. The heart monitor went insane. Kuon's fist bumped against his chest, then again and again, as the hot, torn breathing danced over his tongue. A sharp knee stabbed Yugo's side, but it only inflamed his arousal.

"No." Kuon groaned into his mouth. Yugo's head gyrated. His hands fumbled over Kuon's hospital gown seeking for slits to sneak under. He wasn't sure what he was doing, but more than anything, he needed Kuon to become his, no matter the cost. Sharp teeth sunk into his tongue, and coppery flavor flooded his mouth. Managing to turn his face away, Kuon growled, "No, Yugo. Stop!"

Blood on fire, Yugo tore the annoying fabric, as lightning flashed right behind the window, illuminating the painful contortion of Kuon's mouth.

BOOOM. The thunder resembled a gunshot, and then another instant flash blinded Yugo. A tactile, vivid memory resurrected. Once again he stood on the frozen pier, squeezing the icy grip of the gun. His fingers shook as he pulled the trigger... and then... the burst of blood and the motionless body... the surprise in the dark eyes a moment before the flutter of lashes hid the irises... the swirling snow and the quicksilver of the river.

Yugo's fingers tangled in the fabric, and an angry fist collided with his cheek, throwing him back. The sobering pain cleansed his blood, washing his body in freezing cold.

"What the fuck are you doing?" Kuon asked in a thick voice, panic and fear controlling his expression. A palm over his mouth, Kuon blew out a long breath.

Yugo didn't reply. He imagined the white room, and a locked up Kuon going crazy in silence. Fights, violent sex, bloody kisses, chains, and raw skin under handcuffs; hatred in Kuon's eyes, all the things that used to excite him. He blinked in the gloom, feeling exhausted instead. The memory changed to one of Kuon's rare smiles and the passion of his willing submission; the smoldering lust in his eyes, and the heat of Kuon's eager mouth around his cock. The memory of their short road trip emerged in front of his eyes, providing him a vivid recollection of Kuon gripping the wheel while listening to his directions. Trust and excitement on Kuon's face stirred the weird longing in his chest. And then Rick's words came to mind. *'He deserves to be happy, but people like you don't understand things like this.'*

"Kuon, have you ever been happy with me?" The words came out strained.

Tearing Yugo's palm off his mouth, Kuon exploded, "Who do you think you are? Coming in here right after the surgery… What did you want to do, rape me while I was out cold? How low can you get?"

How low? I wonder… A sad chuckle escaped Yugo's throat as he imagined Kuon going back to Rick's apartment, living a life that didn't include him. When his eyes healed would Kuon let him get close? Yugo didn't think so. Fingers sinking into his slicked-back hair, he got up from the bed. *I guess I really hit rock bottom, huh?*

"Don't you have any fucking pride?" Grabbing a pillow, Kuon threw it in Yugo's direction. Flipping in the air, it hit the floor a few feet away from the door. "You can only force people when they are at their weakest. At least give me a chance to defend myself. I hate people like you the most!"

Every word Kuon said sunk into Yugo's core. His gaze jumped from the painful twist of Kuon's mouth to the crumpled sheet in his fist, took in the rapidly rising and falling chest under the blue hospital gown, and the white plastic eye shields taped over his eyes.

"Is that so? You hate me this much? I guess, no matter what I do, you'll never…" Yugo swallowed the unspoken words against his dry throat. He took a deep breath and closed his eyes, shedding his unnecessary, confusing feelings. His mind calmed, so did his pulse as a decision formed in his heart. "Then, there is no point in holding back."

HEAT AND ICE, ONE AFTER ANOTHER, washed over Kuon's body. Ignoring the rapid beeping of the heart monitor, he asked with his tongue numb, "What are you talking about?"

"Don't worry, I'll be gentle," Yugo said. The mattress sagged under his weight as Yugo's knee brushed against Kuon's hip. A hand collided with his shoulder, and the mattress bounced under Kuon's back the same moment as cool fingers seized his left forearm. "I promise, you will enjoy it."

"Enjoy it?" Kuon asked; the blood rush clearing his head from the remaining sedatives. The warmth of Yugo's fingers cupped his cheek as the fire of a kiss inflamed his lips. Clenching his fist, Kuon threw another punch forward. Knuckles hitting flesh, he forced words through gritted teeth. "Don't fuck with me! Coming here, feeding me this bullshit, and you expect me to lie on my back and spread my legs for you? Go to hell!"

Kuon froze as soon as the words left his mouth. A long-forgotten fear chafed his nerves. Yugo hated rejection. He'd never let it slide. Tensing, he expected the counterblow or for Yugo to launch forward and pin him to the bed, but the man pulled back. Kuon shook his head, confused.

Why doesn't he do anything? That never happened before.

More than ever, Kuon wanted to see Yugo's face. He couldn't help wondering what kind of expression he wore, and if he was furious, hurt, or something else. His impotency and helplessness agonized.

A deep sigh preceded the screech of a mattress as Yugo sat on the bed. Minutes stretched, thickening the heavy, uncomfortable silence.

"I guess this is it..." Yugo finally said, his voice low and quiet. The beeping of the monitor increased. "I won't bother you anymore, Kuon."

"You don't make any sense..." Yugo's words rebounded against Kuon's mind, never sinking in. He shook his heavy head, but the gesture only caused a headache.

"I'm thinking about moving back to Sicily. It has a better geopolitical location for my kind of business anyway. I've considered it for a while. You don't need to be afraid. I won't mess with your life anymore. You can do whatever you want, date whomever you want, even marry that woman."

"Is that so?" Kuon's lips stretched in a smile of disbelief as the strong feeling of déjà vu hit him.

It's happening all over again, like a twisted loop of fate. I'm an idiot... he thought, stupefied. Fingers, fumbling over the cool sheets, couldn't find rest. *How come I never saw it before? All this time, he waited for the surgery.* The thought seared his cheeks. *Has the reason for his visits always been guilt and pity? He barely touched me, and even when he did, it was nothing like before. Back then, he never cared if I wanted sex or not. He just did what he wanted... because he desired me.* Kuon moved his shoulder, trying to accommodate the uncomfortable thoughts. *That's right. After all, why would he want this broken body, when he can have anyone? So many scars... Who in their right mind would ever want to touch them?*

From the beginning, it was all about the surgery. This is why he got mad when I gave up those corneas. He tried to buy his way out of guilt and didn't want to wait. Maybe, after all, he does have shreds of conscience. A soul-slaughtering memory of Yugo's reaction to his eyes slashed through his chest. *He couldn't even stomach seeing me. And now, what was that? A half-assed attempt at a nostalgic fuck?* Kuon couldn't stop a slight headshake of disappointment. "So you have messed around enough and got bored? Just like before."

"Huh?"

"I'm an idiot…" Kuon laughed, sour saliva filling his mouth. "Is it fun? Do you enjoy fucking with my life?"

"What are you talking about?" Surprise and concern mixed in Yugo's voice.

"Do you get high when you mess with me? Do you enjoy breaking into my life and fucking with me over and over? Why can't you find another victim? I can't believe you came here after the surgery, tried to rape me while I'm drugged, and now you tell me this? You know what? Go to hell, Yugo."

YUGO FELT LOST. He'd expected to see relief, a splitting smile on Kuon's face, anything, but this weird aggression he couldn't explain.

Feeling like an idiot, he countered, "Fucking with your life? You're the one who is fucking my brain out! I tried to be nice. I gave you space. I gave you time. I never forced you. I waited for you to acknowledge me, but you never did. I asked you to stay with me of your own free will. You refused, and I tried to respect that. I could have locked you away the moment your foot touched Austrian soil. I could have made you mine long ago like I wanted to. Instead, I'm tolerating you living with another man and kissing a woman because I'm trying to respect your fucking feelings. But the more I wait, the more people surround you. Every time I visit, you tell me to go away. And now when I'm about to do that, you tell me I'm fucking with your life? What do you expect me to do? Stay silently by your side for the rest of my life and wag my tail while that woman takes you away? I'm not your fucking Hachiko! I'm done waiting, but don't worry, I won't force you anymore."

"Fuck you! You can't come here and tell me all this after what you've done. Where was your oh so understanding bullshit two years ago?" Kuon snapped. "You have no right to do this to me now!"

"Then what do you want me to do?" Yugo yelled. "Come on, say it. I'll do whatever you want."

"I don't know!" Kuon screamed back.

"No matter what I do, you're never happy." A burst of indignation splashed darkness all over Yugo's soul. He grabbed Kuon's wrist and jerked the younger man closer. Their noses inches apart. "I'm tired of guessing what I should do to make you want me, but the truth is, it doesn't matter what I do…" Yugo pushed a breath out, trying to control his anger. "Give me a call when you realize what you want from me because I'm done trying to understand you."

Pushing Kuon away, Yugo got to his feet. Closing his eyes for a second to gain his composure he moved to the door, but something held him back. Turning around, he sighed. Resting his head on his bent knees, Kuon clutched the tail of his jacket in his fist.

"What is it, another impulse that means nothing? What do you want from me, Kuon?" Yugo didn't recognize his voice, it sounded so low and hoarse, accompanied by the staccato of the tiny beeping and the background rattle of the heavy rain.

"I don't kno-ow, but an apology would be a good start." Aggression drained from Kuon's voice, but something else lingered in the stretched vowel. Yugo wanted to hear more.

"What for?"

"For ruining my life, to begin with? For raping me? For locking me away for eleven months?" Kuon lifted his head, seeking Yugo's face with his strapped eyes.

"No. I never regretted that…"

Kuon's cheek flinched, as he dropped his hand, the beeping fast and furious. "I see…"

"I'd do it all over again. The only thing I've ever regretted was letting you go." The beeping halted, stuttered. Kuon tore the clip off his finger and threw it aside. A long, piercing signal filled the air. Kuon's face flipped through expressions. Annoyance, hurt, anger, then something else Yugo failed to read.

"Turn it off!"

Approaching the machine, Yugo yanked the plug out of the socket. The sound died, and silence flooded the room. Minutes stretched, and only an occasional rumbling of thunder and the pattering of rain disturbed the repressed quietness.

"Herr Leiris?" The door flew open, and a nurse rushed into the room.

"He is fine. Leave," Yugo ordered, squinting at the bright light showering in from the corridor.

Kuon faced the door. "I'm fine. The machine was annoying."

"Leave," Yugo pressed. "Klor is aware that I'm here."

Conflict bled through the nurse's mousy features before she backed out of the room. The door closed, bringing back the silence and darkness.

"I don't think I can forget that…" Kuon said after what felt like forever. "And you're right. It doesn't matter what you do, because I don't know what I want, but it's certainly not this. Not when you use my state to force me. If this is how it's gonna be, then I want nothing. I'm fucking blind! I already feel helpless enough, don't you get it?"

Yugo sat by Kuon's side, watching his mouth tighten in a colorless line. Kuon's behavior confused him, yet something in Kuon's words gave him hope.

"Okay." He crept closer. His nose brushed against Kuon's shoulder as he rested his forehead in the crook of his neck. "How about I tell you what I want?"

"No." Kuon pulled back, but Yugo clasped his hands around his torso, pressing their chests together. "Don't do this."

"I want you."

"Shut up. I don't want to hear it."

"I missed you. I couldn't stop thinking about you."

"Are you for real? Do you think you can seduce me with cheap lines after you tried to rape me?" A short laugh broke out from Kuon's chest.

"Kinda… Am I succeeding?" Yugo moved his face up, freezing an inch away from a kiss.

"No." The corners of Kuon's mouth dropped, as he nervously licked his lips. "Stop messing around."

"You said you want things sweet. I'm trying." Yugo smiled. "I want to kiss you so bad, but if I do, you'll say that I forced you again, so you have to do it first."

"Are you delusional? Let go, or I will hit you." Squeezing his hand between their chests, Kuon slammed his palm against Yugo's face, then shoved the man back.

"Hit." Yugo breathed into his palm. Catching Kuon's hand with his own, he pressed his tongue to Kuon's wrist, licking a trail up to his fingers. Kuon tensed when Yugo nibbled at his index finger but didn't pull away.

"Stop."

"I'm not doing anything," Yugo murmured. The skin between Kuon's index and middle finger tasted like soap. Giving it a long lick, Yugo took his middle finger into his mouth and gave it a light suck. Kuon swallowed. A shiver ran down his body, reverberating in Yugo's tongue. "You became even more sensitive. I wonder if the lack of vision did it?"

"Shut up," Kuon breathed. "I must be not right in the head for even considering you."

"Is that so? Why did you stop me then? Did you expect that we would be friends, or I would patronize you?"

"No."

"Maybe you want revenge? Do you want to kill me, make me suffer?"

"No." Kuon tried to yank his hand out of Yugo's grasp but failed.

"Then what?" Yugo nibbled at the side of Kuon's palm, expecting an answer. When minutes stretched, and Kuon said nothing, Yugo groped over the blanket, feeling Kuon's groin. "Isn't it because you want me too? You can stop this at any moment. Push me away, and I will leave. Or be honest and say what you really want. You're hard and shaking, but I barely touched you."

A flash of lightning lit Kuon's aroused face, and Yugo leveled their lips, waiting for Kuon to decide. His head swam from the intimacy, as thoughts rushed through his mind. *The truth is you don't want me to stop. You want me to force you, so you don't have to make a decision. You want an easy way out and an excuse for your pride, don't you? But if I do this, you will forever run away from me. If I don't, will you choose me?*

Yugo's pulse spiked as the fear of rejection rose with every passed second. The more he waited, the clearer he understood that no matter what Kuon said he would never be able to leave him alone, not when he'd heard sparks of acceptance in Kuon's words. "What will it be, Kuon?"

CHAPTER 14

"Fuck it," Kuon growled; his facial muscles contorted, betraying his inner war. He didn't know why his body reacted to Yugo's touch. Why his heart choked with blood every time the man spoke to him. His mind kept screaming that it was merely the afterglow of Stockholm syndrome, but at that moment, he didn't care. For the first time since their small ride, Kuon felt alive again. And that realization made a dent in his wall of denial, as he couldn't help but admit that Yugo's touch magnetized his body. The sound of his voice raised the small hairs on his nape and arms. When Yugo was around, his every cell tensed in attention, and Kuon failed to say what caused it—conditioning or lust.

He'd had many women in his life. Wanting to forget Yugo's touch and check his sexuality, he'd let Rick kiss him too. He liked Kristina, and a part of him was sure that he could be happy with her and Nelly, but none of them made him feel this suffocating need to be touched; none of them made him feel alive. *Why does it have to be you? I must be insane for letting you into my life again. Why did you have to say all this shit, as if you care? I was finally moving on, why the hell did you do this, and why did it make me happy? I'm an idiot… A murderer, a rapist, a drug lord. No morality, no code, no rules. Why, of all people, does it have to be you?* Yugo's breath tickled his lips, gravitating him.

"Fuck it," Kuon repeated, giving up. Grabbing the flap of Yugo's jacket, he breathed the words into Yugo's mouth, "I will so regret this."

His teeth clanged against Yugo's smile. Fingers, feeling the familiar warmth and relief of the ripped body, tingled. The smell of heady cologne muddled his thoughts. His blood pressure, elevating, set his body on fire and erased the last remnants of rationality. He didn't want to think anymore, didn't want to try and understand Yugo or himself, didn't care what was wrong or right, and if this had a future. He just wanted to quench this thirst Yugo's touch instilled in his body.

The coppery taste spiked his senses as he bit down on Yugo's lip, then sucked onto it, submitting to the momentary insanity. His hands shook when he ripped Yugo's jacket off the man, fisted his shirt, and tore the fabric open. The sound of the buttons hitting the floor and scattering around joined the pattering of the rain. Kuon didn't care. His head swam when his fingers touched Yugo's chest.

BA-DUMP, BA-DUMP, BA-DUMP drummed under his finger pads. Kuon froze, listening for Yugo's chaotic breathing burning the insides of his mouth and the suffocating, impossible fullness extending in his chest.

"Kuon…" Yugo's hands tore the hospital gown off his shoulders. Hot lips skidding over the side of his face found his neck, and Kuon sucked in a sharp breath as strong teeth sunk into his collarbone. Over and over, Yugo kissed, sucked, and bit down on his neck, imprinting his presence into his skin. "You're an idiot indeed… You had a chance. Not anymore. There is no way I'll ever let you go. You belong to me, you hear?"

Kuon blinked behind the eye shields, trying to process the words, but the meaning eluded him. Scalding heat engulfed him, evaporating the last resistance from his body. Giving up, he concentrated on the shaky touch of Yugo's cold fingers. Trailing up Kuon's forearm and neck, Yugo's fingers followed the burning track left earlier by his lips. Throwing the blanket away, Yugo's knee brushed against his inner thigh. Kuon arched his chest, seeking more sensation.

"I haven't touched you yet, but you're leaking already," Yugo rasped. "When was the last time you touched yourself?"

"I can't … remember."

"Have you slept with anyone after me?"

"No." An electric impulse pierced Kuon's body as Yugo's lips closed around his cock. A maddening urge, blazing through his core, burnt out his thoughts. Crumpling the sheets in his fists, Kuon groaned, feeling the upcoming, unstoppable orgasm tightening his balls. "I'm going to…"

Yugo lifted up. His palms slipped under Kuon's knees, pulled them up, folding his body in the middle. Kuon yelped, as his knees pressed to his chest. Getting comfortable on the bed, Yugo tugged Kuon's ass closer. Shame flooded Kuon's mind when the hot tongue lapped over his anus and balls.

Twisting his upper body, he grasped the pillow on his left with his right hand. He'd already forgotten how embarrassing sex with a man could be, and how shameless Yugo's touch was.

"No, stop!" Kuon's voice vibrated with desperation, but the scorching lips only sped up. "Wait-wait-wait-wait! Ahh…"

A white flash blazed through Kuon's darkness as a powerful electric discharge shot through his core. His stomach tensed, hips rocked in the air, and hot liquid spurted all over his chest and stomach.

"Wow!" Yugo's breath chilled Kuon's wet ass. "I only licked your hole, and you instantly came. You really didn't touch yourself much, huh?" Yugo murmured, pulling back. Cool fingers pressing to Kuon's chest smeared the sticky substance over his heated skin. "So thick…"

Shuffling up, Yugo pressed a flat tongue to the base of Kuon's cock and licked a path up to his stomach, cleaning him up.

THE TANGY TASTE IGNITED YUGO'S LUST.

"Shut up." Turning his face away, Kuon covered his mouth with his forearm. The darkness hid his expression.

The painful need to see more infected Yugo's mind. The rare flashes of lightning weren't nearly enough to provide Yugo with the whole picture. Reaching out to the switch, he turned the lights on.

Kuon jolted from the low click, blood draining from his face.

"No. Turn it off." His voice weak, when his palm slapped the plastic rail of the bed searching for the switch. The line of his mouth, soft a moment ago, twisted in a painful grimace.

Yugo sat back on his haunches as his eyes took in the picture. Kuon's chest, smooth two years ago, was covered with ragged welts of healed wounds and grooves from what looked like shell splinters. Yugo's mouth went dry as he trailed the bullet hole on the right side of Kuon's chest, beneath the collarbone. Painfully familiar, it felt weird under his fingertips, as if it still throbbed with ugly memory. Yugo blinked, switching his attention to the other marks, the ones he never knew existed. A raised scar from a stitched wound glowed with never faded red on Kuon's left shoulder. Another one from a bullet marred his right biceps. A long, thin scar from what looked like a knife stretched from his right side to his lower belly, and a spider web of a weird, red scar decorated his left side, above the hip. Yugo hated them all. He felt robbed, cheated, as he didn't even know they existed. His eyes burned from the dry air as he couldn't stop staring.

Kuon slapped Yugo's hand away from his chest and plastered a fake smile on his face. "Not what you expected, huh? Sorry to disappoint, but I'm not all that pretty anymore."

He tried to sit up, but Yugo pushed him back.

"You fool. I gave you freedom and look what you did with it? How dare you let someone else maim you when you already belong to me?" Anger flooded Yugo's chest. "Remember well; no one can stain your body but me. You hear?"

Slanting forward, Yugo sunk his teeth into Kuon's shoulder and sucked on the beading blood. Kuon jerked, hissed, and tried to push him away. "Hurts…"

"Of course, it hurts. I'm going to make your scars raw and let them skin over with my marks." Giving the fresh bite a long lick, Yugo sunk his teeth into the bleeding flesh again.

"So fucking selfish…" Kuon sucked a sharp breath, but this time he didn't push the man away.

Red hickeys bloomed all over Kuon's chest by the time Yugo's mouth skidded down to his hip bone. Spreading his legs wider, Kuon turned his face away. His semi-hard cock clung to his stomach. A trail of dark hair stretched from his pubis to his crotch, where his balls tightened with renewing desire.

Tearing his mouth away, Yugo peeled his torn shirt from his shoulders, then kicked off his shoes. The belt flopped in the air as he tore it out of the loops and undid his pants.

"Can you turn off the lights? I feel weird because I'm the only one who can't see." Kuon licked his lips, goosebumps prickling the skin on his arms and legs.

"No fucking way…" With his elbow against the pillow, Yugo breathed, attacking his mouth with a painful, biting kiss. His free hand slipped down Kuon's stomach, fondled his hot balls, before inching down to the crack. Giving a light massage to the tight entrance, he forced a single knuckle in.

A shaky inhale vibrated throughout Kuon's body as his head whipped to the side. An agonizing curl of his lips revealed his clenched teeth.

"So fucking tight…" Yugo's vision throbbed in rhythm with his drumming heart. "Have you played with yourself here?"

"No…" Kuon's stomach convulsed, beading with perspiration, as Yugo's finger slipped into the warm insides. "Yugo, I can't. I haven't… not since you."

A tsunami of blood slammed into Yugo's head, as Kuon's words obliterated his self-control and sent an impatient tremor down his limbs. Without thinking, he shoved another finger into the tight hotness of Kuon's body and muffled the pained groan with a kiss. He licked the slick teeth, played with the bottom lip, before snaking his tongue into Kuon's mouth. Gentle and lazy, Kuon's tongue barely reacted to his kiss, as painful breathing quivered at the back of his throat.

So fucking hot. For a moment, Yugo was sure he would cum before he got inside. Breaking the kiss, he hissed, "Shit."

Lips tasting salt from the side of Kuon's face, he withdrew his fingers. Spreading Kuon's thighs apart with his knees, he pushed his hips forward, rubbing the rough fabric of his pants against Kuon's erection. His cock, painfully hard, twitched under two layers of clothes. "I don't think I can hold back. Give me your hand."

Not waiting for the reply, Yugo grabbed Kuon's palm and guided it into his pants. Fingers, tangling in his pubic hair, wrapped around his length. Using his other hand, Kuon tugged onto Yugo's pants.

"Take them off..." Kuon's impatient whisper inflamed Yugo's ear. Hooking his thumb in his waistband, Yugo pushed his pants down. Their cocks collided, and the first drop of precum rolled out of Yugo's slit.

"Fuck..." Yugo managed through the red heat of arousal. His fingers, wrapping around Kuon's hand, increased the pressure over their joined cocks and set the rhythm. His thumb, circling their crowns rubbed Kuon's slit, and he pushed his nail inside. A suppressed moan escaped Kuon's throat as the fingers of his free hand sunk into Yugo's butt cheek.

"You belong to me. You better remember this well," Yugo whispered, chasing after Kuon's Adam's apple with his mouth. His impatience grew as he remembered how beautifully Kuon's pupils used to dilate with pleasure, bleeding into the dark brown irises. His heart constricted as he wanted to tear the eye shields off Kuon's face to see his heavy lids, hooded with lust.

A shaky moan hit his sweaty temple, as Kuon reached forward with his upper body. His blind mouth searched for a kiss, as his bottom lip twitched with an unspoken plea. Unable to resist, Yugo ran the tip of his tongue over the seam of Kuon's lips again, joining their mouths.

"Now, please..." Kuon said in a husky growl, tearing away from the kiss. The sticky precum, fusing together, drenched from their joined fingers to Kuon's stomach. Their cocks swelled and pulsed as small convulsions took hold of Kuon's joints. "I really can't... Yugo..."

The room swam in front of Yugo's eyes, melting, vaporizing. Heat flooded his core and rose to his throat and his head, shuffling his thoughts. The thick clouds of lust tunneled his vision as all his attention was directed to the powerful squirming body under him. Holding his breath, Yugo thrust his hips forward, fucking their fists.

"Yugo… now…" Kuon panted, digging his fingers in Yugo's shoulders. Dark red spots popped all over his neck and chest; the same color flooded his face. Opening his mouth, he chased for air, suffocating. His heels stabbed at the back of Yugo's thighs as his head tossed over the pillow, spewing sweat all over the light blue fabric. His body tensed for a brief moment before the jolts of pleasure rippled through him. He hissed, bit his lip, and hot liquid shot into Yugo's fist. The grip of his fingers weakened, and he stilled over the soaked sheets.

Yugo's cock was painfully hard as he smeared the slippery remains of Kuon's second orgasm over his length. The sensation changed as Kuon's cock deflated and now he was rubbing his pumped flesh against the immense softness. It took less than a minute before his balls tightened, and every muscle clenched in an agonizingly-sweet spasm.

When the last contraction left his body, he reluctantly got up from the bed, strolled to the bathroom, and fetched a wet towel. When he came back, Kuon was snoring with his limbs spread naked and wide over the crumpled sheets.

THE AIR, DRENCHED WITH freshness, smelled like rain. Dew flared with the entire spectrum under the bright sun, as the morning birds chirped in the thick, bright foliage. Throwing the occasional glances up to the clear sky, Rick ambled toward the hospital. It wasn't even eight yet, but he didn't have the patience to wait any longer, and with his busy schedule, he barely had free hours even in the early morning or late at night. Nodding to the nurse on duty, he passed the elevator and rushed up the fire stairs. Excitement demanded he move, and spending even a minute in a small metal box seemed like torture. On the floor, he froze. The soft smile that had tickled his lips all morning dropped from his face as a security guard, dressed in a black suit, propped up against the door of Kuon's room.

He shrunk back behind the corner. It took him more than thirty minutes but waiting paid off, as the guard strolled to the bathroom. As soon as his back disappeared behind the door, Rick jogged to Kuon's private room and flung the door open.

Shock and disappointment stunned him as an invisible vice of frost seized his heart. Two naked men slept on a narrow medical bed their long limbs entwined—the man he loved with his whole heart and the man he loathed with all his soul.

His focus jumped from the handprint bruise on Kuon's shoulder to the multiple bite marks and hickeys that decorated his torso, then to a huge bruise on Yugo's cheek, and his clothes that lay over the floor, surrounded by a bunch of scattered buttons.

The older man startled and peeled his eyes open. His sleepy gaze sobered under Rick's murderous glare. Yugo's brows rose, as he lifted his head from Kuon's naked chest. He opened his mouth to say something, but Rick didn't intend to listen. Eyes burning, he shut the door and rushed back to the staircase. The chaos of his thoughts condensed and swirled, making his head spin. His stomach roiled, and his throat closed up, as a need to vomit the sticky, disgusting jealousy crumpled his muscles. The sight crushed and defeated him, breaking the spine of his hope.

WHY HIM? WHY HIM? WHY HIM? The mourning drums beat in his head as he stumbled out of the hospital. Feeling drunk, he flattened himself against the wall and gulped the thick air. His chest hurt, larynx closed, and temples pulsed with pressure.

I will never accept it. I will never hand Kuon over to him, not in my life. Not to him. Even if I have to kill him... Thinking like this, he closed his eyes, seeking for the inner strength that would allow him to smile in Kuon's presence again.

FOR A LONG MOMENT, YUGO STARED at the closed door before he lifted himself off the sleeping Kuon. Placing his feet against the chilly floor, he pulled on his torn clothes and, granting Kuon a long look, he threw a cover over his naked frame before leaving the room. Fishing a cellphone out of his pocket, he dialed Greg.

"Wait for me in the parking lot. I don't have much time."

THE SWEET AFTERGLOW OF THE PAST NIGHT washed Kuon's blackness in the warm glow of satisfaction. He still felt Yugo's lips over his body, and the bite marks over his scars throbbed, but even those unpleasant sensations made him happy. He yawned and rolled to the other side.

OBSESSION OF THE EGOIST

Sleep fled his body; he jolted upright when the realization hit him. He was alone in the narrow bed.

"Yugo?" he croaked as his voice betrayed him. His pulse spiked as the first shiver of fright sneaked down his spine. The silence aggravated, and to disperse it, he called again, "Yugo!"

Fingers running over the crumpled sheet, found the torn out lace of his hospital gown and a few buttons. Picking up one of them, he fisted it as hard as he could. His chest hitched, as muted laughter shook his body. Growing stronger, it gained power and volume, turning into something unstoppable, uncontrollable, painful.

His hysterical fit stopped as abruptly as it started. Clenching his teeth, he said into the reigning nothingness. "Oh, god, I never learn…"

CHAPTER 15

Greg's black eyes widened, and he whistled as Yugo got in the car. "Have anything to say?" Piercing him with a hard stare, Yugo slammed the passenger door closed.

"I can see Kuon's right hook is still great. How did it go?"

"How do you think it went if I stayed till morning?" Glancing up at the rearview mirror, Yugo hummed and rubbed the blue bruise coloring his left cheekbone. "Did you bring my clothes?"

"Yes, Boss." Grabbing a garment bag from the shotgun seat, Greg passed it to Yugo. "Gustavo called."

"Yeah? What does he want?"

"A new batch arrives tomorrow. He wanted to talk through the redistribution between the smaller bands in Bratislava. So he wants to know if there is a change in the current obligations. Also, the Department of Home Affairs wants a sacrifice. Gustavo needs to pick a scapegoat. You know he's bad with making those kinds of decisions."

"Tell him to drop by tonight. I don't have time now. Kuon will wake up soon."

"Also, payday is coming. The Minister of Defense requested an audience."

"Can't Rudolph handle it?" Annoyed, Yugo fumbled over his torn shirt, seeking a cigarette pack, but found nothing. He snapped his fingers a few times, looking around. Greg opened the glove box and, pulling out a new pack, offered it to Yugo.

"He asked for you. It has something to do with the Al-Amin and the United Nations."

"Schedule him for tomorrow. Book a conference room in the Royal Hotel, but don't give him the address until tomorrow morning. Tell Tobias to tag along."

"Right, Tobias… He called as well."

"Can't they fucking solve their problems?" Yugo unwrapped the pack and, fetching one smoke, he squeezed it between his lips. Lithe fingers stroked the lighter, and blue-gray smoke streamed up from the tip of the cigarette.

"He can. He said something about 'breaking the little shit's arms' if you don't hurry."

"Damn…" Throwing a glance up at the hospital windows, he said, "Hurry up and drive. He better be home."

"OH-HO-HO…" TOBIAS' FACE STRETCHED with a mix of amusement and excitement.

"Lend me your bathroom," Yugo grounded out, stepping out of the private elevator of the Myhive Twin Towers. The spacious anteroom of Tobias' private floor greeted him with a faint smell of sandalwood and a merciless cold light. Passing the security guards and a gray secretary desk, Yugo pushed Tobias away with his shoulder and entered his private quarters. Throwing the garment bag on the low leather couch, he looked around. The change in the atmosphere was dramatic. The light and fluffy carpeted floor and the heavy ebony wood of the ceiling and walls were divided by wide wall screens that monitored the foyer and the outside perimeter of the building.

"You're missing buttons. You know, it's hard to say if you spent a very wild night or got knocked out cold on the floor," Tobias said, drawing Yugo's attention to his half-naked body and bare feet. Wearing only sweatpants, Tobias ran his hand over his naked belly toward his neck, before he scratched the back of his head; his hair was a morning mess. "That makes me wonder…"

"Leave it," Yugo said.

"You know I can't do that. Seeing you in this state is priceless. Seriously, I can't miss the opportunity." He hummed, closing the door behind Greg's back. "So I take it the reunion with your puppy went well. There is still passion."

"I said, leave it," Yugo repeated, adding a fair amount of warning to his tone. "I don't have time for this, so get to the point."

"Fine!" Throwing his palms in the air, Tobias granted him with a wide, crooked smile.

"Where's Mio?"

"I wish I knew."

"What does that mean?" Yugo scowled.

"The little shit broke into my computer, hacked my crypto wallet, then disappeared."

"Really?" Yugo's lips stretched in a smile. "Attaboy!"

"Aren't you a little too happy about it?" Tobias scowled, folding his arms over his toned chest.

"Why wouldn't I be? He hacked your Fort Knox when you were sooo proud of it. He isn't all that useless after all." Yugo couldn't control his pride and granted Greg a blinding smile.

"Well, now you owe me twenty thousand Bitcoin. The little shit hacked into one of my accounts and transferred everything to one I can't access. He already sold a quarter. I tried to track the money, but he transferred it into Monero, which is untraceable."

"Did you hear?" Laughing, Yugo turned to Greg. "Mio fucked Tobias. Who could imagine?"

Greg snorted and turned around. It took him a moment to glue a mask of dispassion on his face, but the corners of his lips kept twitching.

"Fuck you both," Tobias said. "Is this why you forced him onto me?"

"Partly. Don't worry, you will get your money back," Yugo said, as the last spasms of laughter left his body.

"Oh, I'm not worried," Tobias promised, eyes cold, passionless. "But you should be because I will skin him alive as soon as I get my hands on him."

"No, you won't," Yugo said, peering into the ever-tiny pupils.

"I so will."

"No," Yugo affirmed, keeping his voice calm. "You will do nothing. You pretend you know nothing. I'll make sure Mio credits you back with interests when it's all over. Think of it as an investment. Shouldn't you be proud of your protégé?"

"I'm not. It's Mio. You better start worrying about what he will do with this money and the information he got from me."

"Information?"

Tobias approached the sofa, grabbed the remote, and the image on one of the screens on the wall changed. On the black and white footage, from the back, Mio's flaxen hair glowed white as he furiously typed something on the PC. Tobias fiddled with the remote and the part of the screen, right above Mio's ear zoomed, showing part of the display; the copying process running full force.

"I don't know exactly what he copied, but judging by the time it took, I'd say everything."

"Whatever he does, do not interfere. Let him believe you don't know anything."

"You want him to think I'm fucking gullible and keep disrespecting me like this under my fucking roof? No way."

"For the first time, he's trying to accomplish something. I want to see what he is capable of and his potential. You can always punish him later, but now I want to see him in action." Tobias squinted, so Yugo added, "Why do you hate him so much anyway? When Mio was a baby, you adored him."

"Because back then, I thought he was mine!" Tobias said in a low voice, as his eyes peered through Yugo.

"What?" The merriment drained, Yugo sobered up, processing the information. His thoughts spiraled out of control as he remembered how they first met. *Milana brought him in…* Despite having no connection to the family, Tobias was a frequent visitor in their house. Feeling like an idiot, Yugo breathed, "My fucking god…"

"Milana and I were an item until your father decided to marry her off to make peace with the Scarsi family. We kept seeing each other even after she got married. She said she was using protection with her husband, so the chances of him being mine were high."

"When were you going to tell me?" Yugo asked, fishing a cigarette pack out of his chest pocket.

"Never? What's the point anyway? She's dead, and he isn't mine. Please, don't smoke in my house."

Cheek flinching, Yugo crumpled the pack in his fist. "How do you know he isn't yours?"

"When Mio was ten, I couldn't help thinking that there was very little of her in him and nothing from me, so I ran a DNA test."

"So you hate Mio 'cause he isn't yours?"

"No. I hate him because he has bad blood."

"Watch what you say," Yugo warned. "He is a Santelli."

"No." Tobias held his gaze, unblinkingly. "He is a Scarsi. A lying, backstabbing little shit with no code. No matter how you try to groom a scavenger into a predator, he will remain a scavenger."

"He is still my nephew and Milana's son," Yugo said through gritted teeth; Tobias' upper lip twisted. "Anyway, why opening your cards now?"

"It's not a secret anymore, so I figured I'd better tell you before Mio spoils all the fun, and I miss that expression on your face." Despite a wry smile and challenging look, Yugo noticed how Tobias hid his palms in his sweatpants' pockets.

"What's on the hard drive?" Yugo asked. When Tobias didn't reply, he pressed again, "What's on the damn hard drive, Tobias?"

"Why don't you ask your nephew?"

"I will," Yugo promised, his head buzzing with thoughts. *Why the hell did Mio never say anything?* Yugo's mind trailed back to their last encounter. *He acted odd. Was it because he got the hard drive? And I brushed him off...* He remembered the pale face, and how Mio had asked him for a talk. *Fuck my life. What's on the damn drive that got him this agitated? Why did he steal from Tobias? Where is he now? Does he intend to give me the damn drive?* "But I don't have time for this. Why don't you just cooperate for once? If Mio has it, I need to know."

Tobias' expression didn't change, but his lips paled. "It's my privacy, Yugo."

"Not anymore. Is there anything I need to know about? Anything work-related?" When the blond didn't reply, Yugo added all the warning he could muster into his voice, "Tick-tock, Tobias!"

The colorless eyes shot a weird look at Greg, then back at Yugo. He sighed, "Maybe."

"Give me a copy." When Tobias said nothing, Yugo threw a glance at the watch. *Fuck...* "Listen, sooner or later I'll have it anyway. Why don't you spare us all from the excessive work?"

"Fine..." The emotionless word left Tobias' lips. His gaze bored into Yugo's pupils. "But not for free. I'll give you the hard drive, but in exchange, I get to use your intelligence team whenever I need it. Greg included. Your team operates from your house, right? It means I will come and go as I please."

"You're delusional if you think I'll let you do that." Yugo snorted. "Mio will give it to me for free. I just have to ask him."

"Ask." Tobias grinned. "But you're the delusional one. Mio will trade it for a place in your bed." He raised his hand in the air and waved it. "Bye-bye puppy! I'm only asking for the assistance of your intelligence network. The choice is yours."

"Intelligence," Yugo finally said. "Not my database. And they will run your every query through Greg."

"Deal."

"Give the hard drive to Greg. I need to change." Picking up the garment bag from the couch, Yugo stomped to the bathroom.

STANDING IN THE SHARP SHADOW of the hospital building, Rick watched a black jeep park. All morning the shocking picture didn't leave his mind. The more he thought about it, the more he realized that the morning scene didn't look like a lovers' reunion, it looked like a fight that ended with rape. Needing to clear his suspicions, he'd tried to see Kuon but the security guard, propping up the wall of Kuon's room, wouldn't let him in, which only reassured him in his rightness.

The bright sun glinted off Yugo's raven hair. His dark gray suit and black shirt looked stuffy in the morning heat. Darting a glance at his watch, the man breathed, "Eleven already... Fucking Tobias."

"Boss, do you want me to go with you?" Poking his face out of the window, another man, *probably a bodyguard*, asked. Rick squinted. Through the thick glass that reflected the parking lot, he could tell a murderer, even if he wore a business suit. The thought that if this man were to tag along, Rick's plan would go to hell darkened his mood even more.

"No. Better make sure all the preparations for Kuon to move in are finished." Rick couldn't suppress a smile as Yugo rejected salvation. Jolting back into the thick shadow of the corner, Rick watched Yugo examine the hospital building and the parked cars, before striding toward the main entrance.

Slipping through the automatic doors into the well-conditioned building, Rick pushed the door of the staircase and rushed upstairs. The knife handle burned his palm.

NUMBNESS SATURATED. For some time Kuon concentrated on breathing, but even this simple process was painfully-difficult, exhausting. The surrounding nothingness frightened him more than usual. Darkness, emptiness, loneliness, fusing in a vortex, overflowed his emotional pool.

Bastard... He bit his lips, trying to stop them from twisting in a painful grimace. *Does he think he can mess with me whenever he wants and throw me away right after? What am I, a fuck-toy? A disposable pleasure device?*

The more Kuon thought about it, the more he realized that Yugo had never clearly confessed.

"I don't get it… Did I misunderstand him?" he whispered only to dispel the clouding darkness. *Where do I stand? Who am I to him? A toy, nostalgic fuck, pity case, lover? Whatever I am, that didn't stop him from leaving. Isn't it like before?*

The earthquake of unsettled emotions trembled in his fingertips when he covered his strapped face with his palms, feeling used, powerless. His eyes burned as the pulsing pressure at the back of his head intensified, and ripples of chill rushed through his body. Tugging the blanket over his head, he scraped his nails down his face.

Serves me right. A couple of sweet words and I spread my legs for him. I should have killed him!

"ARGHH!" Kuon roared in helpless agony, trying to calm his bruised ego, but anger prickled his eyes.

"YOU CAN GO," YUGO THREW to the guard as he entered the room. He pushed the door closed when alertness prickled the hairs on his arms. At first, he didn't realize what spiked his adrenaline, then he heard heavy breathing and noticed the silhouette of a shaking body rolled up under the covers.

"Kuon?" Darting to the bed, he threw the blanket away. "Are you in pain? I'll get the doctor."

On his side, Kuon propped himself up on one elbow. The thick shock of hair fell over his eye shields when he moved his chin to his shoulder.

"I am … in fucking pain," Kuon said in a gravelly voice, as he sat up on his haunches.

Cold fear, starting under Yugo's tongue, streamed down his throat as he wrapped his arms around Kuon's torso, trying to lift him. "Hold on, I'll get you to the…"

"Bastard!" Clashing his teeth in the air, Kuon threw a short jab forward.

Ringing filled Yugo's ears as he pulled back, blinking away the black flies. The heat and pain blooming on his cheek spread all over his head, and the room swirled.

"That's not the greeting I expected," he said, rubbing his pulsing cheek, but his heart lightened. Kuon seemed to be fine; aggressive, but fine. Then why had his body language suggested the opposite? "What is this all about?"

Waiting for the room to stop, he placed his hand on Kuon's thigh.

"Don't touch me!" Kuon slapped his palm away, then grabbed the flap of his jacket. His other fist bleached white as he held it ready to crash down on Yugo's face again, but in a moment, his determination seemed to vaporize. A heavy air puff crashed against Yugo's neck as Kuon dropped his fist and leaned into him. His sweaty forehead bumped against Yugo's shoulder.

Confused by Kuon's behavior, Yugo hummed.

"Where have you been?" Kuon breathed angry words out. "I'm gonna kill you!"

Dipping his chin, Yugo couldn't help a smile as Kuon let out another angry puff. Every heartbeat radiated through his chest with buzzing heat, but he couldn't say if happiness caused it or Kuon's punch had granted him with a concussion. "Why? Did you miss me?"

"I thought…" Kuon didn't finish.

"Thought what?" Yugo mused.

"Never mind." Kuon pushed away, his face turning red. "Why did you leave?"

Wanting to see more, Yugo tilted his head. Having no idea what's going on in Kuon's head, he felt both amused and confused. "Why? I went out to change my clothes because someone shredded my suit to pieces."

"You should have woken me up… Do something like this again, and I'll kill you with my bare hands."

"Oh, I see," Yugo murmured. Never before had a pathetic death threat, said in a low, vibrating voice, made him so happy. He had to bite his lip to choke the laughter. "So, you're grumpy because you didn't get your morning kiss? Let me fix that."

He leaned into the man, but the slam of Kuon's palm against his face shoved him back.

"Fuck off!" Kuon grumbled, but the aggression left his shoulders. Pulling Kuon's hand away, Yugo drew closer.

"Kuon?" He froze an inch away from the strapped face. "Open your mouth."

"Wha…"

A slight resistance preceded the submission, as Yugo locked their mouths, but in a moment Kuon leaned into the kiss. His hands found Yugo's jacket and crumpled the collar.

Yugo smiled, getting high. The intoxicating feeling of victory soared when the black-eyed man, who stood in the doorway holding a long military knife, and whom he'd been watching from the corner of his eye for the last five minutes, stepped back out, shutting the door.

A PANDORA'S BOX opened in Rick's chest, releasing all the evils in the world into the swirling chaos that his soul had become. His eyes, rebelling against his will, refused to look away from the anguishing scene. He wanted to run away, but his body, frozen to the spot, didn't want to move. When Kuon leaned into the kiss, he let out a long, silent breath, before turning around and leaving the hospital, because he wasn't sure what he would do if he stayed longer.

"ALLOW RICK INTO THE ROOM," Yugo told Greg as he leaned back onto the passenger seat. The noisy city streets bled into the forest backgrounds as they drove west. Undergoing all kinds of check-ups, Kuon had to stay in the hospital for another few hours, but Yugo couldn't wait longer. The hard drive burned him through his pocket, inflaming his curiosity and impatience.

"Boss?" Greg shot up a questioning glance in the rearview mirror. "Why? Didn't you want to get rid of him?"

"I changed my mind. Kuon will have a hissy fit if he thinks I'm isolating him again," Yugo said, closing his eyes for a second. "I've tolerated him for so long; I can wait one more day. Tonight Kuon will move in with me, so there is nothing to worry about. Also, his attachment to Kuon is kinda charming. They've known each other for what, two years? They even live together, yet Kuon said they never fucked. Rick wanted to slice my throat today, but retreated as soon as he realized that Kuon isn't being forced, which made me think… He is like a loyal dog who will rip out the throat of anyone who would harm Kuon. He will never do anything Kuon hates, because he is scared to lose that fragile connection they have, and that makes him harmless to me. He will be waiting for Kuon to choose him, which will never happen. If not me, Kuon would rather choose that woman."

"That's cruel." Greg allowed himself a smirk.

"Anyway, since he is no threat, he can stay for a while, if it makes Kuon happy. Maybe I will put him to good use one day."

Greg said nothing more, and Yugo's focus dissolved into the

background as his mind drifted. Unhurried thoughts warmed his chest with the memory of the last night, then he sobered as he remembered Mio. *Twenty thousand Bitcoin is a lot of money. What the hell is he doing?*

"Aren't you disappointed?" Yugo asked as soreness itched in the depth of his chest. Trying to figure it out, he dug deeper into the invisible raw spot.

"Huh?"

"Mio. What was he thinking, stealing from Tobias? It's one thing to hack his PC, and another to steal… And such big money… How much is it, two hundred million euros? Why does he need so much? Tobias never forgives or forgets anything. He will rip him apart…"

"Do you want me to track Mio down?"

"Yes." Yugo nodded. "I want to know what he is doing before he does it. Make sure you know where he is and where the money goes. If the game is too dangerous, I want to be able to stop him before it goes too far."

"Got it."

Through the thick foliage, he saw the familiar silhouette of his mansion and the thick blanket of wild grape covering the front. Watching it cling to the white stone, Yugo wondered why Mio never told him that he'd gotten the hard drive?

Greg parked. When the engine died, Yugo got out of the car and, entering the mansion. His palms moistened when he rushed upstairs and into the small, hidden room at the back of his bedroom, then connected the hard drive to the computer.

Attention spiking, he flopped down on the seat.

TWO HOURS LATER, WHEN YUGO'S back ached from sitting in the same position, the door opened, and Greg entered the small monitor room. The tray he carried emitted a strong coffee aroma.

Placing a small porcelain cup of ristretto on the desk, he said, "Anything?"

"Everything… Politics, military officers, police, Rudolph, even you and me." Yugo breathed, before opening a video file. "Now, explain this to me… Only you and I had this footage. You said that all the copies were destroyed."

Greg squinted, staring at the screen, where the younger version of himself was wrapping his hands with boxing tape. Behind his back, by the concrete wall, a man sat on a stool. His hands were tied to his torso, and a sack covered his head. The younger version of Yugo unhurriedly smoked behind the prisoner. Turning the video off, Yugo faced Greg. His inquisitive glare boring into the deadpan eyes.

"I'm waiting."

A heavy sigh broke out from Greg's wide mouth. He scratched his ear, scrunched his mouth, then ruffled his short, black hair; his usually expressionless face puzzled. "I didn't know he still kept them."

"Care to elaborate?"

"After Milana's death, Tobias severed ties with us, but from time to time he accepted my calls. At some point, he confessed to running the investigation and asked for assistance, but he wanted to keep his name out of it, which was understandable. We exchanged information. That's how we got that Interpol file. His work in the criminal intelligence department came in handy many times. I used to consult him a lot. He couldn't find peace and asked to see the footage for his moral satisfaction, and I needed help with behavior analysis and background checks. That's it. After we lost the last lead, he quit Interpol and started his small weapon business. He was good, so I offered him work with us."

Yugo's sunk his canine tooth into the side of his thumb, processing the information. "Just like that, you trusted him…"

"You forgot that before working for you, I was Milana's bodyguard. I've known Tobias for a very long time." Greg said, staring at the floor. His wide shoulders slumped as his wide mouth disappeared into a thin line.

"You dumb fuck…" Yugo breathed, dismissing Greg with a hand motion. "Track Mio and get my car ready. I'm going to collect Kuon."

THE CONSTANT CHECKUPS EXHAUSTED Kuon, and he prayed for the day to be over. The plastic eye shields substituted his bandages, but his vision didn't improve. His eyes became sensitive, raw, and photophobic. Expressing his fears at the pre-release check-up, he received a cheerful reply that his vision could remain almost non-existent for a week or two before it would gradually return.

The morning, spent with Rick, stretched into an agonizing silent hell. The man acted distant, and his rare replies were short and reserved. Kuon knew that something gnawed at him, but couldn't bring himself to ask. He could guess the reason. A need to explain himself wrenched his nerves, yet he couldn't help procrastinating, as if waiting would change anything. When the doctor confirmed his discharge, it became impossible to postpone the inevitable.

Sitting on the bed with his hands wrapped around his knees, Kuon sunk his nails into his palms. A few times he opened his mouth then shut it, until he finally managed the weak, "Listen, Rick... I need to tell you something."

"I already know everything. You're covered in hickeys," Rick uttered, gathering Kuon's things. "You're moving in with him, right? Can't be helped."

The coppery mixture of sour saliva and blood filled Kuon's mouth as his tormented lip broke under his canine tooth.

"I'm sorry. I didn't mean to..." Kuon rose to his feet and outstretched his hand, wanting to touch Rick to stop the insurmountable, invisible gulf growing between them with every second of silence.

"Please, spare me from this talk," Rick cut him off. He didn't touch Kuon's outstretched arm, didn't make a single step toward him. "Don't make it even more complicated. I'm already doing my best here."

"I understand..." Kuon mumbled, sitting back on the bed. Listening for Rick to go through the room and collect what little of his belongings he had here, Kuon hunched forward. His guts in knots, as he searched his mind for anything he could say to make it better.

"Don't overthink it. I'm not mad," Rick breathed. "When you break up with him, you know where to find me."

Kuon couldn't suppress a chuckle. He opened his mouth to reply when the door to the hospital room creaked, and someone stomped in.

"Ready?" Yugo's low baritone shifted the atmosphere. Awkward, Kuon dropped his chin. When a warm palm cupped his cheek, and hot lips planted a kiss upon his, Kuon frowned.

"Oh, dog, you are here. Sorry, I didn't notice you." Yugo's voice picked up smug notes, and Kuon clenched his fists, pain blooming in the places where his nails sunk into his palms.

"Yugo!" Kuon growled, investing all the warning he could muster. The way the man marked his territory annoyed him to no end.

Ignoring him, Yugo wrapped his fingers around Kuon's biceps and tugged him up and forward. "Come on, get up."

On his feet, Kuon listened for the noises of the hospital life to become louder. The sound of boots approached with a low screech of metal wheels, and Kuon wondered who that could be. The steps didn't belong to Rick or Yugo, they didn't belong to a nurse either. They sounded heavy as if the person was massively built. Yugo tugged him, disorienting him, as he tried to draw a mental picture in his head. Following the guidance of Yugo's demanding hand, Kuon took a few steps forward but halted.

"Long time no see, Kuon." A deep, rusty voice, coming from behind him, sounded familiar. A huge hand landed on his shoulder, and something bumped against the back of his knees. The pressure of the palm intensified, and Kuon realized that the man wanted him to sit down. He reached back and grabbed the handle of the wheelchair before slumping on the seat.

He let out a sigh, relieved. "Indeed. Hi, Greg."

The spinning motion made him whip his face to the place where he thought Rick stood. Everything happened so fast; the wheels spinning under him seemed only to increase the speed.

"Rick..." He managed. "I'll call you."

"Sure," Rick's voice sounded dull as if coming from a deep hole. "No problem."

Kuon hung his head, letting Greg take him away from the hospital room and the only friend he had.

I'm the worst...

EPILOGUE

"Come on in," Yugo murmured. Holding Kuon's hand, he slowly led him forward. When the texture under them changed from thick, bouncy carpet to hardwood, Kuon didn't need eyes to realize where they were. The sweet scent of tobacco and heady cologne suffused the air, the soft notes of dried wood, vanilla, and smoke laced within. There was only one place on Earth that smelled like this—Yugo's bedroom.

Blazing flashes of memories of hot, sweaty nights spent in the room washed his darkness in red. So bright, so vivid, he could hear his own moans in his head—embarrassing, shameless. Kuon shook his head, trying to chase away the rising heat in his stomach.

It's been a long time... He had an urge to touch something, anything, that would remind him of this place, and Yugo, as if reading his thoughts, let go of his hand.

Kuon's mental projection grew vivid, feeling more like an odd dream than reality, and he needed something to make them real. He took a step forward, then another one and his foot caught in the thick fur of the huge wolf pelt. For a moment, he didn't know how to feel. The sensation it stirred filled his mouth with a bitter taste. The memory of the rape, scattered cutlery, and how he fisted this fur trying to maintain his sanity invaded his mind. Escaping the captivity of the vision, he turned left and made an uncertain step. When his shin hit something soft, he bent forward and touched the bumpy, cold leather of Yugo's favorite chair. Slanting forward, he trailed the backrest. A raised scar he'd left with a meat knife differed from the ostrich leather texture. It stirred a more pleasant memory.

Funny... He smirked as the back of his hand drifted over the leather. Cool and rough, it felt pleasant, familiar. *It's been so long...*

He remembered all the fights they had during those long eleven months. All those bruises and hickeys Yugo left on his body, all the scars, pain, and pleasure they shared. The recollection made him realize that the events would never be repeated. Back then, he was a prisoner, a toy. Kuon's belly fluttered as it occurred to him: this was the first time he'd come to Yugo's place of his own will. Things had changed.

Life is so funny. He straightened up, feeling Yugo's curious gaze on his back. It was so obvious as if Kuon could see his cold, gray eyes following his every move. As seconds ticked by, Kuon's awareness of Yugo's presence became stronger. His imagination ran wild as he felt the elusive touch, caressing his arms, as if Yugo's hands trailed his limbs close enough to stir his body hair, but not to touch the skin.

"Welcome home, Kuon," Yugo whispered as his hands broke the tiny distance and caught his shoulders. "Welcome home."

**TO BE CONTINUED IN
PURSUING THE EGOIST**

ABOUT NERO SEAL

Journalist, poker player, casino events manager, designer, and SEO specialist, Nero Seal tried it all before committing to the idea of being an M/M fiction writer. Living in one of the most homophobic countries in the world, he has a lot to say. Being an avid traveler, he creates his imaginary worlds on the places he's been and the people he's met.

Characters always talk in his head, forcing him to write their stories, using his 49 kinks as the ultimate weapon of allure. When the voices in his head aren't slaving him around, he is drawing, hiking, and procrastinating important things in favor of momentary gratification.

SOCIAL LINKS: https://linktr.ee/NeroSeal

ALSO BY NERO SEAL

EGOIST SERIES:
LOVE OF THE EGOIST
ACCEPTANCE OF THE EGOIST
OBSESSION OF THE EGOIST
PURSUING THE EGOIST

REAPERS SERIES:
IBLIS' AFFLICTION
IFRIT'S VENGEANCE (COMING SOON)

SHORT STORIES:
AND AFTER DEATH…
UNDER THE YEW TREE

Made in United States
North Haven, CT
24 May 2025